PRAISE FOR ANDREA HURTT

"COLORFUL, DESCRIPTIVE, FASCINATINGLY PROVOCATIVE... Andrea Hurtt's *Masquerade*, is a WONDERFUL story about relationships and consequences. Just when you think you know what happens next, you realize THAT YOU DON'T! Not by a long shot, because that's what deception is... a mind trick that lets you think you've got it all figured out. At least until everything unravels. This is a FANTASTIC first novel and I can't wait to see what stories Andrea Hurtt weaves next."

— DEB WHITE- STAFF WRITER FOR *NERDS AND BEYOND*

INCOMPLETE

RAZOR'S EDGE - BOOK THREE

ANDREA HURTT

PIECE OF PIE PUBLISHING

Piece Of Pie Publishing

11923 NE Sumner ST Ste 826515

Portland, OR 97220-9601

Cover by: MGDesigns

Editor: C.A. Szarek

To Bella -
Thank you for being my co-author. I'm sorry I have to remove all your suggestions, most people don't speak cat.

To M-
I couldn't ask for a better lady to give me inspiration for Mia. You are such an amazing woman. I am so honored to know you.

To BSB -
Who knew that a misinterpreted comment on a show could change someone's life. It took me ten years to find my way back to you, but I am so glad I did. Thank you for inspiring me.

CHAPTER 1

"I can't believe I'm doing this alone!" Mia was on her way to see *Next Step*, her favorite band. The group had been popular during her childhood and reunited a few years earlier.

They were now on a US tour with another famous pop band, *Razor's Edge*. They'd share the stage for a night of boy band overload. There was no opening act, no lead; both bands would have equal time on the stage.

There were two concert venues within reasonable driving distance from her house, and she *had* to go. It'd been a rough summer, and the last time she'd seen her boys was years ago.

Mia wished they were alone; she wasn't a fan of *Razor's Edge*, but she'd suck it up to see *Next Step*.

The plan was simple; drive to Minneapolis and attend the first concert, then follow the buses, in case they stopped for waffles, which they were notorious for doing.

Once she got to Kansas City, she'd get a hotel and sleep for a few hours before attending the second concert, then drive back home.

Fate had stepped in while she was speeding along Interstate 35. Her phone pinged the sound for Twitter. She'd it set to notify her when certain people she followed posted, like all the boys in *Next Step*.

"Hey, Siri," Mia said, activating her phone assistant. "Read me that message."

"Eddie Williams and Nathan Hunter of *Next Step* to throw after-party in Minneapolis."

"Are you kidding me?" she screamed at the windshield. Eddie and Nathan were two of the gorgeous men from her childhood. She'd had posters of them, and the others in the band, plastered on her walls as a teenager. "Hey, Siri. Can you get me tickets to the *Next Step* after-party in Minneapolis?"

"There are three levels of tickets," the computer-voice said.

Her heart raced.

"The VIP for Eddie's party is already sold out. Would you like information on Nathan's VIP party?"

Her stomach lurched when Siri stated the cost. The tickets were twice as much as her concert ticket. Mia had settled for general admission and hoped she'd get to see the guys from a distance.

Downtown Minneapolis gave her a little trouble. It wasn't easy finding the venue, and traffic was backed up because of a baseball game, making it even harder to tell where she needed to go.

Mia finally found a parking garage and walked a few blocks to the arena. It was a slow walk, despite her excitement. She'd sprained her ankle just two nights before the concert, so she was stuck with an ace bandage and flip-flops because she refused to use crutches.

She found her 6th-row seat. When the light show started, she really got excited. At first, Mia dreaded when it was *Razor's Edge's* turn to perform but actually enjoyed it. Unlike most concerts, where one band performed at a time, this concert mixed it up with one band singing a song or two then relinquishing the stage to the other and trading off, and also both singing a mix of songs together.

It was a fun way to keep all the fans interested. She appreciated the ten talented men from two different bands, singing their hearts out for the fans that adored them. She tried to look at *Razor's Edge* with new eyes. Had she been missing out on something all the years she'd scorned them? Perhaps Mia had.

The five men on stage, Blaze, Nick, Dwaine, Thomas, and Scott, were extremely talented. Attractive. She caught herself singing along to songs she'd heard on the radio but hadn't recognized they were *Razor's Edge*.

When Joe from *Next Step* took center stage, her cheeks flushed with heat. There was something about his voice and those baby blues that made a girl melt.

Joe was the youngest member of *Next Step* and the closest to her age. She'd always held a special place in her heart for Joe.

Then... there was Eddie.

The bad-boy from *Next Step*, Eddie's singing voice was nothing special, but his presence on stage made up for all of that. He tore off his black tank top in the middle of a song, exposing his rock-hard abs, sending the crowd into a frenzy.

There was so much testosterone in the air that night, it was hard for a girl to keep calm.

Mia felt like she was fourteen again with her hormones raging.

♭♪♩

ON STAGE, with the lights shining and stage rotating, Scott had brief glimpses of the bands adoring fans. He kept his eyes moving, rarely landing in one spot.

While singing *Unfinished*, the lights landed just right on the face of a woman, the only one not singing along with the song.

He couldn't take his eyes off her.

She wasn't a great beauty; most wouldn't notice her in a crowd. But… there was something that drew him to her.

They finished their song and headed backstage, allowing *Next Step* the full attention of the crowd.

Scott turned to the closest bandmate, Nick. "Man, it finally happened."

"What did?"

"I saw a girl in the crowd."

"Dude, how many years have we been performing together? There's like twenty thousand women out there. If you haven't seen them before, you need your eyes checked, old man."

Scott sighed. "It's not like that. There was something about this *one* woman. Look for yourself when we go back out there. Stage right, about five or six rows back, near the end of the runway. She's a dirty blonde, wearing a red dress."

"Dirty, huh? My kind of girl," Nick teased.

"Ugh!" He just shook his head. His friend and bandmate pretended to be a bad-boy, but he had an amazing wife who kept him grounded.

When they took the stage again, Scott watched her, taking more time than the simple glance before.

She was slender and tall, taller than the girls on either side of her. Her honey-colored hair was coiffed up on her head. Her retro makeup, with dark eyeliner and bright cherry lips, was visible from the stage. She wore a red top with a V-Neck but he couldn't tell if it was a dress.

She really wasn't his type. He usually went for women with darker skin and hair.

Scott tried to keep his focus on the blonde woman, hoping to make eye contact.

The choreography didn't make that easy since he was moving all around the stage, but it seemed like every time he looked at her, her eyes were cast in Eddie's direction.

The final song played and all ten of them were lifted in the air on the stage platforms at either end of the runway.

Scott had a perfect view of the crowd below.

They reached the highest point and his eyes locked with the woman in red for a brief moment.

To his great dismay, her attention drifted away, and the show was over.

"I'll never see her again," he whispered.

When Mia exited the arena, she needed to head back to her car for another dose of Advil and to freshen up her make-up. If there was any chance of seeing Eddie or Joe, she wanted to look her best, and the concert had gotten her all sweaty.

She took her time going to the bar the party was at. It would probably take a while for the guys to get there, and she didn't want to sit around waiting.

The streets of Minneapolis were busy with foot traffic from all the fans leaving the concert and the baseball game.

Mia passed several bars before she finally stood outside the doors for will-call tickets at *Club Epic*. She worked her way up to Jimmy, Eddie's promoter.

"Hey, Jimmy! Good to see you again. It's been years. Are there any tickets for Eddie's VIP Still available?"

A hint of recognition flashed across his eyes, but it passed as fast as it came. "No. Eddie is sold out. Nathan still has VIP tickets left; they're an extra $125 each."

Her face rushed with heat. "Thank you, but that's a little out of my budget. I'll stick with general admission." Mia didn't want to tell him Nathan was her least favorite from *Next Step*. He was too cocky.

The promoter turned to the girl beside him, who was helping with the check-in. "She gets a black wristband."

"Thank you," Mia said. She slowly went into the club, hoping to find a place to sit.

The music blared. Dwaine and Nick, from *Razor's Edge,* were DJ-ing.

She sighed, and disappointment washed over her. Mia had come here for *Next Step*, not the other band. She wanted to spend the rest of the evening with her boys. *Not* the band that she'd shunned years ago.

A slow breath escaped her lips. She was trying to open her heart up to them. The concert had been really good, and she couldn't help but admit, they were amazing performers.

Her animosity had been so strong for so long that it was hard to overcome.

Mia slowly took in the scene. The lights flashed as they moved around, spotlights hitting people's faces, illuminating the joy and excitement in the room.

The club had two levels. The main floor had the DJ booth on the back wall and a bar on each sidewall. At the front of the club was a set of stairs that started at the base of the dance floor and led to the second. Halfway up the stairs, it split in two, creating a Y on the staircase.

There was no seating on the main level where the dance floor was, so she took the stairs to the right and headed up. Her foot ached, and she searched for somewhere to sit.

The upper level was rather empty. There was a black couch up against the far wall where only two girls were sitting.

"Do you mind if I rest here for a minute?"

The ladies nodded and went back to their own conversation.

Relief made her release a breath, the moment she was off her feet. It didn't last long. Mia's muscles pulsed, bringing her injury back to the forefront.

I really need to ice my ankle a bit.

Reluctantly, Mia gave up her seat and trudged to the bar. She waited for her turn when a man moved up to stand beside her.

The bartender quickly finished with the woman he'd been

helping and promptly acknowledged the man instead of her.

Etiquette had always been important to Mia, and although she didn't want to be rude, she'd been standing there longer and her foot demanded service. "Excuse me, but I do believe I am next." She didn't look at the man beside her.

The bartender glanced at the guy like he needed his approval.

"Of course. Ladies first." A sultry voice responded.

The bartender looked back at her, his expression displayed slight annoyance.

"Can I get a cup of ice, a shot of Pineapple Whipped Vodka, and a bottle of water?" Mia ignored the jerk's attitude. It was her turn.

The bartender moved to get her order, and she finally spared a glimpse for the man standing beside her.

She probably should apologize. "I'm sorry. I didn't mean to be so rude." Mia gazed into the sweet blue eyes of Nick Ford, the baby of *Razor's Edge*. She expected her heart to skip a beat or something.

He was famous, after all. He did nothing for her, despite his stunning good looks.

Nick smiled. "It's cool."

The bartender returned with her drinks.

She pulled her card out to pay, but the band member signaled for the server to put the drinks on his tab.

"Oh, you don't have to do that," she said.

"It's my pleasure." Nick turned to the bartender. "Can I get a Corona?"

Mia struggled to get a hold of the bottle of water, shot glass, and the plastic cup.

Nick grabbed his beer and her cup of ice. "So, where to?" he asked.

"Oh, um," it caught her off guard. "I was sitting over there." She pointed with the shot in her hand to the now-empty couch.

Nick went with her toward the furniture, and Dwaine was

still spinning tunes below them. The Latin Lover called to his bandmate on the microphone, yelling for him to get his ass back to the DJ booth.

The *Razor's Edge* guy ignored him and set the ice on the small table beside the couch. "So what did you do?" he asked, indicating her foot.

"I sprained it a couple of nights ago."

"And you came to the concert and the after-party?" Those baby blues went wide.

"I couldn't very well miss *Next Step*. I've been a fan since I was fourteen."

"Ouch!" Nick laughed.

Dwaine paged him again, his voice echoing through the speakers and over the music.

He sighed. "I better go. Are you gonna be here for a while?"

What's happening?

She nodded.

The guy smiled and headed back to the DJ booth.

What am I doing? Fraternizing with the enemy?

Mia had added the after-party to her plans because of *Next Step*.

What was becoming of her disdain for *Razor's Edge*?

She picked up the shot and downed it. It burned the back of her throat, and it zinged sweetly on her tongue.

Do you think he'll come back?

Mia tilted her head side to side with each conflicting thought.

Will it bother you if he did?

No.

Scott had made the nasty comment about *Next Step*. The rest of the guys weren't part of it.

I shouldn't have held it against them all.

Next Step chose to go on tour with them. They didn't have an issue with the other band.

Maybe she should let it go. It was probably past time.

CHAPTER 2

Mia iced her foot for a while, before considering a little exploring. She traversed the upstairs to figure out what the roped-off sections of the bar were.

She was the only one with a black wristband.

This is the general admission area. Why does everyone else have yellow ones?

She didn't let the ache in her ankle stop her from heading across the club to one of the only bouncers she could find. "Sorry to bother you."

The man before her was giant.

"Can you tell me why my wristband differs from everyone else?" Mia held up her hand. The black plastic dangled from her wrist.

The guy crossed his thick arms, and the massive muscles in his biceps went rock hard. "The black wristbands are for Nathan's exclusive VIP party. Through there." He pointed to the roped-off area behind him.

"Thank you."

He removed the velvet rope so she could enter.

Her heart played havoc against her chest. She might not be a big fan of Nathan's, but the other band members would probably venture into the area for access to the bar.

At least she hoped they would.

Mia's bandage was coming loose, and she needed to re-wrap it. She borrowed the corner of a full couch to fix it. She'd just unwrapped it and rolled the bandage when she heard a masculine voice above her.

"Oh, no! Sweetheart! What happened?"

Tall, dark and handsome, Nathan Hunter from *Next Step* stood in front of her. His chocolate eyes shone with pity, and he knelt next to her.

She was grateful he wasn't Eddie or Joe; the two men from the band she'd fanned over for years. Speaking with Nathan was easy. "Don't laugh. I slipped on a spilled drink at a bar a few nights ago."

"Damn. That sucks."

"You're tellin' me."

He offered his hand.

She took it, and surprise washed over her when he pulled it to his lips, placing a soft kiss on her knuckles.

He looked back up into her eyes. "I'm Nathan."

"Mia." She could barely get out. She was grateful she hadn't blurted something stupid, like, "I know."

"What a beautiful name."

Before she could answer, Eddie called his name from the DJ booth.

Nathan stepped up to the railing and looked over.

"Man, stop macking on all the pretty ladies and get down here," Eddie hollered.

He laughed and turned back to her. "If you'll excuse me, it seems I'm being paged."

Mia got dirty looks from the girls she'd crowded on the couch, so she sought out another seat. She wouldn't last much longer, if she had to stay on her feet all night.

She found a recently deserted table on the balcony that over-looked the stage. Unfortunately, it was two steps down from where she'd been.

Stairs were the hardest to handle with her bum ankle. She held onto the railing and managed to get down, although her poor cup of ice was crushed as she went.

The table was high-top, with three bar stools around it.

Mia sat in the chair on the right so she could rest her left ankle on the middle one. She could hear Nick singing, *"Overheated"* from his album.

Eddie rapped along, while Nick sang the melody, pumping up the energy in the crowd.

Nathan and Eddie were up next, singing *"Selfish"*.

She noticed a small postcard-size flyer on the table. She picked it up.

"A NIGHT WITH NICK AND DWAINE."

It seemed the after-party had always been a *Razor's Edge* event. Nathan and Eddie had crashed it, she figured. That was why tickets had gone on sale only that morning.

The dull ache in her foot pushed forward. It would be a good time to ice her ankle again.

Mia unrolled most of the bandage, leaving just enough fabric to cover the bare skin. She propped her foot up, twisting her body, so she could hold the cup of ice to the worst part, the outside of her ankle, where it'd turned eight shades of ugly.

"That doesn't look comfortable," a silky voice commented on her awkward position.

"It's not," she replied, glancing up. "But it's better than nothing." She did a double-take.

One of the guys from *Razor's Edge* was before her.

Not just *any* guy.

Scott Ralston.

She almost fell out of her chair.

Mia despised him with a passion.

Yet he stood before her, wearing a sincere smile.

She'd been a *Next Step* fan since she was fourteen years old. Her heart belonged to that band, and the five guys that made it what it was.

She'd fought for them when the media had tried to belittle them for their talent, calling them lip syncers when they weren't. She'd been the outcast in high school when they were no longer 'cool'.

They'd been her teenage world.

When the TV channel, MusicOne, had done a documentary on the massive success, fall, and rebirth of *Next Step*, they'd interviewed the new top pop bands and how the former had affected their success.

Scott Ralston had talked shit about *her* band.

Mia had turned her back on him then. And *Razor's Edge*. The only reason she'd come to the concert was *Next Step*. She hadn't expected to enjoy the 'enemy'.

She tried to keep from clenching her fists, so she tugged at her skirt to cover the red petticoat that was peeking out from her full circle skirt.

"So, what'd you do to it?" Scott asked.

"Sprained it." She didn't really want to talk to him, but her mother's voice in the back of her head was telling her to be polite.

"You sure it's just a sprain? It looks pretty bad." His brows furrowed in obvious concern.

It'd been years since that documentary, and Mia needed to let it go. But could she?

She took a deep, calming breath before speaking. "The doctor originally thought it was broken, but the X-rays didn't show any fractures." She looked back down at her cup, which was crushing, as she tried to mold it to the shape of her foot.

"Well, that's good at least. Let me see if there's something I can do to make you a little more comfortable."

She didn't answer, and he walked over to the bar.

Don't come back.

The shot Mia had taken was just enough alcohol to fuel her fire. She didn't care how sweet he was acting.

He'd always been a pompous ass.

Scott returned with a bag of ice in one hand, and a glass of red wine in the other. He took the cup of ice from her and gently placed the bag on her foot, arranging it so it covered the top and side of her ankle. He then sat in the empty chair. "You don't mind if I sit with you for a while, do you?"

His voice was kind, but she couldn't stop thinking about how much his past words had hurt.

"Sure, Next Step *paved the way. But at what cost? We had to crawl out of the rubble they left behind. They made it so much harder for bands that came after them. Our lives would have been better without them."*

Without *Next Step*, there would've been no *Razor's Edge*. The man who'd brought the five boys together who made up *Razor's Edge* had literally decided he could make another band like *Next Step,* only better.

Next Step had saved her life. They'd kept her from dark places when everything had been against her.

Hearing Scott say the world would've been better without her favorite band had crushed Mia, and any respect she'd had for him.

Now there she was, years later, and *the* Scott Ralston was sitting across from her, treating her kindly.

"I don't care if you sit." She tried to keep the venom from her voice.

"Thank you." The enemy boy-bander scanned the crowd.

"No one's coming to join us, if that's what you're looking for. I came solo, that's why I am sitting alone," Mia said.

Scott scoffed. "Why would you come alone when you're obviously injured?"

"I wasn't going to miss this, no matter what."

"Yeah, it seems like a pretty cool party."

She caught his gaze, and he fidgeted on the chair, then looked around the room again.

She could feel his nerves.

Good. He should be uncomfortable.

Sucking back a sigh, Mia scolded herself. There would be no way he'd ever know the reasons for her animosity. *She* should be the better person. She made herself extend her hand. "I'm Mia, by the way."

His grip was stronger than she'd expected.

"Scott. But I'm sure you already knew that."

She nodded. Could do little else, since she was sitting with the man she'd hated for years.

"Dude! I didn't know you were here. I thought it was just Dwaine and Nicky's party we were crashing," Eddie said joyfully, as he joined them. "I was on my way to get something to drink."

"What's up?"

The men gripped hands and bumped shoulders.

Shock stole Mia's breath.

How did this happen? Guys from both bands, right here? Was she dreaming?

This wasn't something that happened every day.

"Well, I couldn't leave you guys with all these beautiful women," Scott said.

"You certainly have found yourself one right here. Maybe I should just stay here all night." Eddie winked in her direction.

Her heart fluttered. Could she be so lucky?

She couldn't help but stare at the man that'd been such a big part of her life.

Eddie Williams, with his buzzed brown hair and eyes with hints of gold and chocolate, could sweep any girl off her feet. He had a raw sexual appeal and used it to his advantage.

Mia's ice pack shifted and she reached over to fix it. Her movements brought Eddie's attention to her.

"What do we have here?" He pointed to her foot.

"I jacked up my ankle Wednesday night when I went out for my birthday."

"Did June Cleaver trip on her apron strings while baking cookies?" he teased, clearly making reference to her dress style and pearls.

"Hey, you never said it was your birthday!" Scott's voice shot up in an obvious complaint.

"It was a couple of days ago. I slipped on a spilled drink and hit the concrete floor. I wasn't even wearing heels at the time. It hurt like a bitch, but I wasn't gonna miss this party, no matter what."

Eddie glanced at Scott and smiled. "So, are you gonna ask Betty Crocker to dance or can I?"

Mia's chest tightened. What she wouldn't give to be in Eddie William's arms. She'd dreamed of that so many times.

He was a breath away, and there was nothing she could do.

She tapped her fantasy man's arm. "Did you forget something? My ankle's messed up. No dancing for me."

The *Next Step* member smiled a wicked grin. "Where there's a will, there's a way." He extended his hand.

She shifted in her seat to be able to fully face him.

"Trust me." Eddie smiled seductively.

Mia frowned but stood up to follow him. She hobbled up the steps, clutching him for balance.

The boy bander moved a few feet from the steps. He slid his hands around her waist.

She lifted her foot slightly so he wouldn't hit it, and he took the hint, moving closer, wrapping a hand under her knee and hitching her leg up over his hip.

They quickly got into the rhythm of the sultry dance.

True to his word he protected her foot.

Their bump and grinding was very sexual, yet somehow innocent.

Mia felt like he was holding back. Had her foot not been injured, their dancing would have been so hot.

Eddie held her in a way that gave his body full access to hers, but he didn't take advantage of the situation.

Mia wished he would.

CHAPTER 3

S cott couldn't believe he was sitting there, watching his buddy dance with the woman he'd come to see. When Nick texted him that the girl from the concert was at the party...and alone...he'd *had* to come over.

Now she was getting hot and bothered with the *wrong* man.

He wished he had balls like Eddie, but no one had as much audacity as Eddie Williams did.

That was why he was so popular. It wasn't the silk of his voice, like he was known for, or the goofiness Thomas eluded.

Raw sexuality. None of the other men in the two bands had it like Eddie. It'd never bothered Scott.

Until now.

When the song ended, Eddie helped Mia back into her chair. He leaned into her. "I need to go sing, June Bug. But I'll be back for you." He stood up to his full six-foot height and turned to his buddy. "Hey, Scott? Are you coming down to hang with us?"

Scott looked longingly at Mia. He wanted to talk to her, but he couldn't help but see the joy in her eyes when she'd danced with Eddie. He didn't want to compete with his friend over a woman he'd never see again.

When he looked at his bandmate's expression, there was nothing there. Eddie had danced with Mia for her, to give *her* an experience. Not for himself.

Scott took a long sip from his wine, giving him time to think before he answered.

Screw it! We'll never see her again, and I just want to talk to her.

He set down his glass and replied. "No, thank you. I came out to chill tonight. I'll just hang with this lovely lady for a while."

"I don't blame you, I'd stay here with her, too, if I could." Eddie turned to face the blonde. "It was so good meeting you, June Bug. Until next time." He flipped a half-assed salute and took off for the steps.

Scott was used to having the fans fawn over him. All the guys were. But...there was something about *her*.

Mia wasn't acting all crazy, like some fans did.

He stared while they continued to sit at the table. Her eyes were everywhere but on *him*.

He was grateful, at first. It gave him a chance to study her, the delicate curve of her jawline, the rosy flush of color in her cheeks.

Damn, she has some serious eyelashes. And they're real!

He'd seen enough women with fake lashes in his line of work.

She picked up her drink, and he couldn't help but wet his lips at the sight of her mouth opening slightly to take in the top of the water bottle.

Scott shook his head to clear his thoughts. Now was not the time.

Why not? This is the perfect time.

She set down her drink and shifted her body, allowing her to look over the railing.

He followed her gaze to see Eddie arriving back on stage.

Damn it... I am Scott Ralston. The big brother of Razor's Edge. *Why isn't she flirting with me? I need to try harder. Maybe she's into one of my 'brothers'.*

"So, um, what is your favorite *Razor's Edge* song?" he prompted.

"I don't have one."

He stared. That was no help. "My favorite is, *I'll Be Your Shelter.*"

"Never heard it," Mia replied, taking another sip of her water.

How can she never have heard of it? Every RE fan knows that song.

Then it hit him.

Maybe she's a Next Step *fan?*

He let out a deep sigh before turning to look at Mia. "So... Is Eddie your favorite?" he asked, trying to determine where he stood.

"Excuse me?"

"It's just that you kept looking at him all night, during the show, so I assumed he's your favorite," Scott continued.

"I met him once, about two years ago, on my birthday. I just wanted to see if he remembered me. But when we danced, he showed no sign of recognizing me."

Scott smiled inside. He still had hope.

"Wait...what do you mean you saw me looking at him all night? You were watching me?"

Scott tried to keep the conversation on Eddie. "Not to sound cocky or anything, but is there a reason he'd remember you? They do meet a lot of people, every day, and you just said it was years ago." He watched her cheeks flush red.

"*Next Step* had just gotten back together, after splitting over fourteen years earlier. It was one of the very first shows on the Reunion Tour. I'd splurged and gone all out with the meet and greet and front row tickets for the Chicago Show. I wore a red shirt that said, *I'm Here For Eddie.* When he'd walked into the room, he made sure to have me by his side for the group photo. After the picture was taken, Eddie pulled me into his arms and kissed me like I'd never been kissed before. Mint and fireworks."

Her blush started in her cheeks and rushed up, tinting her ears, and into her hairline.

"So, it was something amazing." Scott tried to hide his disappointment.

"No. It was just a kiss."

"It must've been amazing for you to keep it in your mind."

"Just a kiss," Mia repeated.

He shifted in his chair to face her better. Without asking, he reached for her hand, resting beside her bottle of water, and placed his over it. He stared into her eyes for a moment, trying not to look at her lips.

She'd shared a kiss with Eddie two years ago, and she'd carried it with her.

What he wouldn't do to have a kiss like that, one she'd never forget. Her lips were calling to him like nothing he'd felt before.

He could imagine enticing her mouth to part so he could taste her.

Their kiss could be fire, filled with heat they didn't know they could share.

Scott began softly rubbing his thumb across the sensitive skin of her hand, bringing her full attention to him.

Mia pulled back in a hurry, her cheeks flushing crimson again.

"I'm sorry, I, um…" He couldn't finish his sentence, his eyes on her lower lip, half-expecting it to be swollen.

Nathan's voice sounded from down in the DJ booth, talking to the fans, trying to introduce what he wanted to do next. "How many of you wanted to hear *Mental State* at the concert tonight? It's my favorite joint *Next Step/Razor's Edge* song. There wasn't time to add it to the program."

The fans start screaming; indicating they too wished it had been a part of the already amazing show.

It was one of the songs the bands had recorded together but had yet to be performed live.

"Let's see how many of us I can get down here to sing it for you. Dwaine? Where'd you go? Nick? Get your butt back here."

Eddie chimed in, "Scott, you too."

"Scott's here?" Nathan inquired. "He never comes to after-parties."

Scott reluctantly stood up. Now that the fans knew he was there, they'd come looking for him. He glanced at Mia.

He didn't want to be on stage. They'd spent the evening performing in front of twenty thousand people, and he was done.

It'd been a year since he'd come back to the band after taking time off, but he was still struggling with readjusting to the limelight. After-parties were harder than concerts. They were far more intimate.

The only reason he had come to the party was to look for the woman from row six.

He'd found her.

Scott wasn't going to let go.

"Scott. Nick. Don't make me send Rolls to come to get you," Nathan called from the stage.

Rolls was Nathan and Eddie's personal bodyguard. He was a big man who was not afraid to use his "rolls" of muscles to drag someone's ass around.

He sighed, and reached for Mia. "Come on, beautiful. I'm not letting you outta my sight."

"Where are we going?"

"On stage," he said, practically dragging her down the steps.

"What? No!"

Scott could feel her hesitation in the way she pulled back from him, yet it wasn't enough to make him stop continuing forward.

"I really don't want to be in the spotlight."

"Just wait here, on the side of the stage," he said. He stepped toward the huddled band members. Although it was singing over full tracks, they wanted it to sound good, and selected who would sing the missing guys' parts.

The five of them stood in a line; Dwaine, Nathan, Eddie, Nick, and Scott when they began to sing the song. The guys fed off each other, picking up dance moves.

When Scott hit the chorus, he walked over to Mia, who was still hiding in the shadows. He took her hand and backed up slowly, pulling her out into the light.

The other guys followed his lead, pulling girls from the crowd to bring up with them.

MIA WAS grateful the other men had brought women up to join them, too. She couldn't have handled being the only girl on stage.

When the song ended, all the chosen girls got hugs from the guys before returning to the crowd.

She took advantage of the others' exit and moved into the sea of hot bodies. She stared up at the dark-haired man from the crowd below.

Mia hated that her thoughts always went back to her first crush. She held a special place in her heart for Eddie, but as she stood there looking at Scott, she had to admit, he was very handsome.

Yes, being kissed by Eddie had been amazing, but it wasn't like she was the only girl he'd kissed that night.

While they'd been sitting at the table, she'd studied the enemy boy-bander. He'd seemed disappointed that she liked Eddie. She'd seen it in the way Scott's shoulders slumped slightly, and the tone in his voice had altered. She needed to get over her childish grudge.

His comment on the documentary hadn't been toward her, yet Mia had reacted as if it'd been a personal attack. There he was, a grown man and he'd chosen to talk to *her*.

She'd known what she needed to do.

For herself.

For Scott.

When she'd agreed to let him sit with her, it was only to see what would happen. Mia had expected him to be a jerk. She'd needed him to be the asshole she'd always assumed he was.

This nice guy act was throwing her off.

Could there be something more?

She tried to slip further into the crowd to blend in with the other women.

It wasn't that she hadn't enjoyed spending time with Scott, and was trying to change her opinion of him, but *this* was like a dream.

She wanted to keep it safe. If she stayed, it could shift, like dreams did, into a nightmare.

Mia stayed to the side, just in his view, but far enough away to make her feel like any other fan.

The night began to wind down, and the members of *Razor's Edge* that were present; Dwaine, Nick, and Scott, sang a song from their first album, *Designs of Love*, one of the few Mia was familiar with.

The bridge of the song began to peak, and Scott moved to the very edge of the stage. He surprised her by jumping off the stage, rushing through the crowd to reach her, then pulling her into him.

Her hands landed on his chest, as she tried to steady herself, trying to keep off her left foot. She could feel his heart pounding, and her hands warmed from the heat of his skin.

Without warning, Scott leaned down and kissed her softly.

Mia's ankle didn't hurt anymore. Her injured foot went into the air behind her like a romantic foot pop.

People hooted and hollered, of both happy, and those that were jealous, but she didn't care.

His tongue probed gently, causing her body temperature to rise.

It took Mia a moment to catch her breath when Scott finally let her go.

She'd come to Minneapolis to see Eddie and Joe and the other guys from *Next Step*.

Yet, she ended up kissing the guy she didn't like.

Was it fate?

Or a sick joke?

The guys thanked everyone for coming, taking the time to sign some autographs as people left.

Mia slipped away to go back upstairs to get her purse left at the table. Luckily, no one had bothered her things.

♪♫

"DAMN, WHERE'D SHE GO?" Scott looked around. The room was chaotic, as staff guided people out the door, but the girls in the club were still trying to move up to see the guys one last time.

"I don't know. You look around down here, and I'll check upstairs," Nick said.

Dwaine turned toward him, his expression concerned, since Scott was craning his neck in various ways. "What's up, Scott? Is everything all right?"

"The girl Eddie was dancing with earlier, the one I brought on stage; well, I can't find her," Scott said, and continued to scan the crowd.

"So?" Dwaine asked.

"I...I want to say goodnight." the older bandmate said, lamely.

"Oh, man! You're not falling for a fan are you?" Dwaine teased.

"No! She's... different. I wanted to say goodbye."

"Uh, huh. Sure you did."

"What're you talking about? You married the president of your fan club."

"Point taken. So what does she look like?" his friend asked.

"Did you see the girl in the red dress?" he asked, thinking that would be the easiest way to start.

"Yeah. Couldn't miss her. Who goes to an after-party dressed as a 50's housewife?"

"Yeah, that's her."

Scott's phone buzzed in his pocket, taking his attention. He pulled it out. He'd gotten a text from Nick.

Found her. Upstairs.

Scott headed for the stairs.

Dwaine followed.

They strode up to Mia, side-by-side.

"What? You thought you could leave without saying good-bye?" Scott asked.

"No. I thought I'd better get my purse before they throw me out of here."

Scott gestured to his buddy. "Dwaine. This is Mia. Mia, this is Dwaine."

They shook hands.

"It's nice to meet you," she said.

"Likewise." He laughed as did an obvious once-over of her full outfit. "Okay, I have to ask, why would you wear a dress like this to an after-party?"

Mia's cheeks flushed red like earlier.

Scott had to admit that he liked the color on her pretty face. It made her seem even more innocent than her clothing choice did.

"I just started a photography business, doing WWII style pin-up photos. I thought it would be fun to go to the concert as a model. I was hoping it would get me noticed." She brightened again and Dwaine chuckled.

"Well, it worked! No one can miss you. You look like June Cleaver from '*Leave it to Beaver.*'"

"Eddie called me that earlier tonight."

His buddy pulled his phone from his back pocket. He looked

at the screen. "Speaking of Eddie... He wants to know where we are. He said he needs us." Dwaine walked away.

Scott couldn't help himself; he pulled Mia close, being mindful of her foot. "Don't go too far. I need to talk to you before we leave."

MIA'S HEART TWISTED. Here she was, in Scott Ralston's arms. For the second time.

A man she had hated for almost half her life. How had her night ended up like this?

She'd come to Minneapolis to see *Next Step*. Then ended up with *Razor's Edge*.

That seemed to make it all the more thrilling.

Security was very pushy about getting everyone out of the club.

Mia limped extra, trying to buy a little more time. She even stopped and pretended to fix her bandage. She kept looking toward the stage for the guys, but they were nowhere to be found.

When a tall, big security guy began pushing to get her out the door, she didn't have a choice but to leave.

Mia stepped out into the hot sticky night and reality came back.

She was back to being like every other girl in the club. Fans there to see the big stars.She sighed.

Well, it was fun while it lasted.

What if there could be more?

Would I want it?

I don't know.

CHAPTER 4

B *uzz. Buzz. Buzz.*
    Mia grumbled as her alarm went off. She'd arrived in Kansas City at eleven a.m. She was grateful she was an Elite member of Crowne Plaza's rewards program, because they allowed her to check in early. She'd immediately passed out, but not before setting an alarm.

She grumbled at the obtrusive sound but got up.

After a nice, hot shower, Mia blow-dried her thick hair and set it in hot rollers. She ironed her dress before styling her locks and applying makeup in her vintage look.

Tonight, she was even more excited.

Once in the venue, she found her third row seat. She was on stage left at the end of the runway. The house lights went down, and the screams went up.

Mia stood. The curtain dropped, and ten guys stepped out onto the main stage to sing.

They moved halfway up the shaft, but not far enough that anyone could see her in the crowd. She hoped, anyway.

Her heart hammered so hard her knees wobbled. She might

need to sit down. This time, she really listened to the other band, looking at them with new eyes.

Damn, they really looked good.

The song ended, and *Next Step* moved off the stage so the *Razor's Edge* could sing.

Once again, they only made it halfway down the shaft.

The anticipation was torture.

The song ended, and the guys switched.

Next Step moved swiftly down the shaft, three remaining at various places on the stage, but Nathan and Eddie moved to the head.

Nathan sang to no one in particular when he moved to go from one side of the stage to the other.

Eddie came to the other side and stood next to Nathan as the other three members moved up the stage to end up at the head.

Her childhood heartthrob looked down and made eye contact with Mia.

He smiled in obvious recognition and blew her a kiss.

Heat rushed her face, as if she was still that fourteen-year-old girl. Her heart raced, but attention from Eddie just now didn't even touched the organ's condition when Scott had kissed her at the club.

She was so confused.

The song was over too soon, and *Razor's Edge* was sneaking up the small stairs on the side of the stage, just a few feet from her.

The lights were low, so there was no way the men could see her.

But she could see them.

Mia couldn't take her eyes off Scott.

He was looking stage-right, where she'd been sitting the night before.

Scott moved to the very end of the stage in their choreography but still wasn't looking in her direction.

Dwaine, however, was. A mischievous grin spread across his face when he made eye contact with her.

She quickly put a finger to her lips in a shushing motion. She didn't want him to say anything.

He nodded.

Next Step took the stage again, and Mia found herself eager for the other band to return.

That was so different from the night before.

The guys finished, and *Razor's Edge* came back out.

They all had on white satin suits.

Mia just wanted to run her hands over Scott's chest, to feel the soft fabric against his hard muscles. Heat threatened to consume her.

She didn't want to feel like this.

She wanted to go back to hating him.

The stagehands put four bar stools on the runway, placing a long-stemmed rose on the seat.

When the song ended, Blaze started talking about needing to find some girls.

Nick had already found a sweet little girl, who looked around six, to bring on stage.

Blaze was looking for a girl up the shaft, and Dwaine turned to Scott.

"Bro. I have found the perfect girl for you," Dwain said into the microphone.

Scott just looked at him, as if confused.

"But you gotta look that way." He pointed away from Mia. "Cover your eyes. No peeking."

Scott made a show of covering his eyes, and laughter rippled through the captive audience.

Dwaine darted off for the stairs on the side of the stage, close to Mia. He pointed, letting the security know who he wanted.

If her heart had been pounding before, that was nothing

compared to the jackhammer she had in her chest now. This was it...

She carefully slid out from her row, trying not to get her foot hurt.

Dwaine took her hand, leading straight over to where Scott stood. "Okay, you can look now."

The crinkle on Scott's brow revealed his wariness.

Scott turned slowly, with obvious reluctance. His shock was very clear. It quickly flipped into a smile that lit his whole face.

He embraced Mia, lifting her off the ground as he swung her around. He set her back on her feet and led her to the stool to sit like the other girls.

I can't believe I am here!

What did that hug mean?

Is he happy to see me?

Razor's Edge was singing *Let Me Mend Your Broken Heart*, and Scott took the rose, sliding it down Mia's cheek.

She'd seen the other fans sitting up here before, and they always blushed. None of *them* knew his lips were soft, like the rose petals caressing her sensitive skin.

Scott played with her, leaning backward over her knees like she was dipping him.

Toward the end of the song, the guys walked their girls to the head of the stage and sang on bended knee.

When the boys stood back up, and the song ended, reality came crashing back.

Mia was in front of twenty-thousand screaming fans being serenaded by a man she'd once hated.

Once?

Do I still hate him?

No.

She rushed off stage as fast as her sprained ankle would take her.

Next Step took the limelight when it got close to the end of the show.

Mia couldn't believe how distracted she was, barely paying attention to the band she loved, her mind floating back to Scott.

After the concert, she waited for the floor to clear more, so she didn't have to worry about getting stepped on in the stampede of exiting women. She got nervous when a big buff guy in a black security shirt approached her. She stood, expecting him to yell at her to leave.

"You Mia?" he asked in a deep baritone voice.

"I am."

"You're supposed to come with me." He walked toward the head of the stage. He got a few feet away and looked back.

Mia hadn't moved. She couldn't make her feet work.

"Mr. Ralston sent me to get you," he said.

What?

Curiosity got the best of her. She let him lead her through security to the backstage area.

He took her to a hallway of closed doors. Each door had a laminated paper taped to it. The top of each paper read NS-RE and underneath said what the room was for.

They labeled the first door, *Quiet Room*. The following was *Next Step*.

The man passed that door and stopped in front of another one, *Razor's Edge*.

He knocked hard.

It took a moment, but when it opened, Thomas was standing there, still dressed in a KC Chiefs jersey, their last costume change. "Sorry, we didn't order any Girl Scout cookies." He pretended to close the door on her, then yanked it back open. "Or would it be a Betty Crocker cake?" He laughed when he stepped back to allow her into the room, the door left open behind them.

"Really? That's what you're gonna go with? Baked good?" Mia

tried to keep a serious expression but could feel the smile creeping on her lips.

"At least it's not another stripper. Hope would kill me if Eddie pulled that stunt again. Good to see you again, Mia. Please come in," Nick said.

She took in the room, from the ugly gray leather couch in the center of the room, to the folding table up against the wall, littered with the remnants of a six-foot sub and potato chips. There was a rack of clothing to the right, and a door that read "locker room."

What am I doing here?

"It's a good thing you're blonde," she heard from behind.

Mia faced Blaze, the dark, brooding, tattooed member of the band, as he walked into the room. "Excuse me?" she squeaked.

He chuckled, deep in his stomach. "My wife, she's not really the jealous type, but always gets nervous when she hears there're ladies in our dressing room."

"What does that have to do with my hair color, which isn't blonde?" Mia jutted her shoulders back in defense.

"Sure looks blonde to me. But…I digress. No offense. I just don't like blondes. So Grace won't be pissed."

"Good for your wife? And my hair is sandy, not blonde."

Her argument with Blaze ended abruptly.

Warm lips met with the bare skin of her exposed shoulder.

She whirled, her hand raised to inflict pain, but stopped just before striking Scott.

"Why would you slap me?" he teased.

"I didn't think it would be you."

He cocked his head to one side, his eyebrow hiked up. "Who else should be kissing you?"

"Eddie, maybe…" She regretted it the moment the words left her lips.

Scott looked down.

"I'm sorry. I shouldn't have said that."

He met her eyes, but he seemed suddenly shy. "Eddie remembers you," he said.

As much as she wanted her childhood crush to recall their kiss, it didn't seem to matter anymore.

Why?

"We were talking this afternoon, after the huddle and he came up to me. 'Chicago' he said. I must've shown my confusion because he continued, 'That girl, June Bug. I kissed her in Chicago. That's why she looked familiar.' I just nodded and walked away."

Mia smiled at his obvious jealousy.

He didn't see it; he was gazing at the other side of the room.

I don't believe in love at first sight.

Why is this happening?

It's not love at first sight, dumbass. You've known his face for years.

Maybe I should give him a chance?

Duh.

She shook her head to clear her argumentative thoughts.

Mia put her hand on his cheek to force him to look at her. "I don't care."

It didn't matter anymore.

She could *feel* it.

She should be confused about it, but it all seemed *right*.

Without giving him a warning, Mia wrapped the hand that'd been on his face, around to the nape of his neck and pulled him to her.

Their lips met awkwardly.

He hadn't been expecting it, so it didn't go like she'd hoped.

Scott smiled at her gesture, wrapped his arms around her waist, and kissed her deeply.

"You could have Eddie if you wanted," he said when they broke apart.

"I don't want Eddie. I want you. Scott Ralston. No titles, no fame. Just you."

Not caring that there were people in the room, she let Scott envelope her, their bodies fitting so perfectly together.

She kissed him with a passion from deep in her stomach, until her legs wobbled.

Mia was just a girl, and he was just a guy.

When they finally came apart to catch their breath, Nick tapped Scott on the shoulder.

"Come on, bro. We need to get to the club before it closes."

"Shit!"

She glanced between the two guys. "Another after-party?"

"Technically, only Dwaine and Nick have to go. Blaze spends his nights with his wife and Thomas is, well, I think he is too shy to mingle. I usually head back to my bus and read. But tonight... I have an excuse to party."

CHAPTER 5

Club VooDoo, in the Power and Light District, was the hottest place to be in Kansas City.

The men climbed out of the shuttle, heading into the club first.

Mia had suggested the boys go into the club without her so it didn't start gossip.

She followed a security man through a different door; he handed her an all-access lanyard.

She held it up, looking at the picture of the five guys in black and white. Bright red letters said the date, the venue, and *All Access*, in all caps.

The club was packed with *Razor's Edge* fans. The room was a basic rectangle shape, with one long bar on the left as and the proscenium stage at the head.

Nick and Dwaine had already taken the stage.

Mia scanned the area for Scott but didn't see him.

The large security guy that'd walked her in was still behind her. He leaned his in. "Off to the right side, they blocked an area for *All Access* people only. Your lanyard will get you in there."

She nodded, and he took off to follow his other charges. Mia took a few steps toward the area then stopped.

I need to get some ice first. I haven't iced my foot since yesterday.

It was throbbing, and it was likely swelling all over again.

In the back corner, away from the stage lights, Scott sat at a table with three extra chairs. He smiled at Mia, limping toward him.

He stood, holding her chair and helping her get comfortable.

She propped her foot up, and set the bag of ice on the swollen appendage.

Nick took a break from DJ'ing and joined them at the table. "Hey, lady," he said Mia. "Are you having fun?"

"I guess," she replied, unenthusiastically. She hadn't intended on her voice reflecting how she felt, but it happened.

The pain in her foot was getting the best of her.

He laughed. "Tell me how you really feel."

"Sorry, I'm just exhausted," she continued, feeling the need to explain.

"I bet," Scott said. "How did you get here so fast?"

"Drove," she replied, then yawned.

"You didn't drive all night, did you?" Nick asked, concern lacing his voice.

"Couldn't miss your next show, could I?" Mia smiled sweetly.

"Have you had any sleep at all?" Scott asked.

"Yeah, I slept for a few hours at the hotel before the show."

There was loud screaming coming from the fans.

"Let's get this party started," Eddie called from the stage.

Eddie, Nathan, and Joe had shown up to crash the party. Again.

They sang a few *Next Step* songs and a few of their own singles.

Eddie and Joe walked up to the table.

"Well, if it isn't June Bug," Eddie said. "I didn't expect to see you again so soon."

"I'm confused," Joe said.

"Last night, she was in Minneapolis. I call her June Bug because she's dressed like June Cleaver."

"June Bug? I like it," Joe said, tapping his chin with his index finger. "So does that mean you have dinner on the table, and greet your husband with a kiss and a martini when he comes home?"

"Um, no," Mia said, "First, I'm not married..."

"Really?" Joe pulled out the chair to sit but obviously hadn't spotted her bag of ice. He jumped back out of the seat. "Holy crap!" He picked up the obtrusive item with his thumb and fore-finger, moving it to the table. "That's the first time I got goosed by a bag of ice. Why's it here, anyway?"

Scott laughed.

Mia was sure her face was eight shades of red from embar-rassment.

"It's for my foot," she explained, holding her ankle out in front of him.

"Ooh, what d'ya do?"

"Sprained it."

"Mind if I take a look?"

She shook her head.

The guy from her childhood heartthrob band sat in the chair, the ice now gone, and placed her ankle on his lap. He carefully unwrapped the ace bandage, resting her calf across his leg.

Nerves made her tummy flutter, but Joe's fingers were gentle.

He pushed on the first pressure point.

Mia sucked her breath through her teeth as white-hot discomfort shot up her shin.

"Sorry," Joe said, but his fingers kept gently probing.

Soon she was putty in his hands. The pain eased, at least for now.

"Come on, Joe, we gotta go," Eddie said.

Nathan had a microphone in hand, and he was gesturing for them to return to the stage.

Joe gently set her foot on the chair and stood.

"How'd you do that?" she asked, breathless.

He smiled down. "A little trick I learned on *Dancing With The Stars*."

Eddie waved his fingers in front of Mia's face. "Good to see you again, June Bug!"

Joe laughed. "Eddie, I swear you could come up with a nickname for everyone."

"That's not true. Only the ones I've met."

He smiled and led them back to the stage.

BEFORE LONG, the crowd had grown massive, and the music was dance-worthy. It was only songs by the two bands.

Mia was resting comfortably when one of the only *Razor's Edge* tracks she knew, from their first album, played. She was excited she was familiar with one tune playing that night. "Oh! I love this song!"

Scott jumped out of his seat. "Would you like to dance?"

His excitement at her joy made her really think hard about risking herself with him.

Could I have been wrong all these years?

Mia looked at Scott.

Really *looked* at him.

She'd never noticed his eyes were green. All these years, she'd thought they were brown.

His hair was so dark brown it looked black. It was long enough to spike on top, but in the back, there was only enough to run her fingers through. He had a strong jaw, and the thin goatee was attractive, drawing her eyes to his lips.

Mia wanted to kiss those lips again and again.

She'd never wanted someone like this before. Her body was

calling out for him; singing with beautiful vibrations over her sensitive skin.

She took his hand, and he helped her to her feet.

She quickly learned just how good bad boys could be. This was not something she could've imagined experiencing.

Especially with a member of *Razor's Edge*.

Scott leaned in, sliding his hand up her calf, along the outside, until he reached the knee. He lifted her leg, resting it on the curve of his lower back.

Her red petticoat was trying to peek out.

Scott slowly grinded with Mia, pushing the hem of her dress up higher on her hip, so that more of the red showed.

She couldn't help but picture them both naked, making love to the rhythm of the music. Her body fit perfectly up against his; being a tall lady only helped form their puzzle.

Mia looked down at her feet, heat sufficing her face, and other unmentionable places.

She felt it. The stirring he caused.

He was undoing years of dislike, without even knowing her negative feelings.

Dancing made her feel like he could've taken her right there, and she wouldn't have minded.

Scott met her eyes, his smoldering. He brought his lips close to her ear. "Do you feel it?" he asked, speaking words of the song playing.

The heat of his breath sent shivers into her hairline.

He brought his lips to the bare skin of her neck before pulling her in tighter. His kiss was full of fire, the heat filled them both.

Their lips parted, and they both drew in deep breaths, but before they could connect again, Mia was yanked away.

A fan grabbed the back of her dress and pulled.

She wobbled on her foot, since Scott still had the other one. Mia landed hard, and agony shot everywhere—her butt, her upper thighs, and her bum ankle, making her eyes sting.

Girls instantly surrounded Scott, leaving Mia on the floor.

Pain, confusion, then anger washed over her, but she couldn't get up on her own. Her foot was worse for the wear, it felt twice its size.

The huge bouncer she'd met earlier was quickly on them, pulling the girls off of Scott, and forcing space between them.

Scott grabbed Mia's hand and lifted her to her feet.

Security stayed in tow, as he led her to a secure door, and into a small room.

There were two couches, and he took her to one. "You okay?"

"Yeah, just embarrassed," she whispered and sat to get off the double-injured ankle.

"You have nothing to be embarrassed about. You didn't start it," Scott said. His voice was laced with venom.

She shook her head, looking down at her hands. She wasn't worried about her fall; not really. Mia was usually all about etiquette, and she'd just been making out with him in public.

This is totally not me.

Scott placed a warm hand on her cheek and sighed. "I'm glad you weren't hurt. But…" Crimson crept into his cheeks, up to the tips of his ears.

"But?"

"That kiss was worth it."

She smiled. Couldn't help it. Her face warmed from it, and the sweet tension building in her stomach.

"There's that beautiful smile." He leaned down, kissing it away.

She melted at his touch.

How can I be this attracted to someone I'm supposed to hate?

Behind the closed door, they could still hear what was happening on stage.

Joe had slowed things down a little. He was singing a love song from his solo record.

Nathan joined in harmony with him.

Scott stood and offered her his hand, pulling Mia in close, their bodies pressing together in that perfect fit again.

She pressed her cheek against his and sang along softly in his ear. Joe's song was one of her favorites.

"You have a good voice," Scott said.

Her cheeks heated all over again. "You know he wrote this song for 9/11," she said, trying to change the subject.

Scott studied her. "Mia, will you stay with me tonight?" he asked, unabashed.

It took her off guard, this honest question.

He looked so lonely; it broke her heart.

"Yes."

Scott kissed her tenderly.

The song ended, and they headed back to the main area of the bar.

"Hey, you're walking better," he said.

"I don't know what Joe did, but it really helped."

"Joe?" He pointed to the man on stage.

"He said it was something he picked up on *Dancing With The Stars*. I don't know if he got hurt or someone he knew, but it feels better."

Nick came bounding over to them. "Hey, bro. The guys want to do *Mental State*, again. You game?"

Scott hesitated, but Mia squeezed his hand.

"Please, sing for me! I love your voice." She batted her eyelashes.

"Ah, how could you say no to that?" the blond man teased, trying to convince his friend.

Scott sighed. "Okay, but only for you."

She smiled, and he followed Nick up on stage.

The guys sang *Mental State* as their closing song.

They all signed autographs, and talked to the fans before the bouncers cleared the crowd out.

Mia felt weird having one of the *Razor's Edge* security team standing with her, waiting for Scott to return.

She understood his need to protect her, after the fan incident, but she kept looking down at her feet awkwardly, not sure where else to land her eyes.

They left through the back door and got into the shuttle.

Surprise washed over Mia when they pulled up to the Crowne Plaza. "How did you know I was staying here?" she asked Scott.

"I didn't. But that's helpful. Now it will be easier to get your luggage." He pulled a key card out of his pocket.

"You got a room?"

"Yeah. I sent my man over there to book it and take my things. When I knew I wanted to ask you to stay with me... I didn't want to presume we'd be in your room."

"I... um..." She didn't know what else to say.

Scott saved her by taking her hand and helping her out of the van. "What's your room number?"

"2675."

They rode the elevator to the twenty-sixth floor.

Mia paused at the door and spared Scott a nervous glance.

"You don't have to stay with me if you don't want to," he said.

She smiled and put her key in the door.

WHY DIDN'T I pack a sexy nighty?

Mia was so glad Scott had waited outside, because her movements were frantic as she dug through her stuff.

What's he gonna think when I show up in my mickey mouse pajamas?

She laughed.

If you're planning on 'sleeping with him,' he'll have you stripped down to nothing before he'll even notice what you were wearing.

Mia stuck her head out the door. "Do you just want me to meet you back at your room, after I have a shower?"

He smiled. "You can take a shower in my room. I promise not to look." Scott added, "much," as a whisper under his breath.

"Okay, gimme a sec." She shut the door, and dashed to the bathroom to brush her teeth before pulling together a few things she'd need to get her through the night.

Scott knocked on the door. "Is everything okay?" he asked, probably because she was taking a while.

Mia opened the door and took a step out. She had a few things in her arms, including her Mickey Mouse pajamas.

He touched the hem of her pajama pants. "Mickey Mouse? Really?"

For the hundredth time that night, her cheeks burned. "Yeah. I'm a Disney Dork," she said, trying to make a joke; more for herself than Scott. The moment it slipped past her lips, she wished she hadn't. Hadn't he worked at Disney before joining *Razor's Edge?*

What was up with her?

This was not the first time this trip she'd said something she didn't mean to. She couldn't make eye contact, as she tried to change the subject. "So what room are you in?"

"It's down there a little further, but on the same floor." He took her hand, leading her a few more doors down and across the hall.

Mia was nervous as she followed Scott into his room. Her palms were sweating and she could hear the rush of blood pushing through her veins. Her heart was working overtime

He sat in the middle of the king-sized bed, then laid back, stretching his arms above his head before he tucked them under his head.

She stood awkwardly by the bathroom. What was she supposed to do? She needed a shower but was afraid he'd walk in on her. On purpose?

Scott gave her a look, which turned into a double take. He popped off the bed and came to her.

Mia held her breath as he ran his hands up and down her arms.

"Baby, what's wrong? You look like you're afraid I'll eat you."

She swallowed. What could she say? She felt like a silly schoolgirl.

"Mia?"

She finally met his eyes. "It's nothing. I just..." she didn't want to continue, worried about how he'd handle this. Would he think there was something wrong with her, that at her age she still hadn't had sex?

He pulled her over to the bed and sat her down, then took a seat facing her.

"It's obviously not *nothing*. I know you haven't known me very long, but you can trust me." Scott made air quotes when he said, 'nothing'.

Mia whispered the words she didn't want to say. "I'm a virgin." She looked down at her hands in her lap, restlessness bubbled up from her tummy. She wanted to bolt back to her room.

Scott took one of her hands and brought it to his lips. His facial hair tickled her delicate skin. "Mia, I didn't ask you to stay with me tonight just so I could have sex with you."

She met his very green eyes again.

He stared deep into hers, and it made her belly flutter for a different reason. She couldn't look away.

"Not that I'd object to it." He smiled, teasing her, "But I asked you here because you make me feel comfortable. Like whoever I am, it's okay to just be myself with you. I know we'll be moving on with the tour, and you have a life to go back to but I want to spend every minute I can with you."

Mia was still hesitant. Could she believe him? He was a hot

guy, after all. "So you don't mind if we don't..." She wrung her fingers over her lap.

He laughed. "If someday you're ready and I'm lucky enough to be that guy, it would be an honor. But I'd never pressure you."

She smiled, more relieved than she'd ever admit.

"Now, go get your shower so I can enjoy holding you for as long as possible."

Mia took an extra-long time under the hot water. She shaved her legs and brushed her teeth again.

While the water rushed over her body, she made the decision that *this* was the right time.

Scott didn't want to pressure her, which made her want to do it all the more.

She couldn't believe that she wanted to share something so special with someone she'd hated for so long.

How did I get here?

He had no clue about her past feelings. *He* had nothing to prove to her, yet he'd treated her so kindly.

There was definitely more to this man than she'd ever given him credit for.

Mia left her clothes in the bathroom and walked out in nothing but a small towel that barely covered her.

Much to her disappointment, Scott was fast asleep.

He had the covers up over his hips, but his chest was bare.

Still feeling that inner boldness, she only put on her underwear. She climbed into the bed and reached over to shut off the light.

CHAPTER 6

M ia awoke to a big surprise.

Scott's warm bare chest was up against her naked back. He had one arm resting across her, his hand gently holding the breast that touched against the mattress. His *Good Morning America* pressed against her lower back.

She'd been resolved the night before to lose her virginity, but now, in the morning, with his erection firm against her, it hit Mia how ready she *wasn't*. She quickly got out of bed and dressed in her Mickey Mouse pajamas. Mia gathered her stuff and headed for her room. She'd snuck out, but she couldn't help it. She'd apologize later.

An hour later, she stood in front of the bathroom mirror, fully dressed in a pair of tight-fitting light-colored jeans, her black flip-flops, and a white halter top that had a beaded diamond in the middle.

She'd already finished her makeup, and she had curlers in her hair; Scott could show up any time, so she wanted to get ready fast.

A knock sounded and she dashed to the door. It was Nick, not Scott.

"Wanna get lunch?" he asked.

"Uh…" Mia peered around him, but didn't see her tall, dark and handsome beau.

"He's gonna meet us down there."

"All right. Can you give me just a moment?" She pulled her curlers out as fast as she could to hurry and join Nick.

All she could think about as she wretched them from her hair was how hurt Scott must be. If the situation was reversed, her feelings would be hurt.

No. She'd be pissed.

When she stepped into the hall and her door shut, her heart jumped.

She'd left Scott alone, no note, but having his bandmate come get her for lunch had her stomach in knots.

"So, uh, why are we here?" she asked while they sat at the restaurant waiting for Scott.

"Lunch, or course."

"I get that, but why are we here, you and I?"

"Scott called and asked if I'd go get you and see if you wanted to have lunch with us. That's all," Nick said.

She glanced at him, trying to judge his expression. He didn't look shrewd or suspicious. But he did have a lift to his left brow.

He's hiding something.

What? No.

Then why is he here, and not Scott?

The waitress brought two glasses of sweet tea, breaking her internal debate.

"Why didn't he just come to me, instead of sending you?"

Nick shrugged, then picked up his drink and took a gulp. "Yuck! They don't know what real sweet tea is! Have you ever had real sweet tea?"

"I don't know. Why did he send you, Nickolas Ford?"

"Jeez, using my name and all. I don't know why he sent me,

maybe he thought you needed a blond like yourself to brighten your day. I don't know."

The rumble of Mia's stomach shifted the weight in the room and sent them both into laughter. "I'm so sorry! I haven't eaten since... um..." She cocked her head to one side, trying to recall her last meal. "I think it was the chicken biscuit yesterday morning before I checked into the hotel."

"We need to feed you, then. Scott will understand. Speaking of, it shouldn't be taking this long." Nick sounded...worried. "Why don't you order an appetizer, and I'll go check on him." He vacated his chair and headed out on swift feet.

She played with the straw in her drink, twirling it around before finally taking a sip.

Nick was right. This wasn't real sweet tea.

She flagged down the waitress and had her replace the tea with lemonade.

Mia smiled when the two guys walked up a moment later.

Scott looked like he had something going on, but his face relaxed when he looked at her. He pulled his chair close to hers, leaned down and kissed her so gently, almost timidly.

The waitress was back the moment he sat.

They didn't get to talk much; they were too busy eating.

After lunch, as they all piled into the elevator, Nick spoke. "So, Mia, what is the chance of you coming to Tulsa for tonight's show?"

She frowned.

"That is a great idea! Can I have one more night?" Scott piped in.

"I'd love to, but I don't have tickets or a hotel reservation, and I gotta get home to my pets."

"Tickets aren't a problem. We get comp tickets for each show, and you'd go the VIP route."

Mia beamed.

"The hotel isn't a problem, either," Scott said. "We have the next day off so they already have hotels lined up for each of us."

The elevator door opened, and they all stepped out.

"I have nothing to wear, this is my last clean outfit. It's for driving home in." She really wanted to go, but should be realistic.

Scott smiled. "That 50s dress?" he said. "And that smokin' red petticoat?"

"Yeah, no... I wore them to the Minneapolis show and the after-party. I gotta clean them before I wear them again."

"Not a problem," Scott said. "We have a team that does all the clothing. Although we have multiples of each outfit, they wash each night. Can you imagine the smell?" he teased, fanning under his nose.

"But all the buses and semi's have already left... right?" Mia asked.

"Oh, yeah. But we could get them cleaned during the show for you to wear to the after-party."

"Another after-party?"

"We have one in almost every city. It gets exhausting. But with you there..." he teased again.

They slowly walked down the hallway toward Mia's room, making plans.

"Where's your phone?" Scott asked.

Mia pulled it out of her back pocket and unlocked the screen before he took it. She heard his phone make a buzzing noise from his pocket.

"There, I sent myself a text, so we have each other's numbers. I don't know why I didn't do that sooner. That way we can keep in touch, in case you get separated from the bus."

After a quick kiss, they split up to go to their rooms and pack.

Soon enough, she sat in her car, waiting for Scott to text, singing to Nathan's CD she'd bought. Her cellphone finally indicated a message.

. . .

SCOTT: *Hey, baby. Are you ready? We are on the buses, just waiting for you.*

MIA: *Ready. I'll meet you on the corner.*

WITHIN MINUTES, she was circling the block around the *Sprint Center*, waiting for the buses to leave.

When they finally started moving, she stayed behind them.

The next four hours went by with little happening.

Mia wished she could hear Scott's voice.

As if he'd read her thoughts, her phone rang.

She glanced at her screen on the console and saw it was him. So grateful she had bluetooth, she answered the call through the car speakers.

"Hey, baby. I just needed to hear your voice."

Heat rushed her face, and she smiled, even though she was alone. "I was just thinking the same thing. We're almost to Tulsa, in case you didn't know."

"Not a clue. I normally just sleep while the bus gets me to the next place. Half the time, I don't even know where we're going until we're there."

"Must be nice," she said, wishing it was that easy for her. It'd take her days to recover from her lack of sleep. "So, what happens next?" Mia was worried a little worried security might turn her away when she got to the venue.

"The bus driver already knows to inform them you are with us. They'll most likely put a sticker on the windshield to mark your car as part of the tour."

"Okay. Cool."

Just then, they exited the interstate.

"I better let you go and pay attention to driving in a town I don't know."

"Okay, baby. See you soon."

Mia held her breath as the security for the *BOK Center* asked for her ID. She pulled her driver's license out of her purse.

He wrote all her info on a clipboard. He stuck a temp sticker in the upper left corner of her windshield and signaled for her to move forward.

Her heart pounded while they directed her to park. She shut off the engine and sat there for a moment. What should she do now?

Mia's face seared when she mustered the courage to exit her car. She stood there, leaning against the inside of the door, and Scott emerged from the bus.

He looked around, like he was expecting someone other than her. His gaze landed on her, and his entire body language changed.

Scott walked with the fluidity of a predator, straight for her, his eyes locked on hers. He didn't stop at the car door; instead came around, pulled her to him until her breasts slammed into his hard chest.

He kissed her like he had at *Club Epic*.

It made her melt. Mia hoped he had this kind of passion later in the night, when they'd get to be alone again.

SCOTT COULD FEEL the smile creeping onto his face.

Things seem to be going well.

Even after the way his day had started, with an unwanted phone call, a reminder of a past he was trying to forget, he was still on a path that'd make a difference in everyone's lives.

I should tell Mia.

I can't keep it a secret much longer.

His friends had been telling him for so long that he needed to let go of his past or it would keep coming back to haunt him..

Scott was finally listening and had a reason to change.

He could only hope things kept going well.

I'm gonna tell her.

He spotted Nick out of the corner of his eye, heading inside.

Scott closed Mia's car door and offered his arm.

She slipped hers into the crook and they followed his bandmate.

"Mia," he said, when they were almost inside. "There's something I need to talk to you about."

Before he could say anything, Thomas ran from down the hall. Inches before he would've collided with them, he skidded to a halt, a big smile split his face. "Yeah! Betty Crocker is here!"

Mia couldn't stop laughing.

"Thomas, this is Mia. Mia, Thomas," Scott officially introduced them.

"So how was the drive?" Thomas asked.

"Not bad," she said.

"Our room is down here." Thomas gestured to Scott, then led them down the hall.

"If I leave, can I get back in?" Mia asked.

"I think so," Dwaine said, stepping up behind them.

"Why do you want to leave?" Scott asked. Disappointment swirled low in his stomach. He didn't want her to leave. Ever.

"You guys need to get ready. I'm sure it'd be interesting to watch you do vocal warm-ups, but I thought I could do a little shopping. I saw a mall right down the street. The show doesn't start for a couple of hours, and I'll be back long before that."

His heart skipped a beat, but he took a breath, telling himself to relax. He forced a smile. "Be safe." He kissed her forehead.

Sound check had been grueling. This was part of his daily life on the road, but all he could think about was his blonde beauty, and the dreaded conversation he needed to have with her. They'd barely been back in their dressing room when there was a sharp knock at the door.

His heart hammered when he opened the door to find his woman on the other side. "I was starting to wonder if you were coming back."

"Sorry, but wait 'til you see how good I'm gonna look. I promise it'll be worth it."

You're always worth it.

Scott pulled her into his arms and kissed her. "I just missed you," he whispered.

"May I use your bathroom to get ready?" Mia had to take a breath to get the words out.

He was proud he could take her breath away. "Of course. But don't take too long. We start in about twenty minutes."

She smiled and headed to the bathroom.

When she walked out into the dressing room, all the guys wolf-whistled and catcalled at her.

"Well, you guys sure know how to make a girl feel good." She beamed.

Scott couldn't help but notice the flush of color in her cheeks and the way she averted her eyes. It was clear to him that she was not used to compliments. And they came from the other guys, as well. He wasn't worried. Everyone but Thomas and himself had a wife. They were just being genuine. Scott came to her. "I can't wait to see how this looks under the stage lights."

He looked her up and down, admiring her dress. He watched her face burn even more, matching her petticoat.

"Yeah, I was going to talk to you about that."

"What d'you mean?"

"Tonight, please don't pick me to go onstage."

He couldn't hold back the hurt he felt. It was a great honor to be brought on stage.

Why doesn't she want me to-

"You chose me last night, and it was so special. I don't want to take that away from another fan."

"Betty, you sure do clean up good!" Thomas said, his voice raised. His cousin always seemed to be a little too intuitive.

"Scott, you may have to share her for a dance or two," Dwaine said.

"I don't have to worry too much about that. She's got a bad..." Scott glanced at her foot, her red heels, and paused. "Hey, wait! Where's your bandage, were you just faking it to get sympathy last night?"

She giggled, and shook her head, then walked around the couch, slipping off her shoe. She put her bruised foot on the table.

The guys lean in to examine it.

"She definitely did something to it," Thomas said.

"Joe fixed it last night. I don't know what he did, but it feels a lot better. Still not one hundred percent, but so much better."

A knock on the door paused their conversation.

"Ten minutes guys," the voice through the door said.

Scott leaned over, kissing her bare shoulder. "You better go find your seat," he said. Obvious reluctance laced his words.

"Should I come back here after the concert?"

"Wait 'til the floor's empty and come to the stairs by the head of the stage. I'll meet you underneath."

CHAPTER 7

The concert was amazing.

However, this time there was something different.

Something in the way Scott moved on stage, how he and the other members of both bands would occasionally glance in her way.

She'd never got so many winks, nods, and waves as she did that night from the ten men.

Does everybody know about me?

He did kiss me on stage in front of 20,000 people.

Oh, yeah.

The concert was over what seemed too quickly, and she headed backstage.

Scott and Nick met her under the stage.

Her beau took her hand and led her toward the *Razor's Edge* dressing room.

Mia waved her hand under her nose, teasingly. "I hope you plan on showering before the party, because you stink."

Nick laughed.

Scott winked. "I don't stink, I smell like roses."

She pulled him close. "Don't worry, I'll work you up to a sweat later," she said seductively into his ear.

He pulled back to look at her. His huge eyes betrayed that her boldness shocked him.

She smiled again, going for a wicked one.

They all laughed as they continued down the hall, chatting about the show.

Mia and Scott got there first.

Still holding hands, he opened the door with his empty hand.

They were laughing at each other about something Thomas had done during the show.

Scott brought Mia's knuckles to his lips. He looked up and froze.

Mia glanced at him, then back to a stunning woman.

Why had her new man gone so pale?

She was tall and dark-skinned, and her long black hair reached just past her mid-back. Her hands were perched on slim hips. She tapped one foot, black stiletto shoes made a loud click each time it hit the tiled floor. Her dark eyes filled with rage.

Nick almost ran into Scott. "Oh, shit," he whispered when he peered around them. "We should go this way." He tugged gently on Mia's free hand.

"What is going on?"

"Marissa's here." Nick pulled harder on her hand, but Mia couldn't move away; Scott still held tight to her other hand.

"Who?"

"She's Scott's ex-fiancée," Nick confessed. He scrunched up his face and rammed a hand through his hair, as if something in the room smelled bad.

Scott hadn't said a word. Just stared at the very attractive girl.

"His...what? *Fiancée?* You knew he had a girlfriend and you let me spend the night with him? Why didn't you tell me?" She turned her eyes back to the room, unsure she heard the 'ex' right, and went into full panic mode. Bile rose up to ravage her senses.

Her eyes filled with a brightness that threatened to blind her. She blinked to clear her sight.

How could he do this to me?

Marissa took a step toward Scott.

He dropped Mia's hand then and physically turned to look at her. "I am so sorry," he whispered. Then he whirled to face his fiancée. "I thought you weren't flying out to meet up with us until St. Louis?"

"After our conversation this morning, I thought it was clear I'd better come and make sure you didn't screw up again. I don't need the press to find out you did something stupid, right before we're supposed to get married," Marissa spat. Her eyes were narrowed to slits.

Even though they were no longer touching, Mia could feel Scott shrinking back. His whole demeanor changed like he was becoming a different person.

But Mia didn't care. He'd lied to her. That was all she could focus on.

She was pissed as all hell. Her blood felt like it was boiling in her body, bringing the anger in her out with fury. She spat her next words with all the hate for him she'd held on to for years.

"You're getting married?"

Scott turned to face her, his skin still white, he seemed to vibrate with intense emotion. He also looked like he was about to vomit.

"Mia, there's been a mis-".

"I almost gave my virginity to you!" She cut off his words, not caring what he thought he needed to say. That time was long gone. She reared back and slapped him as hard as she could. Her palm smarted, but she didn't care.

Mia pivoted on her good foot and headed out of the room. Scott couldn't follow her.

Marissa had stepped forward, and grabbed his arm. "You have a lot of explaining to do, Scott."

She heard the stunning woman's voice, even as she stormed down the hall. Mia bumped into Nick.

She still didn't care.

"I'm leaving. *Now.* How do I get out of here? Where is my car?" Her tears finally made their way down her cheeks, hot and sharp like her budding heartbreak.

How could Nick have been a part of this? He'd encouraged them, and had been by Scott's side every time they'd encountered each other.

Why? And to think, she considered she was falling in love with the tall, dark, man.

"Mia, wait," Nick called after her.

Down the hall, Eddie stepped out of the NS dressing room. His hair was still damp from a shower. He stepped into her path, and she couldn't get around him.

"Move," Mia ordered. She wanted to get to her car and as far away as she could.

Eddied shook his head. "No. Tell me what happened." His voice was even, calm.

"Eddie. Get the fuck out of my way." She was so angry, her tears flowed faster.

Without asking permission, her childhood crush pulled her into his arms while her sobs racked her. He let her cry for a minute before he backed up, and pulled her into his dressing room with him.

Mia let him, then slammed the door closed, letting Nick know it was for him. She wiped the tears away, hoping her mascara hadn't run and given her raccoon eyes, on top of the fact they were all red.

Eddie led her to a couch and sat her down, his arm still around her. "I take it you met Marissa?"

She shoved away. "You knew about her, too?" she cried.

"I knew you were a *Next Step* fan, but I assumed you at least knew some stuff about *Razor's Edge.*"

"No. I knew their names, and a song or two. I hated them for so long. I know nothing past the first album."

It was surreal to be sitting there with Eddie. This was a dream come true, having him hold her, comfort her as her heart broke. She had idolized him and the rest of the band for so long, it was hard to fathom how "normal" they were. But it wasn't quite how she would have dreamt it. She was falling for Scott. She hated to admit it. That was why it hurt so bad.

The man she'd crushed on for so long, wiped a tear from her cheek. "What d'you mean you hated them?"

"Please don't laugh. I'm not a stalker, just passionate."

"Mia, no one thinks you're a stalker. It seems you're quite the opposite, if you don't know about Marissa. Go on."

She took a deep breath and blew it out. Trying to get ready to share her story. "I've been a *Next Step* fan since day one."

Eddie quirked a cocky grin.

"I've always been proud to be a fan. Never once did I let people knock me down for something that meant the world to me. It's not just music and lyrics. It's each of you and what you bring to this world. It's the fans, the sisterhood we created. I'd do anything to keep it safe, protect it."

The bad boy of *Next Step* took her hand and held it with compassion.

Mia's heart skipped, but she made herself keep talking. "When MusicOne did the documentary about you guys, Scott said some rather unkind things about NS. They were still new to the music scene, but very popular. When I watched that, it broke my heart. You paved the way for them, and countless others! I just… I mean…" She sniffled back more tears. She was right in leaving, but it felt like she was being childish about the whole situation.

"You know, they took that entire interview with *Razor's Edge* out of context, right?"

"What?"

"I was there the day they filmed it. What aired, was not how it went down. *Razor's Edge*, Scott, all the guys, they're good friends to us. Hell, I was at Blaze's wedding. And Scott, he couldn't stop talking about you when we were doing sound-check in KC. So my question is... what are you really mad about?"

"Really?" Mia tried to get up from the couch.

He's a cheater!

She couldn't say the words aloud.

He put one hand on her thigh, keeping her in place. "Where do ya think you're going?'

"Home. I'm leaving. I don't want to be here anymore."

Eddie's handsome face sobered. "I don't think driving right now would be a good idea."

She sniffled. He was probably right. She could hardly see through her tears, and her foot was throbbing. She relaxed against the couch, defeated.

"You need to answer me. What're you most mad about? HIs bullshit comment on the documentary years ago, or Marissa showing up? You make it sound like you can't make up your mind. You can't really be this juvenile."

"I'd assumed I'd forgiven him for the past, when I met him in Minneapolis. It felt right to let go. You all were having fun on stage, playing with each other. You wouldn't do that if you held a grudge. I can't hold one if you don't."

"That's right."

"But he shouldn't have led me on if he had a fiancée. It's not cool. Do I give off the 'one-night-stand' groupie vibe?"

"No." Eddie shook his head. He seemed sincere. "But there's some-"

She cut him off. "Then what made him think this was okay?" Mia got all riled up again. The pain in her foot wasn't helping any. She reached down and rubbed at the worst of it.

"Hey, Joe. Come work your magic again," Eddie called. "Her pain is making it hard for her to actually listen to me."

Her whole body melted into the couch when the youngest member of the band massaged her foot.

Joe had always been the one she wished she'd marry someday. Yet, Mia didn't care that his hands were all over her, caressing her skin. Making her feel better.

Scott had changed her.

Forever.

She was numb now.

Nick hadn't really done her wrong.

It was *Scott* who was the cheater. Who'd made her cheat with him. Why would he encourage the two of them?

It made little sense.

Old boy's club?

Eddie moved to stand beside the armchair to her left. She watched him looking over at Nathan, who was leaning against the far wall, silently watching everything play out.

"I think she could use a drink to help her relax." Nathan finally spoke.

"Good idea," Eddie agreed. "Let's take her with us tonight."

"Where're you going?" Mia asked, and arched an eyebrow. She wanted to go home. She *should* go home.

"We have an afterparty to crash."

"No! I don't want to run into Scott," she confessed.

"First, it sounds like he has his hands full right now. I love those guys like my brothers, but sometimes even brothers can be little shits. Like not telling you beforehand about his little problem. Marissa. Second, you'd be hanging with us." He looked over at Nathan, who nodded in agreement. "Normally, I wouldn't be vindictive like this, but, come on. He snagged you in Minneapolis when I called dibs on you."

Mia threw her hands in the air. "Called dibs? What the hell is wrong with you guys? Do you think every girl at your concerts wants to screw you?"

He laughed, resting his hands on her shoulders. "Easy there, tiger. All I meant by that was, I wanted to hang out with you, chat with you, reminisce about that kiss in Chicago."

She gasped and shook her head, then pushed his arms off her. "You didn't even remember it was me until after the party was over and we all left. Otherwise, you would've had a little more grind when we were dancing."

He tipped her head back, looking at her upside down. "I promised I wouldn't hurt you, remember?"

That was true. Mia had to admit she remembered that. "I did buy this dress, and I don't feel like driving. Well, I can't drive, I'm such a mess. Fine, I'll go to the party. Afterward, I can get a hotel nearby and get a good night's sleep before I drive home. Besides, I could really use that drink."

As it turned out, Eddie had been right.

Scott was busy dealing with his own problems. Mia would stick with Mr. Abs.

"So, should we head over there?" Nathan asked.

Eddie walked around the couch and stuck his head out the door. The hallway was empty. "It's all clear." He dashed back to help Mia up.

She followed Nathan and Eddie out through the doors they had come in earlier in the day.

They walked right past Mia's car, to a white, unmarked shuttle.

CHAPTER 8

Mia took the hand Eddie offered her, walking her through the door.

They handed her an *All Access* lanyard.

He took the lead, and headed straight for the DJ booth.

Dwaine was spinning tunes when they walked up. He did a double-take at Eddie's arm around her waist.

She didn't miss the look on the guy's face, or when he pulled his phone out and quickly tapped out a text.

Mia imagined how the conversation went.

DWAINE: *WTF! Why is Scott's girl here with NS? And you're not here yet?*

NICK: *Can this night get any more fucked up?*

DWAINE: *What's going on?*

. . .

NICK: Marissa's here.

ONCE THEY GOT on the stage, Eddie left Mia with Nathan and walked to the edge of the stage. "How's everyone doing tonight?"

Screams erupted from the fans.

Without skipping a beat, he asked everyone to exit the VIP dance floor.

It was a roped off area in front of the stage that only those with the right colored wristbands got to party in.

The girls complained but did as asked.

Eddie went to the end of the stage, scanned the crowd until he found what he was looking for.

Mia followed his gaze.

Standing there all alone, stirring her drink with her straw, was a woman.

Eddie called, pointing to her so the security knew who he was looking at.

The security guy helped the girl move through the crowd, and into the VIP area.

While she stood there alone, Dwaine announced he was going to sing his new single, *Kisses*.

Eddie stepped off the stage, went to the girl, seducing her with his dance moves. He offered her his hand.

This girl was definitely not used to this kind of attention. She blushed as she reluctantly offered her hand in return.

He took it and pulled her close, whispering something in her ear before he spun her around the floor.

The look of joy on her face as they danced warmed Mia's heart. Here was a man that, no matter how famous he became, never forgot who got him here.

Her old heartthrob danced with several girls before he'd obviously spotted what Mia had—and was avoiding like the plague.

Scott and Nick stood on the balcony surveying the room.

Eddie climbed back on the stage. He hollered, "Who wants to hear Nathan's new single?"

Nathan was more than happy for a reason to sing. He went to the center stage as the music started.

Eddie grabbed Mia and walked her to the center of the stage, then left her standing by Nathan. He jumped off the stage in a very Patrick Swayze like move, and the girls in the audience screamed again. He whirled to offer his hands up to Mia.

Hiding a smirk and a frantic pulse, she stepped toward him.

His hands encircled her waist and Eddie lifted her, spinning her just before her feet touched the floor.

"Are you ready?" he asked, but didn't really give her a chance to answer. He spun her around with a grace and fluidity, making Mia look like she belonged on a professional dancing show.

He flipped her over, her skirts flying around, and the red petticoat made an appearance. Eddie moved so well, no one would've known she was so dizzy, and had no clue which foot was where at what point.

She was so wrapped up in trying to catch her breath from her vigorous dancing. It was all she could concentrate on.

Eddie helped her back up on the stage but didn't let go of her hand, spinning her around one more time.

She almost fell, but he caught her in his arms and laid her back, bending at the waist.

He leaned down to kiss her.

A distraction behind them had him throwing a glance over his shoulder before their mouths could touch.

Scott was there.

Mia's breath caught and her heart tripped for reasons other than dancing. Was she excited or angry?

"I believe her kisses are mine. Not yours," Scott said.

Eddie straightened, and pulled Mia up, stepping ever so slightly to the side so she could face at Scott.

Rage won over silly excitement to see him.

Scott Ralston did not own her.

That's it.

"My kisses belong to no one. Yours, on the other hand, belong to your fiancée," she bit out clenched teeth, and her eyes burned with tears. She gathered all her strength to hold them back.

Before they could win over her resolve, Mia ran down the steps on the side of the stage, and headed to the bathroom. Where neither of them could follow.

She pushed open the bathroom door and rushed to the sink. Nausea teased at the edges of her sensing, pushing forward. She needed to cool off, so she turned the knob and dampened her hands.

The cold water on her wrists helped. She brought her hands to the back of her neck and felt a trickle of water travel down her spine. It was good, and the tightness in her chest eased a little.

The door opened and three ladies came in.

One was a chestnut-haired beauty, who was at least six feet tall. Mia looked at her shoes to see if they were stripper heels. Nope. Just standard high heels.

The girls headed straight for her. Next to the Amazonian beauty was a petite woman with chocolate brown hair and hazel eyes. Her smile was inviting.

The third was an average height gal with cranberry red hair in a slinky black dress.

"Are you Mia?" the tall one asked.

"Yes…" She cocked her head to one side, part curious, part confused.

"Hi." The woman stuck out her hand. "I'm Grace. Nice to meet you."

Mia took her soft hand, and the other woman gave a gentle squeeze.

"I'm Blaze's wife."

She nodded. What the hell was going on?

"I'm Hope," the petite one said, also offering a handshake. "I'm

Nick's girl."

"Evey," the cranberry haired one said, giving Mia some room.

"We know it's a little unorthodox, but will you come out of the bathroom with us, please?"

There was something about the ladies that put Mia at ease. She really didn't want to see Scott, but they intrigued her.

Why would these women come to get her?

"Why should I?" she forced out, trying not to pout.

"They're just men. Normal human beings. And like anyone, they make mistakes. The only way to become a better person, is to learn from said mistakes. Please, give him a chance?"

"Why the hell should I do that? I owe nothing to him."

"No, you don't. But Mia, let him explain what happened. It sounds like there was some serious miscommunication. I'd love to give you all the details, but I think that is something only Scott has the right to do."

Mia let the woman's words sink in. Grace was right, even if she didn't want to admit it. So she stepped aside, allowing the other lady to lead them from out of the bathroom, Hope behind her.

She expected to see Nick, Dwaine, Eddie, and Nathan on the stage. Eddie and Nathan had left, and all five *Razor's Edge* men stood in a line.

Scott's eyes found them, as if he'd been waiting.

Mia didn't look at him, she couldn't, but her traitorous desire to stare was a battle she was quickly losing.

He tapped Dwaine's shoulder, then pointed toward them

Dwaine then cut the music.

Nick took a step toward the edge of the stage. "I know this is a little out of the ordinary, for all five of us to be at an afterparty. But we are all brothers, and we help each other out. It seems Scott made a mistake and royally screwed up."

Mia both put her hands on her hips and tapped one foot in irritation. Some grand show wasn't going to work.

Scott had a fiancée who wasn't Mia.

"So," Nick continued, "We're gonna sing a song. We need our friend, Mia, to come up on stage."

She shook her head.

No song would make this okay.

She turned to Grace. "Fuck this."

Hope blocked her, and Grace touched her arm before she could take one step.

"You can do this. For all of us. Please," Grace said.

Mia cast her eyes to the ceiling and forced a breath. She was curious, dammit. She glanced back at the guys on stage, and the girls who loved three of them.

They'd hinted at an 'us,' not just *him*—as in Scott—twice now.

She'd stay, but she wouldn't look at Scott.

There was nothing he could say to make things right.

Mia wouldn't be *that girl*.

"I bet they'll sing *Cheater*," she said sarcastically to the women.

Blaze met them at the top. He kissed his wife sweetly before she took off with Hope and Evey to stand in the back, in the shadows, where *Mia* wanted to be.

He offered his hand to her, and she reluctantly let him lead her to the center of the stage.

Blaze picked up a mic and the intro music began.

The five guys of *Razor's Edge* stood around her.

Thomas and Dwaine went to Mia's left side.

Nick and Blaze were on her right.

Scott stood off to the left.

Mia kept her eyes out straight, refusing to make eye contact with Scott, although her eyes would still disobey her resolve, occasionally wandering his way.

There is no denying the truth, Only an idiot walks away
I made a big mistake

My words were not the best, don't think before I speak
Talked about going separate ways.
I destroyed our love, I never meant to do you wrong
Now here I stand

SCOTT MOVED CLOSER, as if he was yearning to get eye contact with Mia.

She kept looking at either Thomas, or out into the crowd. Tears slipping down her cheeks, no matter how she tried to stifle them.

Asking for a little more
Please, baby, open up the door
I'd bleed and die for you, and I'm groveling to you
Please give me another chance
Baby, Open up the door
I couldn't see what's true, and I'm groveling to you

SCOTT SANG THE LEAD, Nick joined harmony.

If only you would face me, darling
See the man that I'm becoming
Know the fear that I am facing

SCOTT SANG the next line alone, reaching out to Mia, but she still ignored him.

Would you love me since I've changed

SCOTT SANG ALONE, getting down on one knee in front of Mia, reaching out to touch her.

It took everything inside her to remain still and not scoot away. They had a crowd, after all. The song thing wasn't working.

He still had a fiancée.

Asking for a little more
Please, baby, open up the door
I'd bleed and die for you, and I'm groveling to you
Please give me another chance
Baby, Open up the door
I couldn't see what's true, and I'm groveling to you

THEY ENDED THE SONG, Scott on his knees in front of her.

Mia still hadn't looked at him. She couldn't.

When he'd tried to take her hand during the song, she'd pulled away.

She finally made herself meet his gaze, and her gut twisted.

The agony in his deep green eyes was more than she could bear.

So real.

Mia was so angry, but she still cared for him.

What's wrong with me?

He's a cheater.

Not just *a cheater.*

He has a fiancée.

She was entitled to be pissed.

"You can just keep on groveling," Mia gritted out through clenched teeth before she walked off the stage. Angry tears fell as her heart broke all over again.

She headed straight for the bar. "A Dr. Pepper, please."

"Leaded or unleaded?" the bartender asked with a wink.

"Just ice," Mia said.

His expression was curious, his eyebrow arched, but handed over the soda without another word.

She glanced to the stairs she'd seen that led to the balcony upstairs. She needed to get as far away as she could.

The balcony was fairly empty, since most of the crowd was on the dance floor. Mia found a dark corner with a small round bar table and two stools. She sat and sighed deeply.

Did he really think he could make everything better by singing to me?

It only made her more angry.

He has a fiancée.

What does he need me for?

She was so busy dwelling in her own pity party; she startled when someone spoke.

Dwaine stood at the edge of Mia's table.

She jumped. Hadn't heard him come up.

"Can I join you?" He didn't wait for an answer; just pulled out the barstool and took a seat. "Don't worry. He has no idea I'm up here." He spared a glimpse toward the edge of the balcony. "You deserve the truth."

Mia scoffed. What Grace said spilled from her lips. "It should be coming from Scott."

She had the highest respect for Dwaine. He was a devoted performer, and a good friend to those in his life. He'd be honest with her, but if there was a truth to be told, it was only right to come from Scott.

Who was she kidding?

She wouldn't listen to Scott right now.

But she'd hear Dwaine out.

Scott didn't respect her. If he did, Marissa's name would've been the first thing out of his mouth.

"You know I'm married, right?" Dwaine didn't wait for her to answer. "I feel like I'm the most qualified to come talk to you, since I married a fan, and all."

Mia bit her tongue, wanting to snap about being considered a mere fan. It was insulting.

"I won't lie to you; we all pushed Scott to get rid of Marissa. She's not good for him. She continues to remind him of his flaws, instead of encouraging him to be a better man. I'm honestly worried she'll drive him to drink. Or worse." Dwaine paused as if, trying to judge Mia's reaction to his words. "As soon as Thomas, Blaze, and I heard about you, then met you, we knew *this—you—* was exactly what we all needed. I don't want to scare you, but we looked at you as our salvation. You were someone who'd love him for him, not his pedigree."

Mia's stomach knotted even tighter. She picked up her soda and drank it down fast. "I think I need another." Maybe the next one should be *leaded*, as the bartender had offered.

Dwaine looked down at her cup.

"It's just Dr. Pepper."

"I can get you another if you like?"

She nodded.

He left his seat and headed to the bar along the far-right wall, opposite of where their table. While he was away, she left her seat and moved to the railing.

Mia's eyes wandered of their own accord, looking for Scott. She didn't want to see him, yet her heart called out for him.

Dwaine wouldn't lie to her. However, she could never trust Scott again. She hated herself for the feelings she had for him.

CHAPTER 9

S cott caught sight of her looking away from where he stood, on the floor below, just off to the side of the bar.

She must not be able to see him.

The lights behind her lit up her dirty blonde hair, making strands look like molten gold.

His heart twisted in his chest.

Scott had finally found *the one* and lost her.

Dwaine walked up to her and offered her a drink.

She turned away from the balcony and headed back to her seat.

Scott was glad she wasn't alone.

He wished it was him she was with, not Dwaine.

He had to go talk to her.

She deserved to know the truth from *him*, as only he could tell it.

He quickly finished his red wine, set the empty glass on a nearby table before he headed to the stairs.

Scott walked up to the table, and glanced at his friend first.

They exchanged a nod.

Then, his bandmate got up from his seat, flashing Mia an

encouraging smile. "It was great talking to you. I really hope everything works out." Like a dad or big brother would do, he squeezed her hand.

"Thanks for sitting with me," she said before he walked away.

Scott took his seat, his heart thundering with the base from the music spinning below..

She lifted her cup, swirling the ice around. She wouldn't look at him.

Can I fix this?

He sat there for a moment, and neither of them broke the science.

"Mia, please," he whispered finally, his voice thick with emotion. "Look at me." He leaned in, his arms on the little table.

Her voice wavered. "I can't. If I look at you, I might start crying."

He took the hand Dwaine had just touched. "I wanted to tell you about her. I'd planned to tell you right before the show, but Thomas interrupted us. Then you took off shopping. And I...I chickened out," he finished, glancing down; he couldn't meet her eye.

Mia took a sip of her drink.

"All I ever meet is *Razor's Edge* fans. I met Marissa at a show I did at the *O2*. I'd concluded she was the best there was. Being with her was better than being alone. I never knew there was anything better. *She* was the reason I left the band. To start a family. But, she doesn't want kids. She only wants a famous husband, and all that comes with the band. So I came back to my brothers. I've tried to break it off several times, but like a bad penny, she keeps popping back up. Then, you came along."

"You lied to me," Mia said.

"I didn't lie. I just...omitted a few things."

"Omission is the same as lying," she snapped.

"Just so you know, she's gone now. I broke off all ties."

"You shouldn't have left her because of *me*." She couldn't put her finger on why, but she suddenly felt bad for the girl.

"I didn't. I've been trying to remove her from my life for a while. She's my ex-fiance. Has been for a while. Part of what I've been working on this tour is figuring things out for myself. Marissa was trying to make me perfect for *her*. The guys have been telling me that for a while. After I met you, I realized I could be myself with someone *and* be happy. After you left, I told her I'd had enough and she couldn't keep coming around. When I'd said we were done, weeks before I met you, she wouldn't let it sink in. She thought she could keep coming back and make it work."

Mia shook her head and met his eyes. "You were going to *marry* her. Spend the rest of your life with her. And now you're gonna break up with her because of some girl that showed up at your concert?" Anger was swirling in her eyes, heating her neck and cheeks.

"First off, you're not just *some* girl," his voice wavered with frustration and he took a breath. He was getting mad, too. "Have you ever had one of those days where you can't say what you are feeling because you are feeling too many things at once?"

Mia looked into his eyes again.

He could only hope she could see the frustration there. Scott could feel his shoulders were stiff, and he sat up straight.

She took a deep breath. "I'm sorry. Go ahead," she whispered.

Scott looked down at his hands again. "Every girl I've ever dated since we formed the band, has been all about dating a *Razor's Edge* member. It was about who I was, or the money they thought I had. Each show, it was the same thing. Girls were throwing themselves at me. Alcohol flowed like water. It was a never-ending party. But I felt so alone. It was like I was standing in a room full of people, and no one could hear me scream." He looked up, meeting her eyes again.

Mia's breath caught. "Since we're being honest, I really didn't pay much attention to *Razor's Edge*, so I don't know all the details."

Scott sighed, feeling a hint of relief. "I met Marissa a few years ago, at a *Razor's Edge* concert. She was beautiful and fun. Things were good in the beginning. She knew everything about me. Well, everything the media knows. Things seemed perfect. After I proposed and left the band, it changed. It was subtle at first. She started buying clothes for me I'd never wear, or want me to go to places I had no interest in. I thought she was just trying to expand my horizons, but the changes became more drastic, and if we'd argue she'd always throw it in my face I was once a secret alcoholic. The tabloids would have a field day with that news. I have always been the 'perfect boy' in the band. I still have a glass of wine every once in a while, but I stay away from hard liquor. I digress. Back to Marissa. I figured it was better to be with her than to be alone. When I brought up having kids, she freaked out. It's not marriage and a family she wanted, but security from me. Marissa loved nothing more than to sit on the couch in my theater room with a glass of wine and chat on the phone to her friends about her sugar daddy. The guys had been pointing this out for a while, but I didn't want to see it. Who *wants* to be alone? I was afraid that if I was, I'd go back to the bottle."

All he'd wanted in life was so basic, someone to love him *for* him.

After a subtle breath, she took his hands into hers.

He looked her deep into her eyes, trying to read her. "You can't help who you fall in love with," Scott said. "I never meant for this to happen. I keep breaking it off, but she keeps coming back. And I always take her back. In Tacoma, which was back in December, when I saw her last, I told her I was done, again. It's been six months. I thought she was gone for good. Then I saw you at the club when you were icing your foot, and a feeling came over me I'd never felt with *her*. Compassion. All I wanted to do was to make things better for you. You treated me like any other guy. I *wasn't* Scott Ralston from *Razor's Edge*. I was simply...Scott."

She smiled. "So...where do we go from here?"

"Can we go back to the way things were?" Scott asked.

Mia shook her head.

She crushed him.

His heart sank and he felt ill.

"We can't erase what's happened. But I would like to try again," she said, touching his cheek.

A tear escaped from the corner of his eye to trail down to get lost between Mia's fingertip.

"You'd do that? For me? A recovering alcoholic from *Razor's Edge?*"

"No. I'd do it for you, Scott Ralston. Just this guy I met at a bar."

He stood, moved to stand in front of her, and pulled her into a hug. "Thank you," Scott whispered in her ear, holding her, as if his life depended upon it. "Would you do me the honor of dancing with me?"

Mia nodded.

He took her just a few steps away from the little table and twirled her close to him.

One hand landed on his chest, searing him with her heat. She wrapped the other around his neck.

He started to slow dance with her.

"It's kinda hard to slow-dance to something this fast," she teased.

Scott pulled her a little closer. "Does it really matter?"

The balcony was mostly empty, so he had plenty of room to dance her around.

They both sang and laughed as they danced.

Scott pulled Mia so close, he could feel her heart beating through his shirt.

"Thank you."

"For what?" she whispered.

"For looking so stunning tonight." He lifted the hem of her skirt to reveal her red petticoat. He made a sexually charged growling noise.

They both laughed.

Then he was serious. "I'm sorry I hurt you. I won't do it again. I am groveling to you, asking for another chance." He went down on one knee to look up at her.

She leaned down and kissed him. "Let's get outta here."

He didn't hesitate.

The shuttle took Blaze, Dwaine, Scott, and Mia back to the *BOK Center* with plans to continue on to the hotel.

"Meet you guys back at the shuttle?" Dwaine asked.

Scott looked at Mia.

"I have to take my car," she said, apologizing.

"Give me just a moment, I gotta grab my bag. I'll ride with you." He kissed her cheek.

"I need to see if I can get my purse from Eddie's dressing room. I'll meet you at my car."

He watched her rush away, into the venue.

Although Dwaine needed nothing off the bus, he walked with Scott. "I'm glad things are working out for you and Mia."

"She's something special, isn't she?"

"Yes," his buddy agreed.

He was lost in thought while they walked to the bus.

"What is it?" Dwaine asked, climbing onto the bus behind him.

He sat on the couch, running his hands over his face and hair, coming to rest on his neck. When he finally looked up at his friend, worry creased Dwaine's brow.

The Latin Lover leaned against the counter. "Something is still eating at you. What's up?"

"She's a virgin," Scott confessed.

"Oh," he drawled, understanding touching his expression. "That's a big responsibility. You sure you're ready for that?"

"I don't know."

"Is she?"

"She says she is, but I don't know."

"Well, be sure. Sex changes everything," his bandmate said seriously.

"I know."

CHAPTER 10

M ia had butterflies in her stomach as she walked back to her car.

This is it.

After tonight, she'd no longer be a virgin.

Am I really ready for this?

She wasn't exactly saving herself; it'd just never felt right before.

She started the car to wait for Scott, and the radio blared to life. It was tuimdb.com

ned into a local station. Mia reached to switch it off, but the *Razor's Edge* song, *I'm Yours Tonight*, started. The words hit her—really hit her—for the first time.

> *My words could never be more true*
> *Though lost for so long in, inside they were*
> *Oh, yes they were*
> *It took some time to break them all through*
> *I hope you know I am right, this time*
> *I'm yours, Tonight*

I'm yours, always
The feeling's deep, you feel it too
Don't listen to what others are saying
I'm Yours Tonight

SCOTT NEEDED HER, but what was more surprising how much she needed him, too. She sang along to the words, her eyes closed, her head resting back on the seat. As the words exited her mouth, she meant each one.

Right as the song ended, Scott opened the passenger door to join Mia. He kissed her cheek and held her hand as they went to the hotel, the radio still playing.

They grabbed their bags, and Scott took her hand as they stepped into the elevator.

He pushed fourteen, the top floor.

Mia was so nervous she trembled.

He brought her hand up to his lips and placed a soft kiss on her knuckles.

Something within her tightened, then loosened, but she was warm all over. His touch calmed her, letting her know it was going to be all right.

Their eyes locked, and it made her breath catch. Scott's green eyes were filled with passion.

She was afraid hers showed fear, or at least revealed her nerves. Mia wasn't afraid to make love to him; she was looking forward to it. His body was made for those things. She was worried she wouldn't please him.

The metal doors creaked when they slid open.

She was a step just behind Scott. Still holding tight to his hand.

He flashed her a soft smile.

She melted.

Everything was going to be okay; she could tell by his smile.

Mia waited for him to open the door, but he turned to look at her instead.

His green gaze was intense. "You realize, once we enter this room, everything will change, right?"

She cocked her head to one side. "What d'you mean?"

He leaned back against the unopened door. "I can't explain it, but I just know it will. I want to make sure you know now, in case you want to change your mind."

Mia understood what he was saying. Once she had lost her virginity, everything was going to change.

She was ready to walk through the door.

She let go of the handle of her suitcase.

Scott's eyes went wide when Mia put her hands on the door, one on each side of his head.

She leaned in close, their lips almost touching, but not quite. Her body trembled with desire. "I know what I want. I want you to open this damned door."

Acknowledgement darted across his gaze. Without moving from her cage, he pulled the room key from his pocket. He offered it to her, saying without words that it had to be her decision, her action.

Mia placed the card in the slot and let the door open.

The room was beautiful, but her vision was on Scott and what burned in his eyes.

She had to break away from his gaze to turn back to the hallway for her suitcase. She pulled it into the room.

"Are you hungry?" Scott inquired and sat on the bed.

She was grateful he asked. She was starving, and it would give her a little time to get more comfortable with the situation. "Absolutely."

He picked up a menu he found next to the phone. "Room service was available until midnight, and it's almost two. I'm normally not one to use my fame to get what I want, but this seems like a good time to try it."

Mia laughed and pulled her suitcase in further, dropping it by the dresser. She leaned down to get a few things out.

She jumped when Scott's hands reached to grab her skirt and flip it up. She hadn't heard him get off the bed or move.

"God, I love the sight of that red under there. I swear, it peeks out to tease me."

She popped up and wobbled on her feet. "You scared me. I wasn't expecting that." She giggled again, and this time heard her own nerves.

He wrapped his arms around her in apology. "What do you want to eat?"

She just shrugged. "I'm so hungry; I'll eat just about anything."

One of Scott's eyebrows went up. "Oh, really," he teased.

She kissed his nose. "Really."

Scott kissed her and reached for the zipper in the back of her dress.

Mia's heart started racing, butterflies beat wings in her stomach. She was so ready for this, yet so scared.

Halfway down the dress, he stopped unzipping and faced her. He kissed her again tenderly before looking into her eyes. "I think you should eat some real food before anything else."

Mia could see his struggle, too.

They both wanted to get right to the fun stuff, but both recognized they needed to go slow.

Scott reluctantly released her and went to the phone.

She went back to the suitcase while he was occupied with the menu and stardom's demands. She grabbed the pink Victoria's Secret bag she'd tucked in there and hurried to the bathroom.

Mia stood in front of the mirror and stared at herself in the navy blue satin nighty. She'd never felt beautiful before, but at that moment, she did.

She brushed her hair until it shone. Her cheeks were flushed pink with excitement of what was to come.

She brushed her teeth, even though they were going to eat. Mia took a deep breath and shut off the light before stepping out and into her future.

SCOTT HELD his breath as Mia came around the corner from the bathroom.

She was stunning in her innocence.

Marissa was a glamorous beauty, but Mia, she had a beauty all her own.

Maybe it was the way she looked at him. Not with lust or infatuation, but with genuine love and desire.

His body, and his heart, stirred. His cock was already interested, and it tingled, then started to harden.

He'd made himself sit there, waiting for her to come out. His thoughts raced. This time, Scott wouldn't be having sex; he'd do something he'd had never done before.

He'd make love to the woman he loved.

Mia took one look at him, and blushed prettily.

Scott wouldn't apologize, though. No doubt, she'd noticed he was looking at her as if he wanted to eat her, and hell, he did.

He'd consciously perched himself on the middle of the bed, instead of at the edge, so she wouldn't think he'd pounce on her, but he could barely control his hunger.

Slow, idiot. She's a virgin.

Mia took one step forward.

He held his breath in anticipation.

She moved quickly, yet gracefully to stand in front of him.

Scott scooted to the end of the bed to meet her. His knees were just far enough apart that she could step in between them.

He looked up into her eyes. His hands went to the back of her thighs, touching her so tenderly.

Goosebumps covered her, and he wanted to rub them all away.

He ran his fingers gently up and down, from the back of her knee to just above the hem of her slip.

She leaned forward to wrap her hands around his neck and kissed him softly.

Scott put his hands around her waist. He pulled her in closer for a deeper kiss, almost causing her to fall. "Sorry," he whispered and steadied her.

One knee hit the bed, just a breath away from the swelling in his jeans, but he didn't care. He held her there for a moment, their lips together, their tongues dancing in the heat of each other.

Mia moved her hands to his shoulders and pushed him back, so his head fell onto the bed. She pushed against the bed to gain a standing position.

Scott let her have control, putting his hands behind his head to lift it up just enough so he could look her in the eyes when she crawled onto the bed and straddled him.

He looked on, amused, but didn't say anything. He couldn't tear his eyes away from her. She was so hot, and it got him even hotter at the idea that his little virgin could be so brazen.

Mia leaned down to kiss him, and her hair fell forward onto his face.

They both laughed, and she pulled the strands to the side.

Their lips met again, and Scott put his hands on her thighs, moving the satin nighty up.

He explored her soft skin, sliding up over her bottom. He growled when he found the lace of her matching panties.

He was in no hurry, as he kissed her, proud of himself for keeping to the slow pace. He wanted to take his time and be as gentle as possible. Scott tugged her closer, trying to pull her down on top of him.

She hesitated.

He ran his hand through her hair, hooking it behind her ear. "What's wrong?" he asked softly.

Has Mia changed her mind?

"I don't want to hurt you," she said, sitting back on her heels.

"By laying on me?" he asked, frowning.

Mia nodded, and her cheeks pinked brighter.

He smiled at her innocence, but didn't want to hurt her feelings. "Baby, you won't hurt me, I promise." Scott sat up, pulling her closer so she could feel him up against her. He ran his fingers through her long hair again, as and studied her face. "You're so beautiful."

She looked down, as if unable to maintain eye contact.

He lifted her chin and kissed her softly, then lowered them back to the bed.

The rough material of his jeans still separated them. It wasn't very comfortable, especially his crotch. As much as he loved the silk feel of her lingerie, he wanted them naked.

Mia rolled off him. "Sorry," she said. "But this isn't very comfortable." She gestured to his clothes, and hers.

He laughed and kicked off his shoes.

She moved up on the bed, reclining against the stack of pillows.

Scott joined her, hovering above her, leaning down to kiss her again.

Her arms reached for him, and her fingertips explored his shirt until she found the hem. Mia tugged on it, and the muscle shirt underneath. She threw her head back against the pillow and she groaned in frustration.

Scott laughed, then stood on his knees, pulling the shirts over his head. He tossed them to the floor. "Better?" he teased.

She rolled on her side, facing him. She slowly moved her

attention to his pants. She unfastened his belt buckle and unhooked the button.

Scott didn't say a word. Mia could do whatever the hell she wanted to him. This was her show, and it was all at her pace.

She sought his gaze, and he smirked. Like she needed to check with him. He relaxed, one hand on the satin of her nighty, and the other behind his head.

His little virgin's attention was on what she'd partially revealed. His boxer briefs still shielded his erection.

Mia ran her hand up and down the material, feeling his width and girth.

Scott's breathing quickened; he couldn't help it.

She moved back up to lie next to him.

He kissed her again, and she continued to stroke him through his underwear, until he couldn't take it anymore.

He reached over, pulling her on top of him. Scott settled her hips so they could grind, and he could get her excited. He guided her movements, urging her on.

Mia moaned in pleasure. She'd just started locked into his rhythm when there was a knock on the door.

"Damn!" Scott whispered. His balls already ached, and his cock pulsed, demanding more.

She rolled off him, allowing him to answer the knock.

He pulled his pants back over his hips but didn't bother to fasten them. He couldn't exactly yell at room service. He'd thrown a fit to get food after hours, after all. He sucked in air, and opened the door.

A gentleman stood there with a tray of food.

Scott smiled when the smell of maple syrup invaded the room. He took the tray and thanked the man, handing him a generous tip.

Then he set the tray down on the desk and returned to Mia, who was leaning back on her elbows. "Now, where were we?"

"We were about to eat," Mia teased.

Scott let out a sigh, then smirked when her stomach audibly growled. Maybe cooling things for now would help. His cock jumped, sounding its disagreement.

He grumbled playfully and took the lids off the plates. Somehow, they'd eat and he'd have to keep a full tummy from making her sleepy. He really needed her tonight. Selfish? Maybe. But true.

Mia got off the bed and went to stand behind him, and wrapped her arms around his waist. She rested her chin on his right shoulder, tilting her head in so that her lips were close to his ear. "Put the lids back on. It will keep it warmer longer."

Scott loved that she was wicked. He flashed a smile, but obeyed, dropping the two lids back in place. He turned in her arms to face her. "But you need to eat."

"I will. But right now, all I want is you."

He blinked. What?

He couldn't believe it. She was putting his needs above her own.

No girl had ever done that before.

Mia slipped back to the bed, crawling across it.

Scott watched.

She lay back on the multiple pillows at the head of the bed, looking at him with hooded eyes.

He took two steps forward before Mia held her hand up to stop him.

"You might as well take those off. There's no point in having to get up again in a few minutes."

He laughed.

She was right, though.

His clothing quickly hit the floor, and he stood before her in all his naked glory.

Scott mounted the bed, making her his prey.

Mia laughed, and it shivered down his spine.

She reached for him, wrapping her arms around his neck, pulling him closer.

He ran his hands up the outside of her thighs until they found the lace of her panties. In one swift motion, he pulled them off and tossed them to the floor.

He lay beside her, exploring her throat with his lips and tongue, and ran a hand down over her hip to her thigh, then up again. Scott gently moved her nightgown up. He slid his hand between her thighs, separating them to give him better access.

Mia's kiss faltered when Scott parted her folds with a very gentle probing finger. Her breathing became rapid.

She didn't pull away, so he kept going, until her clit twitched beneath his touch. He used the bristly hairs of his goatee to tickle the sensitive skin surrounding her sex. The spaghetti straps of her nightgown fell from her shoulders and slid down her arms, leaving her breasts exposed.

His lips found their way to her nipples.

She gasped, so he kept going.

His tongue moved down her body until his lips replaced his fingers. He twirled and flicked at her until she was panting.

Scott climbed back up her, kissing a trail up her body. He pushed her thighs farther apart with his knee, and settled down on top of her. He rubbed himself gently against her. His cock ordered him to shove forward and join them. Make Mia his.

She was a virgin, and he couldn't do that. He would never hurt her. Being a woman's first was a huge deal.

He had to make sure she was sure.

"You can still say no," he whispered in her ear.

"No. I want you. Now!"

Scott smiled, and dropped one last kiss to her mouth. He moved a little lower, placing himself at her opening. He kept their lip-lock going, slowly penetrating, then withdrawing at the same time.

Mia gripped his back as he slowly moved, inch by inch, further and further inside her.

He didn't want to hurt her. He was so large, and she was so tight.

When she moaned, more pleasure than pain, he went deeper and his strokes got longer.

Soon, she moved with him, encouraging him.

Scott drove himself all the way in, grunting with the pleasure that washed over him.

Her legs curled up around him.

He looked at her face, to ensure he wasn't hurting her.

When Mia met his eyes, her expression went almost peaceful. She reached up, kissing him again, and tightening her legs around him, starting his rhythm, again.

Scott returned her kiss and moved in and out of her.

She felt so good, so tight.

He watched her pleasure build, trying to restrain himself. He didn't want to come until she did. Sweat built on both their bodies, but he didn't care, as long as she never stopped touching him, or kissing him, or letting him inside her.

Mia's sex clenched around his.

Scott hadn't had a virgin in a long time, but he was glad he could give her pleasure her first time. As her inner muscles contracted and relaxed against him, he pulled back, so he could watch her first orgasm.

Her back arched, and she clung to him, her body shaking out of control as one aftershock after another filled her.

He picked up speed, so he could join her. Pressure exploded up his spine and he gritted as he started to come inside her. He tightened his grip on her shoulders, his body going rigid as he released the climax he'd been holding back. He buried his face in her neck as their bodies remained together.

"Oh my God! Is it always this good?" Mia panted and started to relax.

Scott chuckled. What an ego stroke. "I'm glad you liked it." He pulled back to look at her.

"*'Like'* is a serious understatement."

Scott watched Mia devour the plate of waffles and eggs he'd ordered for her. She was still naked, and he could stare at her all night. She was...perfect.

It kind of shocked him she wasn't embarrassed to scarf food down in front of him like that. It made him laugh.

"What's so funny?" she asked, shoving another bite of waffle, dripping with syrup, into her mouth. Some sticky syrup dropped on her chin.

He leaned closer and licked the drop off.

She laughed, then her eyes zoned in on his cock.

He was still naked, too.

Mia gestured. "I didn't think you could do that again, so soon."

He beamed. "I'm a fast reloader."

Her cheeks went pink again.

Scott beamed even wider. He was so happy at that moment. Earlier that night, when all the crap with Marissa had gone down, he'd assumed she'd never see her again.

He'd been such an ass, how had his luck turned?

Never had he planned to be sitting naked with her, eating waffles at almost three in the morning.

He was one lucky son of a bitch.

CHAPTER 11

Mia stood in the shower, letting the hot water rush over her sore body. After the mess they'd made with the waffle syrup, she was all sticky. They hadn't slept at all, so making it through the day would be a miracle. She had a seven-hour drive back to Omaha. But if this was the last time she'd ever spend with Scott, she wanted to enjoy every minute.

"Mind if I join you?" His deep voice resonated through her.

She'd be more than happy if his voice was the only thing she ever heard again. "By all means."

She was grateful for the posh hotel's large dual shower. She'd heard horror stories of sex gone wrong in a shower. Someone was always cold, and there was no room to maneuver. That wouldn't be a problem here. This shower had two heads on each side, and multiple spouts that jutted water in random directions.

"Oh. That feels so good," Scott said, as he stepped into the hot water. "My muscles hurt so badly."

Mia stifled a laugh. She was glad she wasn't the only one.

Although, he had more excuses. He'd been dancing on stage almost every night for over eight months.

She'd made love to Scott twice already, but she'd never get enough of him. She needed to touch him.

She grabbed the soap and lathered it up.

His face was to the water, and his back was to her.

Mia started at his shoulders, massaging as she washed.

Scott moaned when she worked the knots at his shoulders, and down his back.

She stepped closer, her chest smooth to his back, then reaching around to soap his chest. Her hands went down to the top of his hip bone, teasing him, not going any lower.

Scott's breath caught in his throat. He let out a feral growl and turned in her arms. "You are such a tease."

Mia smiled, and kissed him tenderly.

His arms went around her, pulling her close.

She could feel his erection growing. Heat suffused her face, and made its way down her body. She wanted to go again, but could her body handle it? Her nether regions began to quiver. "I need to wash my hair," she said, trying to change the subject. She reached for the shampoo. When she faced Scott, he took the bottle from her hands.

"May I?"

Mia had always wanted someone to wash her hair. He must've seen the look in her eyes when he asked, because he didn't wait for an answer.

He rubbed the shampoo into her scalp.

She moaned in pleasure as the lathers built. She moved under the water to rinse the soap from her hair, her breasts lifted. She conditioned her hair and soon, it was past time they got out.

Scott stepped out first, drying himself off. He offered her a towel, then gently rubbed her down, removing all the water from her skin.

It was a big task, because her hair was still dripping wet. He stood just in time to catch a drop from her hair that was traveling between the valley of her breasts. He caught it with his tongue, causing goosebumps to cover her skin.

He laughed when her nipples tightened into little nubs. His mouth found its way to the right one, and he laved it before closing his lips around it.

Her hands went to the back of his neck, drawing him in closer.

"I need you, Mia," he said, huskily.

"Again?" she panted.

"Always."

♩♪

MIA SAT ON THE BED, in just a towel, listening to Scott brush his teeth in the bathroom. The smell of his coconut shampoo still filled the air. It was an odd scent for a man like him, but it gave her a sense of comfort.

She glanced at his phone, sitting on the nightstand beside her. Another text went off.

He'd been texting while she was busy trying to untangle the knots in her long, wet hair. Scott had excused himself and left his phone behind.

She wasn't intended to snoop, but still worried about the night before. What if it was Marissa he had been texting with?

The message was clearly displayed on the screen.

THOMAS: I think you have a great idea... Omaha it is.

MIA'S HEART SOARED. Did this mean what she could only hope? Did Scott really want to spend more time with her?

She went to her suitcase, trying to get her clothes together, but her heart was racing and her thoughts were scattered. She pulled a pair of jeans and a light blue T-shirt, out before hastily throwing everything else into it.

Scott joined her, opening his arms in invitation.

Mia almost dropped her towel when her arms went around him. His muscled chest held it in place.

"You look like you're in a hurry. Not leaving me, are you? You wouldn't walk out like that, would you?"

Mia would if she needed to protect herself, but she wouldn't admit that. She just looked down.

"Well. I guess it's a good thing you won't be rid of me for a while. I'd like to spend my two days off, going home with you." He stopped, looking into her eyes. "That is…if you want to spend more time with me?"

She brought her hands to the back of his neck, drawing him even closer. She kissed him.

"I'll take that as a yes."

Mia nodded.

"You better get dressed. We should get on the road so when the rest of the crew realizes I'm gone, there's nothing they can do about it."

She laughed. "Really?"

Scott was completely serious.

With her face now buried in the crock of his neck she whispered. "You're gonna walk away from the band, to spend time with… me?"

She could feel the vibrations of his laugh before the sound escaped his lips.

"You make it sound like I'm joining the circus. It's just two days, Mia. Then I'll be back on the road with him. Besides, I wouldn't be the first one in the group to disappear for a few days in the middle of the tour."

She reluctantly let him go and stepped back to look at him. She didn't know what he meant, but took it as a good sign they wouldn't flay him for taking some personal time. She picked up her clothing and got dressed. She brushed her hair back into a ponytail and put on the barest of make-up.

Mia yawned as Scott put their suitcases in her trunk.

"Are you sorry you didn't rest up last night?" he asked.

"It was worth every minute. But I am having problems walking this morning."

His cheeks flushed with color.

She giggled, then covered her hand with her mouth. "How about we just get in the car…"

"So what kind of music do you have?" he asked.

"Um…"

"What?"

"I was going to the concerts, so mostly I have *Next Step* stuff loaded on my phone."

Scott smirked. "Seriously," he said, shaking his head.

"Yeah, it put me in the mood for the shows. I have Nathan's new solo album and *Next Step*'s newest on CD I picked up this weekend, but you're probably tired of hearing those songs."

"Wait, you have Nathan's newest? But no *Razor's Edge*," he teased.

"I got it in Minnesota, and I hadn't decided if I was a *Razor's Edge* fan yet, so I bought his."

He laughed. "Well, as it happens, I know a guy…"

"Really? Do you think he could get it autographed for me?"

"Probably, and maybe even kissed."

"I still can't believe this is happening," Mia whispered, more to herself than to him.

"What?"

"I'm driving home, with the eldest *Razor's Edge* member in my car."

"Why? Can't you see yourself with a pop star?" he asked more seriously.

Mia didn't answer right away. "I guess I'd worry about getting my heart broken." She almost added, 'again'.

"That could happen in any relationship, though."

"True. But, this would be different. When things don't work out with a star, you lose so much. You wouldn't be able to listen to the music anymore, there'd be no more girls' weekend trips to concerts. Not to mention, seeing him on TV and hearing his voice on the radio. There'd be constant reminders."

"I get what you're saying, but you wouldn't be the only one with a broken heart. Think about it from a singer's point of view. There are songs that would be associated with said lost-love, songs he'd have to keep singing. With passion and love. The crowd can't ever know what's really going on."

They drove in silence for a while, and Mia tried to process what he'd said.

If he only knew her past and how much she…

She couldn't even say the words in her own head.

Eventually, she pulled in to a rest stop and headed straight to the restroom. She washed her face.

When she came back out, Scott was leaning against the hood of the car. She went back to him, her arms crossed; she held herself together.

"I'll understand if you don't want to be with me anymore," he said. "But we've come a long way in a short time and I wouldn't change that."

"I'm sorry," Mia said. "It took me off guard. I'm glad you're here. But…" She could feel the tears welling up again. "I keep waiting for the other shoe to drop. This can't be real."

He smiled. "It worried me you didn't want me because I'm a pop star. But you really don't care about that, do you?"

"It's what you do, not who you are."

Scott pulled her to him, kissing the top of her head. "All right then, let's get back on the road, so we can get this drive over with."

Mia smiled.

Once back in the car, he tried to find a radio station, but since they were in the middle of nowhere, there weren't any.

She laughed as he grumbled and handed him her phone. "Here, see if there's anything on there you'd like to listen to. If not, you can see if there's any reception to download from iTunes."

He shuffled through her music. "Really? You have the *Marcerna?*"

"No making fun of my music! There're a lot of good memories with that song."

Scott arched an eyebrow.

Mia chuckled, shaking her head.

He put her music on shuffle as they cruised down the highway, although he skipped all the NS songs.

"Penny for your thoughts?" she asked when the silence was unbearable.

"I was just thinking how lucky I am that I saw you in the crowd that night," he said, taking her hand.

"Why would you pick me?" she inquired.

"How could I not?"

"Well, look at me. I'm not the supermodel type. I'm a hardworking woman with an odd sense of fashion. I'm not the type of girl that a good-looking guy like you would ever pay attention to."

"*I'm* looking at you. What I see is an amazing woman, who has the self-esteem to go out just the way she is, and damn what others think. A woman with beauty and strength she doesn't know she has." He kissed her knuckles. "I see a down-to-earth woman I could easily fall in love with."

Warmth threatened to swallow her whole, and she couldn't look at him. Then again, she'd never taken compliments well. "Oh, I know why your eyes are green." She pushed the tease out to get the spotlight off herself.

"Why?"

"Cause all the crap falls out your mouth before it can fill up to your eyes."

"Oooh," he laughed. "That's brutal."

"I don't get them often but every once in a while..."

They drove on to Topeka, where they stopped for lunch.

They found a quaint mom and pop restaurant off the main street where it would be less likely Scott would be recognized.

Once inside, they chose a booth in the back, and the hostess brought them menus.

When she took their orders, Mia asked if there was a ladies' room, and was directed to the back of the restaurant.

Mia gripped the edge of the sink and stared at herself in the mirror. The black circles under her eyes were prominent, but her skin radiated with an unfamiliar glow. Her lower regions still held a dull, yet pleasant, ache.

What am I gonna do with him at home?

She watched her reflection reddening, her cheeks so bright she fought the urge to pat them cool.

Anything but sex. I think I am gonna walk bow-legged for a week.

She giggled and returned to the table. She wouldn't want Scott to worry and come after her.

When they'd finished eating and were headed out to the car, a teenage girl followed them.

"Excuse me." Her voice was shaky and hesitant. "My friends dared me to come to ask you if you were from *Razor's Edge*."

Mia and Scott exchanged a look.

"Yes, I am."

"Can I have your autograph?" she asked, holding out a napkin and pen.

He took the napkin and pen. "Go get your friends, and we'll take a picture."

The girl squealed, but ran off without her napkin. She returned quickly with three friends, who all handed their phones to Mia.

The girls were full of questions for Scott, and he happily answered while the pictures were being taken.

"I'm sorry, girls, but we have to go. But it was nice meeting you." He moved toward the car, so they didn't have a chance to argue.

"That was sweet," she said, after they'd climbed in.

After an hour of silence, other than the radio, she needed to change her game plan. She couldn't have Scott just sitting around her house for the next two days.

"So, um… do we know…" How should Mia ask?

Scott chuckled. "While you were in the bathroom, I found a flight to St. Louis on Wednesday morning. That's our next show. So you have me all to yourself for tonight, all tomorrow, and just a few hours on Wednesday." His hand found its way to her thigh, and he gently caressed.

"Oh, don't start with that," she teased. "But in all seriousness, what do you want to do?"

"What do you normally do with friends that come to visit?"

"That's easy. The zoo."

"I already spend my days with a bunch of monkeys," he teased.

"So you'll be right at home."

CHAPTER 12

Mia let out a sigh of relief when she pulled into her neighborhood. She was so glad to see her house.

It'd been a very long weekend. Although she wouldn't change it, she was so very tired.

They pulled into the driveway, and she opened the garage. All she could think about was how dirty the catbox was, and worry it would smell bad. Paranoia about dirty clothes on the floor, and how neat her rooms were swirled around in her mind.

It's too late to worry about anything. He's already here.

Mia left her suitcase where it was and hurried to enter the house.

Gibbon was the first cat to meet them at the door.

She picked him up for a kiss and he went straight to her shoulder. She didn't let him up there often, but she'd been gone for four days, so he got in a good snuggle.

Scott just laughed as the cat looked at him defiantly.

The feline was telling Scott he was alpha. Not the human.

Mia quickly gave a tour of her small two-story house. They walked in the foyer and past the dining room. She showed him the living room and kitchen before moving upstairs.

There were three rooms upstairs. The one at the very top of the stairs was her office. Across the hall was the guest room, and further down the hall was the master suite.

Her heart thundered and her face was hot all over again when she showed him her inner sanctum.

She'd share her bed with Scott for the next few nights.

It was one thing to make love to him at a hotel.

But in her own bed?

Once he left, she'd always have the memories.

Every time Mia walked into the room, she'd remember.

It made her chest hurt thinking about it.

Scott glanced out her bedroom window to her backyard. "Holy shit!"

She'd never heard him cuss before.

It was hot.

"You have a pool?"

"I have a pool," Mia said, throwing him a wink.

"Can we?" His green eyes were full of excitement.

"After dinner. I have rules."

He pulled her into his arms. "Rules?"

"Dinner first. I hope you like Chinese."

♩♫

MIA SLID the glass doors in her basement open. She led them into the backyard, and the humidity assaulted them.

"Ugh! How do you live in this heat?" Scott complained. "It's midnight, and just as hot as during the day."

Her in-ground pool was kidney-shaped, with the deeper water at the right end. There was a slide in the middle and small solar lights around the landscaping against the fence.

"Swimsuits?"

She flashed a devilish smile. "Remember, my rules?"

"I thought it was dinner before swimming?"

"No clothes after midnight."

A big grin crossed his face. "I like these rules." said he pulled off his shirt, staring her down as he let the fabric fall to the deck. He urged her into his arms, kissing her. At the same time, he found the bottom of her T-shirt, tugging it over her head.

Nerves danced in Mia's tummy. She'd joked about the no clothes rule, but she'd never done it. Now, here she was, with Scott Ralston, from the boy band *Razor's Edge*, about to get *naked* in her pool.

His touch was gentle when he unhooked her bra. He let it fall, exposing her breasts. He leaned down, kissing them softly, then helped her step out her jeans.

She stood in only red panties.

Scott sucked in his breath. "I could stare at you all night."

Mia put her hands on his chest, and her lips sought his. Her hands slid down, unfastening his belt buckle, then his pants.

He kicked off his shoes, allowing her to remove his pants.

Scott took her hand and led her down the steps into the cool dark water. Both of them still had their underwear on.

She had her arms wrapped around him, and her breasts were shielded by his torso.

The water was warm, but all she wanted to do was go upstairs and make love to him.

She might be new at sex, but seeing him wet, made her body assert a need she was still getting used to.

He released her long enough to immerse himself in the water. When he came up for air, his back was to her.

Mia took the opportunity to jump on Scott.

He grabbed her and pulled her around to face him. He threw them both forward, and submerged them both.

Panic threatened to swallow her whole. Mia clawed at him, trying to get back above the surface of the water. As soon as her head broke through, she moved away from him to sit on the stairs.

He couldn't know. He didn't mean anything by what most would see as playful pool antics, but it didn't matter.

Her heart thundered and she couldn't catch her breath.

"Baby! What is wrong?" Scott asked, rushing to her.

She coughed, trying to calm her breathing. "I can't swim," she sputtered.

"Then why do you have a pool?" His voice rippled, as if he was amused but was trying not to laugh.

"It came with the house. My stepbrother left it to me when he deployed overseas." She coughed again.

"I don't understand."

"My friend's brother thought he was being funny and almost drowned me when I was little. I still have a great fear of my head being underwater."

Scott hovered in front of her, his knees resting on the bottom of the pool at the base of the stairs. He cupped her face in his hands, making her look up at him. "I'm so sorry, I didn't know. Forgive me?"

Mia nodded.

He leaned in, kissing her tenderly.

She slid her arms around his neck and he pulled her off the step, holding her so her head and shoulders were above the water.

"I think it's a good time for a swimming lesson."

She pulled back, shaking her head. "Are you serious?"

"Yes. I don't want you to be afraid of the water."

Mia groaned.

"Look, when the tour's over I'm gonna take you away somewhere for a week, and I'm sure we'll spend a lot of time in the water."

She stuck her bottom lip out, as if she was a little girl, but she didn't care. Water had been a "no thank you" for a long time.

"No pouting, or you won't get your reward," Scott said, sounding a little too much like a teacher.

"I can float and doggie paddle. I just don't like to have my face in the water. I can get by."

He scoffed. "Fine. Show me what you can do. I'll be the judge."

First, he had her float on her back. Then he showed her how to blow out her nose while underwater to avoid getting water up her nose.

Scott taught Mia how to swim like a frog and the breaststroke.

She got tired quickly, but she definitely felt more comfortable in the water.

He was a patient teacher, and never made her feel bad for being scared.

"You ready to go in?" he asked some time later.

"Yeah. I'm starving."

"We just ate."

"Being in the water always makes me hungry."

They climbed out of the pool, and Mia retrieved two towels that she kept in the pool shed on the deck, up against the house.

Scott wrapped her in a towel first, then the other around himself.

She grabbed their clothes as they went in.

Mia fixed them a snack, but her towel wasn't cooperating and kept falling off. She finally gave up, laying it on the counter. She moved around the kitchen completely naked, her hair still dripping wet. She could feel Scott's eyes and heated up from the inside out, but she didn't say anything to him. Knowing he watched her made her feel sexy.

When she joined him at the table, he pulled her onto his lap.

She fed him bites of cheese and crackers and some pepperoni. "Can you just stay here forever?" Mia asked, knowing her words were cheesey.

"I wish I could. I think people would notice if I disappeared off the tour entirely. Again."

"Are you really going to be in trouble when you get back?"

"No, I told them I was taking off for a few days and would meet the tour in St. Louis."

"I don't want you to go."

"Me either, but we'll make the most of tomorrow and I'll call you from the tour."

Mia groaned.

"Now, now. No pouting or you won't get your reward."

She tilted her head to one side. That was the second time he'd mentioned a reward.

Scott slid his hand inside her thigh, setting her body on fire.

She leaned back against him.

He spread his legs, pushing hers apart in the process. Then he explored her when she relaxed in his arms, her breathing becoming more rapid.

Her fingers dug into his skin the more he teased. Finally, Mia couldn't take it anymore. She stood, pulling his towel loose. "Let's go upstairs."

Scott pulled her close, his erection grinding against her, taunting her. He backed her up to the wall, hiking one of her legs up on his hip as he dipped down, and slid inside her.

Mia moaned, and didn't even care that he'd never answered her demand about her bedroom.

He pressed her harder against the wall, gaining leverage, and he pulled her other leg up.

She came almost immediately, trying not to cry out at the pleasure coursing through her.

Scott sped up his pace until he joined her.

"We may need to go cool off in the pool again," she panted.

He laughed, then set her back on her feet. "I think a shower would be more appropriate."

Mia let the water run over her, washing the last of Scott from her body. Her shower was tiny, only one person could fit.

Scott was an angel, and let her go first.

She was quick to wash the chlorine from her hair and skin. When she stepped out, he held a towel for her.

Scott's time in the shower was much shorter, and before long they were in her bed, curled up together.

He was out in no time, breathing deeply against her.

She couldn't fall asleep. In less than thirty-six hours, he'd walk out of her life. What would happen after that? Sure, they might get to see each other every so often, but what kind of relationship was that?

Mia couldn't let him go. Could she?

CHAPTER 13

Mia tossed and turned all night; sleep was elusive. When the sun rose, she was the first out of bed.

She tried reading for a while but couldn't concentrate. An hour later, she made breakfast; pancakes, bacon, and scrambled eggs.

Mia started her Keurig. She didn't drink coffee, mostly tea, and cocoa, but she'd bought a box of Gloria Jean Mocha Coffee when it was on sale.

Scott laughed. "Really? Fru Fru coffee? Don't you have any real coffee?"

"This is real coffee... just chocolate caramel flavored," she threw back, carrying the food over to the table.

"So, what's the plan for today?" he asked, a little too cheerily.

"The zoo, remember?"

Soon, they were walking through the main gates at the zoo. The Desert Dome and Kingdom of the Night were to their left, and just past that was the monkey house.

Straight ahead was the Wild Kingdom, and behind that was the Aquarium and Butterfly Pavilion.

To the right was the Lied Jungle.

They headed into the Lied Jungle after Scott told her to lead the way.

Mia had been to the zoo a million times, so she pointed out all the things she found fascinating. She led them across the rope bridge that had a waterfall beside it.

"Stay right there," she hollered at him when they'd reached the center of the rope bridge. "I'm gonna run to the other side. This is a great photo!"

Mia had just taken the shot when a family walked past.

"Sweetie, do you want to be in the picture? I'd be glad to take it for you. I'm almost always the one on the other side, so I like to help others when I can."

"Yes! Thank you for the offer," Mia returned, handing her phone over to the mother. She ran onto the bridge, causing it to move a lot.

Scott opened his arms to hold her while the lady took the shot.

"I really appreciate that!"

When they moved through the jungle, Mia continued to take pictures. There was a place that had vines visitors could hang from and pretend to be monkeys.

"Come on, just play with me?"

"I'm never the goofball. I always leave that up to my cousin, you know, Thomas."

Mia gave him her best sad puppy eyes. "Please, just this once, give in to your inner child and hang around. Like a monkey."

He finally gave into her, and they both laughed like children.

After the jungle, they enjoyed the Butterfly Pavilion and the Aquarium.

Mia wanted to sit and watch the penguins, but there was too much to see. They went into the Desert Dome.

The upper level was all desert, and the lower level was dark.

They headed into the Bayou in the Kingdom of the Night holding hands.

"Are you homesick yet?" Mia teased.

He arched an eyebrow.

"I grew up in Kentucky, not Louisiana."

"I was talking about the gators."

Scott didn't get her Florida reference, where RE band was created, so she dropped it.

It was almost four p.m. when they finished traversing the whole place.

"So, what should we do for dinner?" Mia asked as they walked back to her car.

"How about if I cook?" he asked.

"You cook?" she asked.

He laughed. "Should I be insulted? You sound so surprised? I'm like a gourmet chef."

She cocked her head to one side, half skeptical, half intrigued. "I guess we can go to the grocery store on our way home?"

"Sounds good to me," Scott said, a wicked smile taking over his face. "Do you have any food allergies?"

"No. I'll eat whatever."

"Careful, I may feed you something you never expected," he said, with a wink.

"Hey, as long it tastes good I don't care."

"Oh, I can make anything."

Mia pushed the cart as Scott filled it. Every time he picked something up, it hitched up her amazement and surprise. They were items that would never have hit her normal grocery list.

When they returned to the house, he went to work in the kitchen.

"You must be fixing something fancy," she said.

He shrugged. "Fancy is all in the presentation." Scott glanced over his shoulder. "After I left the band, I needed something to keep me busy, so I took some gourmet cooking classes."

She smiled. "So I'm sure you were oh, so impressed with my

skills at ordering Chinese and putting together some meats and cheese yesterday."

He leaned against the counter opposite her, kissing her forehead. "It was delicious because you made it with love."

Mia set the dining room with a burgundy tablecloth and her fancy dishes with wine glasses.

Scott stood at the stove, stirring various pots and skillets.

She wrapped her arms around him from behind, and rested her cheek against his back.

He'd said her hasty meal was made with love.

Surely, he'd just meant that as a figure of speech.

They barely knew each other.

Mia enjoyed every minute being with him, and she couldn't have chosen a better lover to bring her into that part of life.

But...love?

No.

She wasn't there yet.

Right?

Scott had a beautiful meal laid out, and lit the candles, creating a romantic atmosphere.

"I can't believe you are going back to work tomorrow," Mia said. Sadness laced her voice, even she could hear.

How did she really feel about him?

It'd been amazing, but reality had to come back.

He covered her hand with his. "Babe, this has been the best three days. I can't thank you enough for showing me..." He looked up at the ceiling. When he brought his gaze back down, his eyes were rimmed red.

She took his hand in hers, and led him upstairs where the rest of dinner was left, completely forgotten.

MIA WAS STILL BREATHING DEEPLY, sated from the lovemaking. Her head was on his chest.

His right hand made circles on her back. Scott used his manicured fingernails to tease her skin. His left hand rested on her lower back.

She had her arms wrapped around his waist, listening to his heartbeat.

"How are we going to survive, being away from each while I finish the tour?" he asked, in an almost whisper.

Mia looked up at him. "We'll figure something out."

He kissed her forehead. "Don't be sad, baby. It's not forever. Just a few more weeks of the tour."

"I know."

Scott crawled out of bed and offered her a hand.

Reluctantly she left the bed, and let him lead her to the window that overlooked her pool.

"Every day I'm gone, I want you to come out here and swim. I want you to think of me while you're doing it so when the tour is over, I can take you away, we can play in the ocean, and I'll know you won't panic when a wave goes over you. Okay?"

She smiled.

He was coming back.

He was making mental plans to take her places.

He wanted to help her get over her fear.

Scott suggested they take one last swim in her pool.

The moment the sliding glass doors were open, he stripped down to nothing and dove into the water.

Mia laughed as he splashed her while she leaned down to get his clothing off the deck. "Paybacks are a bitch, you know that, right?" she teased. She was grateful she had her extra bikini hanging in the laundry room, stiffly dry from the last time she swam, just before she'd left for her crazy road trip.

She stepped outside, trying to spot Scott in the pool. The lights were still off, except for the solar domes in the landscaping. Her eyes adjusted to the semi-darkness when a splash hit her legs. Mia still didn't see him. It wasn't until she stood right at the edge of the pool did she realize where he was.

He'd pressed himself up against the wall of the pool, keeping just enough above water to breathe, but low enough that his head didn't peek over the edge.

Scott pivoted in the water and grabbed her foot. He didn't pull her in, but it unbalanced her enough to cause her to fall in.

When she came up from the water, instead of sputtering, it was smooth, and she sprayed water in his face.

He wiped the water from his eyes and looked her up and down. "Hey! What about the rules?"

She splashed him again. "It's not midnight yet, and I warned you, paybacks are a bitch."

They both laughed before she took off to the deeper end of her pool. She climbed out.

The moment he was close, she jumped in, tucking her knees to her chest, causing a big splash.

This time when she came up for air, Scott pulled her into his arms with a little difficulty. The water was deep, so they had to tread water.

He took off to the shallow end.

Mia swam like he'd shown her before. She could put her head underwater with a little more ease.

When they got to the shallow end, he pulled her back into his arms again. "Look at you. I can see a difference already."

She smiled, and her cheeks went hot. "Well, I have nothing to fear anymore."

He brought his lips to hers.

She sighed as his mouth parted hers and their tongues danced.

His hands reached around her back to the ties to her top. With a tug, they came undone, and the material floated upwards.

Scott broke their kiss so he could toss it to the side of the pool, landing in a small, wet pile on the deck.

Mia pressed her breasts to his bare chest, reveling in the feeling of his warm skin against hers.

Their kissing resumed, but with a new fervor. Their hands explored one another.

He slid his touch to her waist, over her hips, to catch the very edge of her bikini bottoms.

Scott took a deep breath, then went under the water to remove her bottoms. When he emerged, he threw the fabric with the top.

Because of the buoyancy of the water, she could wrap both her legs around his waist with ease. She felt his cock awakening beneath her. She gasped when the soft mushroom head pressed at her most sensitive part.

His kisses became wilder, more all-consuming.

Mia could hardly breathe as passion took over.

In one swift movement, he impaled her.

She cried out as her body took him in, all the way to the hilt. With the motion of the water, she rode him hard and fast. Her body tightened around him as her orgasm built.

His hands almost dug into her waist as he helped her move up and down.

Mia dug her nails into his back when her body exploded with pleasure. Her legs fell away from him, her body going weak.

Scott slipped out of her and moved them over to the stairs.

She sat on the second step, keeping most of her body submerged. She opened her arms to welcome him back, and her legs went around him again. Mia moaned when he entered her again.

He lifted her up one step, so he could bring her breast out of the water and into his mouth.

Her core tightened when he suckled.

Scott released her, letting out a deep groan before he kissed her, and his body was still in motion.

She tightened her legs around him, squeezing him. Another

wave was building within her. Mia grabbed at him, trying to pull him deeper. Her body went rigid as her orgasm rocked her.

Two more deep thrusts, and Scott joined her with a shout. He leaned forward and rested his head on her breasts.

She ran her fingers through his wet hair.

He looked up at her, his eyes appearing tormented.

"Was it that bad?" she teased.

"No. It was amazing. It's just..." He sighed. "I don't want to sound all girly and all, but... I really don't want tonight to end. In your arms, I've realized why my life felt incomplete. I was waiting for you. And I have to let you go."

It was Mia's turn to sigh. "You don't have to let me go. We just have to say goodbye for a little while." She kissed him and their bodies separated. "You know, tonight doesn't have to end. But the pool time does. I'm turning into a prune. Let's go get cleaned up."

Scott smiled, and they climbed out of the pool, grabbing towels from the shed before heading in.

MIA TOOK care of her cats and cleaned up dinner.

Scott was still in the shower when she entered the bedroom. She would've given anything to have a shower like at the hotel the night before.

She slid the frosted glass door just an inch to look at him.

He had his head back, and the water ran over his dark hair and down his back.

She ogled his massive chest and had to suck in a breath. Mia could look at him all day long and still be surprised by the things she observed.

Scott glanced over his shoulder and beamed. "I'd invite you in, but..." He said, gesturing at the small space.

She laughed. "You don't have to explain. I have a hard-enough time trying to shave my legs in there."

He shut the water off and reached for a towel, just as Mia dropped hers.

It was the shortest shower she'd ever taken. She wanted to spend her last few hours wrapped in his arms.

When she stepped out, she expected to find him in bed.

Scott was nowhere to be found.

She slipped on her navy-blue nighty, since she'd had little chance to wear it, and the matching small robe.

Mia checked the kitchen. The door to the deck was open.

Scott sat on one of her patio chaise lounges. He was looking up at the dark sky.

The clouds had rolled in and there were only a few stars peeking out.

She stepped out into the cool night air.

He spread his knees and patted the space in front of him.

Mia took the hint and was more than happy to snuggle up against him.

He'd put on a T-shirt and a pair of boxers, but no pants.

She pressed her ear against his chest, and listened to his heartbeat for a moment, before looking up into his eyes. "You have a concert tomorrow. Don't you think you should get some sleep?"

He kissed the tip of her nose. "Not yet. I want to sit here with you for a while longer. I can sleep on the plane and do warm-ups in the taxi to the venue."

"Speaking of singing…"

Scott waited for her to continue.

"I, um, wondered…" Mia was too embarrassed to continue. She felt his laughter from deep in his chest as she lay in his arms.

"Would you like me to sing to you?" Scott asked.

She smiled.

He looked up to the sky, , then he nodded, as if something had hit him. He wrapped his arms around her, holding her tight as he sang.

His voice seemed to resonate within her, with their bodies so close. It was a part of her.

The words to the song, *This Is The Truth*, took on a whole new meaning.

She didn't know if he'd written the song, but right then, it was as if he had. It'd been written for Mia.

This is the truth
And I will always tell you so
There is nothing that can tear us apart
This is the truth and I hope it'll never change
There is nothing I won't do for you
Complete with you, I am

WHEN SCOTT FINISHED, their gazes collided.

His eyes had been on her the entire time. He leaned down and kissed her deeply. "I love you," he whispered against her lips.

That brought Mia up quickly. "What?"

He frowned, then cocked his head.

"Why would you say that?" She couldn't keep the demand from her voice.

"Because it's true."

She scoffed. "You haven't known me long enough to know that for sure."

Scott pulled her back against him. "Do you feel that?"

"Feel what?"

"My heart. It's beating for the first time."

Mia laughed. "Are you serious?"

"Completely," he replied. "With you, I don't have to hide who I am. You forgave me for something unforgivable. You showed me

I can be me without worry. I know enough about you to know I love you."

Mia stared, speechless. She'd always been a hopeless romantic, the one who'd dreamed about love at first sight.

Here it was, in her hands, yet she was trying to deny it.

She could see it in his eyes.

He wasn't lying.

Scott truly believed he was in love with her.

She placed one hand on his cheek. Then kissed him softly, the brisk hairs of his goatee tickling her soft lips.

He was probably waiting to hear the same words, but they weren't hers to share. So she kept their mouths too busy for her to reply.

Mia pulled the blanket up a little higher over her and Scott. In the darkest hours of the night, she'd gone inside long enough to grab a throw blanket off the couch.

It was almost dawn.

He'd insisted they stay out long enough to watch the sunrise together. She had tried to protest, insisting he needed to get some sleep. Scott won.

She'd dozed on and off throughout the night, her head on his warm chest.

Pink, orange, and blue took over the sky.

Scott pulled her even tighter, kissing the top of her head when she sighed with an appreciation for the beauty of the morning.

Each morning, when she watched the sunrise, it would remind her of this moment.

CHAPTER 14

S cott picked up his cup of coffee, Mia's hot cocoa, and headed upstairs. He needed to talk to her.

He hated to admit it to himself, but he was afraid the upcoming conversation would be the one that turned her away from him.

His heart pounded with the prospect. He took a deep breath as he entered her master suite.

Mia was dressed in denim capris and a top that reminded him of the sunrise they'd just witnessed, with shades of yellow and orange and pinks in a pattern. She was putting on her make-up.

He held out her mug as a peace offering, then he sat on the rim of the bathtub, watching her. "Mia. I think we need to talk."

She paused her eyeliner and looked at him through the mirror. She finished the eye she was doing. "Okay," she said, elongating the word. "What do you wanna talk about?"

"I need to tell you about something."

She waited for him to continue.

When he didn't right away, she put the make-up brush on the counter and stepped toward him. She put one finger under his chin and tugged up. "You know you can tell me anything."

Scott finally met her gaze. "I've never felt like this. It hurts, just thinking of not having you there. I wasn't joking when I told you my heart is beating for the first time. I haven't even left yet, and the pain is unbearable."

She kissed his cheek. "It'll be okay. You said so yourself. Just a few weeks and the tour will be over."

"But in the meantime? I don't know what to do. What if I start drinking hard liquor to ease the pain?"

"Scott, all you have to do is call me. If you think you might have a stiff drink, I don't care what time it is, call me. If you succumb and have a glass, don't hide it. Tell Thomas, tell Nick, tell me, but don't hide it. That wouldn't be the way to handle it. I'll be here for you."

He sighed, a sound of relief.

He'd make it through. The tightness in his chest had loosened just by talking to her.

Scott set his coffee cup on the floor and stood, pulling her into his arms. "Where were you fifteen years ago?"

"In love with *Next Step*," she laughed.

"Well, for once, I am so glad you were. Otherwise, I may never have met you."

SOON ENOUGH, they arrived at the airport. They were running a little late and Mia worried about getting his bag checked in on time, so she dropped him at the United Airlines curb. They agreed to meet at the top of Terminal A's escalator after she parked the car. She was so thankful Omaha had a small airport.

She drove to the parking lot as quickly as she could. Her phone vibrated in her back pocket right when she killed the engine. She pulled it out and laughed at first glance.

. . .

SCOTT: I miss you already.

SHE WAS STILL LAUGHING and couldn't tear her eyes off the text when she stepped onto the escalator.

The sight at the top was breathtaking.

Scott stood there wearing a goofy grin.

Mia threw her arms around his neck and kissed him deeply, not caring there were people watching.

This was her last few minutes with him, and she wanted them to be good.

She leaned into him so only he could hear. "So, is it still called the Mile-High Club if it is in the airport bathroom?"

His ears turned red, something she hadn't expected. "Don't tease me like that. I don't think you have the balls to do that."

She looked down in mock-shame.

He was right.

There was no way she'd ever do that, but it was a funny joke.

They moved away from the escalator and toward his terminal and security.

Mia had resolved to send Scott off with a smile so they joked about his upcoming shows. "You know it's embarrassing when you lay across the girl's lap while you have them on stage."

"Didn't hear you complain."

"I had an advantage over most girls."

He raised an eyebrow.

"I spent the night before making out with a bad boy. After that, being on stage was nothing." She couldn't hide her smile.

Scott burst out laughing. "Oh, I almost forgot! I need a picture." He pulled out his phone, taking a few pictures of her alone, then a few of them together. "You know the saying... photos, or it didn't happen."

"Then you'd better send them to me, too."

"You need to send me the ones from the zoo."

"Deal."

All too soon, they heard Scott's flight was boarding. The airport was small, so he'd breeze right through security.

After one last kiss, he slipped away.

Mia's phone buzzed.

SCOTT: Is this real?

MIA: Hope so. Otherwise, I lost my virginity to my imagination.

SCOTT: You won't forget me?

MIA: I should be the one asking that.

SCOTT: Before I forget, can I get your address?

MIA: Email or snail mail?

SCOTT: Both.

SHE SENT HIM BOTH.

SCOTT: Sorry, the flight's leaving. Text you when I land.

. . .

MIA: Have a safe flight!

SHE COULDN'T STOP her tears. She wiped them away and more would follow.

Mia sat in her car for quite a while, unable to start the engine.

How did I end up here? Falling for a guy I used to hate?

How silly was that?

The heat of the car in the parking garage finally prompted her to turn the key.

The silence was too much.

She plugged her phone into the stereo USB and turned on the music, needing something, anything, to fill her head.

The *Razor's Edge* song *Unfinished* flowed through her.

Pretending You were never here,
Stuck in a world of dreams,
Wishing I could heal my heart, All I do is scream,
Without you I am, Unfinished

SHE WAS unable to shut it off, but didn't want to hear more.

It finished, and Nick's song *Overheated* started while she pulled out of the parking garage and headed home.

Scott was true to his word and sent her a message less than two hours later, letting her know he'd landed safely.

In the following days, he called at least once a day, and sent many texts. He even convinced Mia to follow him on Twitter.

That was weird, in the beginning. He dropped hints about her, without saying anything at all.

He talked about when he'd mysteriously disappeared for three days. His followers kept trying to guess where he'd been. Through Twitter, he kept their memories vivid.

Once a week, they set alarms to watch the sunrise together. If they were in different time zones, like with their shows in the lower western region, Scott rose with her, then went back to sleep for two hours.

When it was his sunrise, Mia listened to him describe all the colors. It was something no one could ever take away from them. Two months after he'd left, and the NS/RE tour was complete, Scott declared he needed to see her again.

Mia had nothing going on, no pressing shoots that couldn't be rescheduled, so she offered to go to him.

He insisted that he wanted to come to Omaha again.

It wasn't until he arrived that she understood why.

Mia was antsy, and her stomach was in knots. She stood at the guest area of Terminal B, waiting for him.

Scott finally walked to her.

Other than herself and a few other people, there were no great crowds, no paparazzi to snap photos. It helped that it was after ten p.m.

"All I want is a few days of normal life, to walk around your house in nothing but my boxers, and not worry about someone trying to get a picture through the window. I just want to be Scott, your boyfriend. Not Scott Ralston, the guy from *Razor's Edge*."

They walked upstairs to put Scott's luggage in her room.

He dropped his bag and stepped to her, moving her hair out of the way so he had access to her neck. He leaned down and trailed kisses along her skin.

Goosebumps went up into Mia's hairline. She was tired, but the moment his lips touched hers, her body switched off the former urge to sleep.

Scott's arms went around her neck, his hands finding their way into her hair.

She normally wore it up, but today had left it free, and it flowed down her back.

"I love running my fingers through your soft, loose curls," he whispered before he gave a gentle tug.

She tilted her head back, exposing her throat.

His kisses resumed from her throat to the neckline of her shirt. When he couldn't go any lower, he grabbed the hem and pulled the opposing fabric over her head.

His hunger was apparent in the way her clothes were coming off before she had a chance to think about it.

Mia stood before him, naked, and not one bit ashamed or embarrassed. She reached for him, grabbing his gray T-shirt and demanded its removal. The garment dropped to the floor to join her clothing.

She grabbed his belt buckle, and couldn't help but notice the bulge his black jeans were poorly hiding. She skimmed her knuckles over him when she worked on the buckle.

Scott sucked in a breath as she took her time unzipping his jeans, one tooth at a time.

He wanted her to touch him; he didn't need to say it aloud, his darkened green gaze begged her.

She slid his pants over his beautiful backside, letting her hands linger for a moment. She enjoyed tormenting him.

Mia lowered his jeans, moving downward with the material. She pushed the denim past his knees and to his ankles, and his boots were still on.

Mia stood back up, slowly, letting her full breasts rub against his already sensitive skin.

He'd started this, but she was going to take over.

She stepped back and moved around him.

When Scott pivoted to face her, he'd placed his back to the bed.

She laughed and shoved him gently, causing him to fall back onto the bed.

He chuckled and arched an eyebrow, asking what she was up to without words.

His jeans had tripped him up, as she'd planned.

He moved up the bed a little, so his knees hit the edge of the mattress. His hands went to the back of his head when she joined him.

Mia straddled him.

When his hands went for her, she pushed them away.

She leaned down, putting one hand on either side of his head, hovering her lips close to his left ear. "Keep your hands under your head. No touching me," she whispered. A shiver of anticipation shot down her spine. She'd never been so bold before, but she'd hold onto the sudden courage with both hands and go with it.

Frustration rumbled from his chest with a deep growl.

Mia ignored him, and brought her body back up, running her hands through her hair, giving him a glorious view of the underside of her beautiful large breasts.

"Damn, I love your boobs. I've always had a thing for large ones, and yours are perfect."

She floated over him, just a breath away from his skin, torturing them both.

She ran her hands across his chest, applying a little pressure with her nails.

He panted when she ran them over his nipples.

Mia brought her lips so close to his, teasing him more.

Scott lifted his head up, pressing his mouth to hers. He caught her lips at the correct angle, but she didn't pull away. Didn't want to.

Her hands went to his cheeks to hold him while she devoured him.

His tongue did what his hands likely wanted to do, explore her.

She lowered herself so she could feel the soft tip of him

pressing lightly against her sensitive core. Mia went a little lower, letting him enter her slightly, then pulling away again.

She laughed when his hands came out from under his head to reach for her again.

She pushed them away. "Back under your head, boy," she teased. "You don't want me to tie them down, do you?"

Scott's eyebrows shot up.

"What?" she asked, biting her lip so she wouldn't grin.

"I, um… I wouldn't expect that from you. It's thrilling." He put his hands back down, lacing his fingers first.

Mia went back to exploring his body.

It was all hers.

She could do almost anything she wanted. Mostly, she wanted to sate her curiosity. She slid her hands up and down his arms, then her nails down the sides of his body, feeling each rib when her fingers moved.

Mia brought her hand inward, toward his belly button, then moved to follow his happy trail lower.

He growled deeper when her fingertips went outward, missing his most sensitive organ. "I don't know how much more I can take," he breathed when her fingertips went up and down the insides of his thighs.

She gently cupped his sac, then gave it a light squeeze.

He sucked air through clenched teeth when she blew across his soft mushroom head.

It moved on its own accord, causing her to giggle.

Mia moved back up so she could look into his eyes again.

The fire there told her he'd had just about all he could take.

She positioned herself above him and lowered slowly onto his erection, all the way to the hilt.

Scott groaned and threw his head back. His hands enclosed her waist and helped her move up and down.

She shoved her hair out of her eyes and moved faster.

The pressure from his fingers was intense, but not painful.

He bucked beneath her, driving himself as deep as he could go.

Mia rode him, milking his body, squeezing him with muscles she didn't know she could use.

His hands left her waist to move up toward her heaving bosom.

Mia cried out when her body exploded. She continued to ride out the pleasure until Scott's hands went back to her waist and he took control.

In one swift movement, he was on top.

He bent her knees, and put her feet on his chest to give him greater, deeper access. He looked her in the eyes, their gaze not breaking, while he pounded into her until his own release crested.

Mia panted when he buried his face in her hair.

"I love watching you move. You've taken control in a very passionate way when I've only before seen the innocence of you. I've changed you. Your body and soul have only ever loved me. And I have to admit to myself, you're the first one my heart has truly loved. It isn't just about the sex, as it had been with others."

She let out a deep sigh. "If we're having confession now, you should know," she said breathlessly, "you've ruined me."

He lifted his head, arching an eyebrow all over again, when their eyes met.

"Well, if one day you decide you're done with me, no other man will ever be able to satisfy me." She was trying, in a twisted way, to compliment him, even though it was a fear she held.

Scott pursed his lips, but didn't answer. He moved off her, completely sliding off the bed. He paced, wall to wall.

Regret smacked her chest. Mia sat up, wrapping her arms around her now bent knees. She hadn't meant to upset him. She took a deep breath. "Scott, I'm sorry."

When he finally spared her a glance, his eyes were filled with disappointment.

She'd been so stupid. She pushed to her feet and ran for the bathroom, tears already beginning to fall.

Mia had to go past him to get to the door. She hoped she had enough space to get around him, but Scott snatched her wrist as soon as she neared him.

He swung her around, catching her in his arms.

She tried to push at his chest to get away, but he held tight. She wouldn't meet his gaze; couldn't take that look on his face again.

"Mia," he said roughly, "Look at me."

She slowly obeyed, keeping her eyes down for as long as she could.

"Don't ever say things like that again. You're my heart, my angel. Without you, there's nothing for me. I didn't know I was lost until you found me. You saved me from the one person who could hurt me the most. Myself. I will *never* 'be done' with you. Can't you see that?"

Mia sighed. It was too quick. They didn't even know each other, did they? He said he loved her, and she wanted to believe him. She did believe him, didn't she?

She was a woman, and insecurities ran in her blood.

He could have any woman in the world, yet he wanted her?

Scott wiped a tear away, then tucked a lock of hair behind her ear. He echoed her sigh before he spoke again. "Mia, I love you. Don't forget that."

She nodded, unable to speak.

He kissed her nose, her cheek, and then her lips.

Mia stared into his green eyes. "Then why did you get upset with me? I thought maybe I'd disappointed you." She had to avert her eyes again.

"No, baby. I was disappointed in myself, that I hadn't done a good enough job of letting you know what you mean to me; that you'd ever think I wouldn't want you. I know you're not ready to say the words, but *I love you*. With all my heart. I felt like I didn't make that clear. As cliché as it sounds, it was about me, not you."

Mia laughed. She'd been silly. Again.

There was something about him that made her think and act like a juvenile far more often than she would like.

She kissed him with the fervor she'd had moments earlier. How could she have ever doubted him?

CHAPTER 15

S ounds came from Mia's kitchen, the clanging of dishes being moved around. She kept her eyes closed, breathing in the scent of Scott on her sheets. It'd been after eleven p.m. when they'd finally made it to her house, and they hadn't gone to bed until after two.

Her body protested the thought of getting out of bed, but nature screamed. She finally glanced at the clock.

It was almost noon. Mia never slept that late.

She quickly dressed in jeans and a pink fitted T-shirt. She headed to the kitchen, still barefoot.

Scott hummed while he put the dishes away. He moved around the kitchen, a mug in his hand. He gasped and jumped when he closed the cupboard, which forced him to face her. "Shit, Mia. You scared me!"

She wrapped her arms around his waist. He was so comfortable in her home, he was putting her dishes away, and it was incredibly sexy. It warmed her from the inside out.

Mia kissed his cheek before releasing him, and heading to the coffee pot. She wasn't normally a coffee drinker, but she needed a pick me up. She could feel his eyes on her. The intensity of his scrutiny made her curious. "Penny for your thoughts?"

"It's just..." He shook his head.

"Come on," she pressed, accidently adding far more sugar to her coffee than needed.

"You're my angel. You saved me when I was so close to the fall. It's like a miracle or something."

She stopped, mid removal of the mug from the cupboard, letting his words sink in.

How much cheesiness can one girl take?

Isn't that what most boy band songs are?

"So you said, last night." Mia laughed, and couldn't keep from grinning. "No offense, but you totally sound like a boybander right now. I can hear the lyrics already."

She looked over at him just in time to see him grin and his eyes look to the ceiling.

"Well, I just might write you a song."

"I think you might need this more than me." Mia handed him her mug.

"Um, thanks? I've already had three cups." His cheeks and the tips of his ears flushed red.

Mia smiled into the mug instead, and took a sip. "Mmm," she moaned.

"Did I wake you?" Scott asked, his voice laced with concern.

"No. I can't believe I slept this late. It's not like me."

"How about we go get some lunch?"

"Anywhere in particular?"

"I haven't been out to eat in so long, I don't remember what 'out' food tastes like. So, I'll let you pick," Scott said.

She drove them to the *Chili's* down the street from her house, and pulled into a spot right in the front.

The place was mostly empty; the lunch rush had come and gone, and the dinner rush was at least three hours away.

The hostess looked at them with interest, like she recognized

Scott, but couldn't place him. She led them to a booth and let them know a server would be with them soon.

A thirty-something carrot-red haired woman stepped up and asked them what they wanted to drink. She did a double-take, then watched them like a tennis match. "Woah! I totally just saw you guys, like a few months ago, in Kansas City."

Scott flashed a wicked grin. "I hope you enjoyed the show."

"Oh, yeah! We were a little envious of the girls that got pulled up on stage, but, oh well." Her gaze settled on Mia. "So, this is why you're in Omaha? The girl you pulled on stage that night?" She sounded excited.

Mia watched in silence, and surprise washed over her that the waitress seemed merely curious.

Scott nodded. He took her hand. "This is my girlfriend, Mia."

She snapped her head to him, then at the redhead, fear and shock filling her.

"Wow," the server said, "It's so nice to meet you." She grinned, and it seemed genuine. "What can I get you to drink?" She took their orders and left them to look over the menu.

"Why did you tell her? I thought we weren't going to share that information for a while?" Mia demanded.

He kissed the back of her knuckles. "Babe. Look at it this way; she knows you're a fan, from the same show she was at. So now she'll think there's a chance for any girl, including herself, to be able to date a *Razor's Edge* guy. All I was doing was exactly what you'd want…giving her a special encounter."

"That's complete bullshit, you know that, right?"

"What?" He sounded confused.

"Is that what you tell yourselves when you impress a fan? That you're giving them a special moment?"

He looked down at his glass, playing with the straw. "Yeah, I guess so."

"That's sweet," she teased.

The server was friendly and helpful for the rest of their meal.

She was respectful and didn't bother them unless it appeared, they might need something.

Scott was more than glad to leave her a nice tip.

For the next two days, they never left the house.

They swam in Mia's pool, made love in her oversized bathtub, and almost every other room in the house, and simply spent time together.

It was weird for her to not be out and about, at least once a day. She didn't have a standard day job, but she was always busy.

When they ran out of milk, she finally convinced him to get out.

They went to the zoo again, the art museum, and saw three new movies while Scott was in Omaha.

He said it gave him a chance to feel like any other guy. They didn't have another fan encounter for the rest of the trip.

They were curled on Mia's couch, watching a movie on Scott's last night with her.

"Come on the cruise with me next month," he said.

"What cruise?"

"Seriously, you don't know about the epic cruises we do every couple of years?"

"Uh, you forget, I'm a *Next Step* fan. I don't keep up with what your band does." She winked, so her words didn't hurt his feelings.

Scott sighed. "It's a boat full of fans, and us, for four nights of partying. With themed parties, concerts, and shenanigans. I think you'd love it."

She cocked her head to one side. "I don't think it would be a good idea. As much as I'd like to go, it wouldn't be fair to take time away from fans. I'm sure you know girls have been going crazy since you broke up with Marissa."

"What do you mean girls are going crazy?"

Heat rushed her face, and forced her eyes from his. "Well, you asked me to follow you on Twitter, so I took it another step, and joined the RE fan club so I could go into the chats and see what fun people have had when meeting all of you. The buzz about you being single is insane. They're all hoping to get a chance to catch your eye."

"You joined the fan club?" Scott threw his head back and laughed. "Now you *have* to come."

"Wait, what? Because I joined a website, I have to go? How did you come up with that?"

"It's the rules."

She sighed again. "I can't go. Besides, it's too late. I'm sure cabins are sold out. I can't stay with you. You need to be 'single'. The fans are expecting it."

"Hello... I'm the big brother of *Razor's Edge*. It's *my* cruise. I'll get you a cabin. A really nice cabin. And you will go."

"But—" she started.

"No buts. Except yours, on the boat."

There was no time to talk him out of it.

He already had his phone out and was texting away.

"Wait until you see what I'm wearing for *80s Hair Band Night*. You won't be able to keep your hands off me."

Mia smirked. "I'd better be able to. Your fans aren't supposed to know about me. Does this mean if I get to put my hands all over you, so do the other fangirls?" She was teasing, or course, but regretted saying it as soon as it left her lips. Again. She had a bad habit blurting stupid things out when he was with her.

Scott didn't answer; just went back to texting.

She set her mug of cocoa on the table and moved closer, setting her hand on his thigh. "Please forgive me. I swear I'm the 'right now, Poster Girl'. I don't think 'Big Picture'. All I think about it right now. Will you please forgive me?" She kissed his cheek.

"You'll make it up to me on the boat. I expect full participation in activities, including the costume parties, and mind-blowing sex with the motion of the ocean."

Mia laughed, slipping into his lap and silencing his demands with a passionate kiss.

The next day, their kisses goodbye were bittersweet.

When Scott pulled her into his warm embrace, her heart skipped a beat.

It would be a month and a half before they'd see each other again, but Mia still cried.

"Have I told you today how much I love you?" he whispered against her lips.

"Tell me again," she demanded.

His reply was in his kiss.

He'd never have to say the words again if he always kissed her like that. Scott's kiss said things his words never could, even though he said it often.

He showed no signs of distress when Mia never returned the words; she just wasn't ready and didn't really have an explanation. She pushed away the guilt rushing up and kissed him harder.

The airport announced the last call for his flight, and she reluctantly left his arms.

She watched him go through security, and before he was completely out of sight, he waved goodbye.

On the escalator down to the main level, there was a woman about her age, with short brown hair, a few steps below her.

The brunette glared the entire ride down.

Mia wiped her tears away, glanced down at her phone, and ignored the girl. It felt weird to have someone she didn't even know staring at her.

When they reached the bottom, the lady slowed and fell into step with Mia. She didn't want to be rude, but she wanted to demand what the hell the chick wanted.

"Does anyone else know you are making out with Scott Ralston?" The woman beat her to the punch, throwing out a demand.

"Excuse me?" She reared back.

"His fiancée might be a little pissed off to know he's in Omaha, making out with some fan. You should be ashamed of yourself!"

Mia burst out laughing, causing confusion and outrage to dart across the brunette's expression. "Are you talking about Marissa?"

She nodded.

"So, I take it you are a *Razor's Edge* fan?" she asked.

"Well, I'd say so, if I knew you were making out with RE's oldest member." Obvious fury coated her words.

"Sweetie. He broke the engagement off with her months ago. Where've you been? Obviously, under a rock." Mia didn't feel bad for the condensation in her statement.

The woman snorted. "Excuse me?"

She pushed further. "I'm sure his girlfriend doesn't mind that he was kissing some 'fan' in Omaha. You should mind your own business."

They reached the door to the parking lot and Mia stopped, waiting to see which way the woman would head. She was done dealing with her.

Something like this was what Mia had feared; pissing off fans when they found out about her.

The brunette went left, and she was relieved her car was on the right side on the lot.

With rushing feet, she fled to the safety of her car.

CHAPTER 16

M ia stepped off her plane in Miami. The butterflies in her tummy threatened to rise from her gut and spill from her mouth.

What are you doing?

The demand had been pinned to her brain from the moment she'd started packing. How could she have let Scott talk her into this crazy adventure?

So many things could go wrong. She'd been obsessing for the short month she'd had to plan everything. Although, Scott had taken over most of her travel plans.

When Mia exited the secure area of the airport, on her way to the baggage claim, she spotted a man dressed in a nice black suit and cap, holding a sign with her name on it.

Scott said he'd send a car for her, but this man looked far too official.

"Hi," she said timidly to the tall man. "I'm Mia Lee."

"Ms. Lee. If I can have your baggage claim tickets?" He held out his hand.

She dug through her purse to retrieve the little white stickers and handed them over.

He took her carry-on luggage as well, ignoring her nervous protest.

"If you'll follow me." The man led her through the airport to a long white limo.

Mia gasped and swallowed hard. Her mouth was dry. This was too much.

"It will take me a few minutes to get your luggage. Please, help yourself to anything in the fridge or cupboards." He closed the door, leaving her in silence.

Curiosity got the best of her, and she opened the fridge.

There was a fruit and cheese plate and an assortment of juices, water, and soda.

She helped herself to the snacks and played with the TV.

When the driver returned, he put her bags in the trunk and climbed in the front.

Mia held her breath. Her nerves were back, and Scott hadn't answered her, "*I've landed,*" text message. Where were they going? Scott said he had taken care of everything.

"I wish I could be there," he'd told her the night before, "But we have a few radio spots we have to attend to, so it'll be a few hours after you land before I can get away."

When they pulled up to the hotel, Mia's mouth dropped open of its own accord.

The Five-Star Hotel was right on the beach. It was something she could never afford. That made her stomach flip. The room would be as much as her mortgage.

The chauffeur opened the limo door. "If you'll please make your way to check-in, I'll be sure your luggage is seen to."

Mia crawled out, almost losing her footing. Embarrassment washed over her, and she avoided his gaze. She nodded, instead of finding words to answer him, then retrieved her purse from the limo and forced her feet to the front desk.

"Welcome to *the Setai*. How may I help you?" the man at the counter inquired.

Mia took a deep breath before she could find her voice. "I'd like to check in. Lee. Mia Lee?"

"Ah, yes. Penthouse Four." He handed her a keycard. "Topher will show you up. If there's anything we need, please let us know."

"Thank you."

A young man in a bellhop uniform stepped beside Mia, and placed her two suitcases on a golden trolley.

She followed him to the elevator, where he used a keycard to access the Penthouse level of the hotel.

They stepped out into the hallway of mint and olive-green carpet. The cream walls and landscape artwork gave a feeling of serenity.

Topher led her down the hall to Penthouse Four. He asked for her key to open the door for her.

The room was enormous. The far wall was all picture windows, and the ocean was visible. The furniture was cream-colored with pale blue accents, giving the whole place a tranquil feel.

There was a square dining table that could seat eight people, and a full galley kitchen.

The bedroom was a separate room. The king-sized bed was on the wall opposite the window, with the ocean still visible. They could lie together and watch the water.

Mia tipped the bellhop before he left.

She stared at the huge shower and immediately and made plans for her free time.

She could've stayed in there for hours, but she needed to have enough time to dry and style her hair before Scott arrived.

Mia had just finished blow-drying her hair when there was a knock at her door.

Scott pulled her into his arms the moment the door opened. "Damn, I missed you."

"I missed you, too. Come to the bathroom with me." She pulled him along so she could finish getting ready.

He sat on the edge of the huge tub while she finished her makeup.

"So, how did it go? Were there a lot of girls at the radio station?" Mia asked.

Scott moved to stand behind her. His arms went around her waist, his chin resting on her left shoulder. He looked in her eyes, through the reflection in the mirror. "Honestly, all I noticed was the noise, not the faces."

She stared back at him. "Scott Ralston! You damn well better see their faces! They love and adore you. The least you can do is to see their faces. Just not their boobs."

He laughed, and she soon joined him.

Scott kissed the side of her neck then stepped back. "I'm gonna hop in the shower." He undressed.

Mia watched him with hungry eyes.

Damn, he has turned me into a monster.

She could spend all day being naked in his arms.

"Don't even think about it," he warned. "We have a party to go to." Scott stepped into the shower, leaving her with her lustful thoughts.

She finished rolling her hair and applying her makeup, but watched him through the reflection of the huge and helpful mirror.

The shower had frosted glass doors, so she really couldn't see him clearly, just his outline.

Mia felt like such a guy while she glanced at him. "So, what's the plan?" she asked while he dried off.

"We kick off the party at nine with a little show, then mingle with the crowd, signing autographs and such."

"Where are you performing?"

"On the beach. They've set up a stage. We had our soundcheck just before I came up here to you. But, I'll keep an eye out for you."

"Oh, don't worry about me. I'm good at going to events solo, and still having a good time. You should have one, too."

Scott hugged her from behind. "I love you, Mia. Never doubt that."

She could only smile at their reflection, still not ready to say those three words back.

Mia was unprepared for what greeted her on the beach; thousands of girls, scantily clad in bikinis, as far as the eye could see.

She felt overdressed, compared to everyone around her, but she didn't let it phase her. She kicked off her heels when she reached the sand and headed toward the stage.

They'd set it up much like the one used on the tour with *Next Step*, but it was much smaller, and had no lifts.

Since she couldn't get close without being crushed, she hung back and just listened.

"How ya'll doing tonight?" an unfamiliar voice called out from the stage. He was answered with screaming girls. "How many of ya'll are going on the boat with us tomorrow?" He waited until the screaming died down a little before his next question. "Who here likes *Razor's Edge*?"

The crowd went wild.

"You want 'em, you got 'em! Please welcome BJ, Thomas, Nick, Dwaine, and Scott to the stage!"

The band came out singing their hit song, *Because We Are Meant To Be*.

> *Even though Solitude is my constant companion*
> *I know my salvation is there*
> *I may be mental, I may even be oblivious*
> *But love at first sight, I believe*
> *How you keep this veil still confuses me*

Forever you are in my thoughts
Your past is irrelevant, move close to me
Because we are meant to be

BRIGHT LIGHTS ILLUMINATED the stage as the last rays of the sun disappeared behind the horizon.

"We just finished our summer US tour, as you all know," BJ said when the last words of the song faded away.

The crowd screamed and Thomas stepped up. "We made some new friends on that tour, and reunited with old friends. Some of them we've really been missing."

Dwaine took over. "We thought, 'hey, why don't we invite them to our party tonight'?"

"No way," Mia said out loud.

Nick walked forward. "Can you give a huge welcome to our brothers from another mother? Eddie, Joe, Nathan, Raleigh, and William, come on out!"

Next Step ran out on stage to join them.

With no further introduction, they went straight into performing the mega mix of both band's songs; the same tunes that'd been the opening of their summer tour.

The screams when they all said goodnight and left the stage were almost as loud as it had been inside the arena where the sounds could echo off the walls.

Mia wanted to go back to the safety of the hotel, before the throngs of women came barreling her way. She went straight to the outside pool bar and ordered a *Sex on the Beach*—it just seemed appropriate—followed by finding a table near the pool to sit at.

She wanted a good view to watch Scott mingle with the fans without interfering. She sent him a text, so he'd know where to find her when the time was right.

"Here you are," a masculine voice she'd know anywhere said from behind her.

She almost jumped from her chair, happy to see a familiar face. "Eddie! How are you?"

He pulled her in tight. "Looking good, June Bug. Let's dance." The *Next Step* boybander didn't give her a chance to argue.

There was a small wooden dance floor in between the tiered pools, where a few people were already starting the party.

Eddie pulled her there and spun her around, causing her to laugh with joy as he moved them around the space.

"You're wearing that red thing, again," he pointed out.

"It's called a petticoat. And Scott loves it."

"I do, too."

SCOTT SEARCHED THE CROWD, trying to find Mia. She wasn't where he was expecting her to be.

When he spotted her, memories of a night he never wanted to remember filled his head.

Eddie was dancing with Mia, just like they had in Tulsa. His friend even dipped her backward, like he was going to kiss her.

Scott darted through the crowd, ignoring the fans grabbing at him for attention. He didn't blame Eddie; there was something about Mia that drew people to her.

She was a people person, making friends everywhere she went. However, his insecurities were creeping up.

Before he'd even made it close to the pool area, everything changed.

A dark-haired beauty in a little blue bikini was trying to get Eddie's attention, to no avail. She must've gotten frustrated and tried to get Mia out of the way.

Eddie had been spinning his dance partner around when the girl stepped up to them and caught Mia off guard.

The girl gave her a shove and Mia fell backward. She hadn't had a chance to see it coming.

The dance floor was close enough to the pool, so Mia fell into the water.

Unfortunately, they were right by the stairs in the shallow end.

For a brief moment, Scott looked for the girl that pushed Mia, but she seemed to have melted back into the crowd, so focused on his woman.

Red tinted the clear water, and dread gathered in his gut. He quickened his step.

Girls around them pushed closer, trying to see what happened. No one had called for help yet, and Scott couldn't get through the people.

His heart thundered. The more he pushed to get to her, the more the surrounding girls held him back, trying to catch his eye. Horror, and frustration built in his chest.

Eddie jumped into the pool. His friend scooped up Mia and gently laid her on the side of the pool. Blood puddled under her head.

Eddie couldn't get her to respond and leaned down to feel if air was coming from her nose. "She's not breathing! Someone call 9-1-1!" He tilted her head back and placed his lips to hers, blowing a breath of life into her.

Scott pushed hard, not caring if he offended anyone and finally broke through the crowd. He ran to Mia's side.

Eddie leaned down and gave her two more breaths.

Scott grabbed her hand and looked up into the crowd. "Someone go, get help!"

Eddie breathed a third time, and Mia began choking and coughing up water. He helped her sit up a little.

Her free hand went to the back of her head. She brought her hand back in front of her and looked at the red staining her hand. "Where's the bitch that pushed me in," she asked, her voice weak.

"That's my girl," Scott whispered to her.

Security worked quickly to get the crowd to move back, so the paramedics had room to get through.

Nick came up with them. "What happened?"

"One of the other girls pushed her into the pool to get to me, I think. Unfortunately, she hit her head on the steps when she went in."

"You pulled her out?"

"Yeah, I was the closest."

"Thank you," Scott said, not taking his eyes off Mia.

"Any idea who the girl was?" Nick asked Eddie.

"No. She looked like any other fan. But she disappeared the moment Mia hit the water."

"That's not good," Nick said, worry lacing his voice, as the paramedics loaded her onto the gurney and wheeled Mia off.

Scott ignored his buddies and held her hand, staying in step with the paramedics.

CHAPTER 17

S cott cringed when Mia had eight stitches put in her head. They'd already X-rayed her lungs and found them clear. The doctor insisted she continue to breathe pure oxygen until they released her.

"I'm fine. Really, I'm good. I just wanna get back to the party."

"Sweetie, you have a hole in your head. Let's not worry about the party," he said.

"But I wanna dance. And have *Sex on the Beach*."

His cheeks flushed hot, and interest made his balls twitch. He leaned in close, hoping the nurse wouldn't hear. "Babe, sex on the beach is really messy. Sand gets in every crevice. It's not as fun as it sounds."

Mia glanced his way, her eyes almost crossed. "I meant the drink, but sex sounds good right now, too." She reached for him, but the nurse stepped up and gently pushed her back down onto the bed.

"She has a mild concussion and might act out of character for a while. Just monitor her. And, um…no sex tonight."

Mia stared at Scott. and her eyes went misty. "They shaved part of my head," she cried.

Scott was torn between a laugh and the gut-wrenching vision of his woman crying. The laugh won, which caused her to cry harder. "Oh, baby. It doesn't matter. No one will see." He looked at the back of her head. "It's only a tiny bit."

"But now I'm ugly! I'm gonna be on a boat full of pretty girls in little bikinis with big boobs and no bald spots!"

Mia wasn't normally shallow, she'd hit her head hard, because this wasn't like her. She really did have a concussion, and the nurse had been right about the out-of-character stuff.

"Baby, you have big boobs. I'll tell you what, I'll shave part of my head, too. Then we'll match."

She blinked, then her mouth rounded. "Hey! Your head is already shaved on the sides!"

They both laughed.

The doctor came back a short time later and finally released Mia. He gave her an ointment with pain relief, an antibiotic to take for a week, and told her to see her family doctor when she got home.

The nurse returned and handed her information on how to care for her stitches, including how to wash her hair.

There were still a few fans hanging out in the lobby when they arrived.

Mia suggested she head in alone, have him go around the block, so it didn't look so obvious they were a couple.

Scott insisted they walk in together. He kept an arm around her to keep her steady.

The six girls in the lobby jumped to their feet and hesitantly approached.

"Are you all right?" one girl asked politely.

"I'll be okay, thank you. Did anyone figure out who pushed me?" Mia said.

All the girls shook their heads.

"If I see her on the boat…"

"We'll ask around! Glad you're still coming," another fan said.

"She wouldn't miss it," Scott said. "But spread the word that we'll kick anyone that gets out of line off the boat. I probably should make sure Ms. Lee makes it safely to her room. Thank you for your concern. See you on the boat."

The door clicked closed in their penthouse. "Do you think they suspected anything?" Mia asked, stepping into his arms.

"No. They just think I'm looking out for a fan that got injured," he said, letting her go and heading to the bathroom to start her a warm bath. "For the rest of the cruise, anyone that saw what happened tonight will think I'm only checking on you like a good star should do. They won't realize you're a huge part of my life."

Mia smiled, but he could tell the local anesthesia they'd given her was wearing off and her head was hurting.

Scott helped her out of her clothes.

It was three in the morning, and she was obviously exhausted.

He got her into the tub, then quickly undressed to join her.

Mia had her eyes closed and must not have realized he was joining her until his hand went to her shoulder to get her to move forward a little to give him room. She'd made a small gasp in surprise.

He slipped in behind her, keeping his knees bent.

She leaned her head back against his chest but instantly hissed at the pain when the stitched-up skin touched. She sat forward, bringing her knees up to her breasts and resting her chin on them.

Scott grabbed the natural sponge and gently washed her back. He worked his way up, squeezing the water over her hair to wash the blood away.

The stitches were low on the back of her scalp, but the blood had soaked her hair.

He kept his touch gentle as he lathered the locks.

A whimper escaped her lips when he accidentally brushed against her stitches.

He rinsed her with a cup of water and helped her out of the tub. Scott dried her off before worrying about himself.

Mia sighed when she slipped into the huge bed, trying to lie only on one side.

Scott spooned her, trying to comfort her. He was waiting for her to start crying again, but she drifted off to sleep. He lay awake for hours, listening to her breathing. It was such a beautiful sound.

He'd spent most of the time at the hospital angry with Eddie, when really he was angry at himself.

There was no reason to be mad at his friend. Scott was also upset he'd made the agreement with Mia to keep them a secret until the cruise was over.

All he wanted to do was be by her side. It'd been so hard for him to see Eddie being the one to breathe life into her when she had been the one to breathe life into him.

She moaned lightly in her sleep.

He gently tucked a lock of hair back behind her ear.

They didn't need to be on the ship until after one pm, so he didn't set an alarm when he picked up his phone. Instead, he texted Eddie.

SCOTT: I wanted to say I'm sorry.

He didn't expect a reply but received one, anyway.

EDDIE: What for, bro?

SCOTT: For being an ass because Mia got hurt.

EDDIE: Hey, no one can think straight when someone they love is hurt.

SCOTT: It wasn't your fault, though. I'm sorry I wanted to blame you.

EDDIE: It's all good, brother. Take care of her and let me know how she's doing.

SCOTT: Thanks. She's all right. Eight stitches and a mild concussion. But they said she's good to cruise.

EDDIE: Have fun.

Scott laid back down, listening to Mia, then slowly drifting off to sleep.

♪♫

MIA WOKE WITH A MASSIVE HEADACHE. She'd never had a hangover like this before. She did her morning cat stretches and slid out of bed, not wanting to wake Scott.

He looked so peaceful sleeping; the pillow curled up in his arms.

She went into the bathroom and was promptly reminded of the night before when she spotted her ruined petticoat on the floor.

Antibiotics and painkillers sat beside the sink.

Just another reminder.

She sat on the edge of the tub and tried to recall what'd happened exactly. She'd make the bitch pay if she showed her face on the boat. All she could remember was her dark hair.

Mia took one of each pill and washed her face. She was afraid of the pain to her head, so she skipped the shower. She dressed in capris and a light-colored top, trying to be quiet. She didn't want to wake Scott.

She put on the barest of makeup and gently pulled her hair back into a loose ponytail, hiding the bald spot the best she could.

Mia went to check her phone, but it wouldn't turn on.

Damn it!

She'd had it in her bra at the party. The device had gone into the pool with her.

I wonder if putting it in a bag of rice would do the trick?

I'll ask the front desk if room service could bring me a bag of uncooked rice.

She set it on the counter, hoping after a few hours the inside would dry and it might turn back on. It was supposed to be water-resistant but she doubted that included a trip in a pool.

She slipped into the bedroom and glanced at the clock. Nine a.m. She needed to get out of the penthouse for a while. Mia put on her light blue sandals, and grabbed her purse, then slipped out the door.

She stepped off the elevator to a lobby teaming with *Razor's Edge* fans getting ready to head over to the shipping dock.

There was a little restaurant across the lobby, and she was starving. She really didn't want to walk through the large crowd to get to the restaurant and was grateful for the tables and chairs that were associated with the restaurant, to her left.

She headed for the glass doors.

She'd barely selected a table when a server came to her. Mia ordered a glass of orange juice, pancakes, and eggs. She wished her phone was working.

I should've left Scott a note.

While she ate, she people-watched. The girls gathering in the lobby were an interesting bunch. They were all sizes, ages, and nationalities.

A server, but not hers, stepped up to the table, a piece of paper in his hand.

"Miss? I was asked to give you this."

Mia took it and opened it as he walked away. The handwriting was neat. It wasn't obviously feminine or masculine. The words caused her stomach to knot, and shot apprehension down her spine.

"You should know, what happened last night was just the beginning. When the rest of the boat finds out about you, they'll all be trying to crack your skull open."

She scanned the restaurant and lobby, as if the author would materialize.

Gazes caught her eyes, but that was all.

She didn't see the server that'd brought it to her.

Fear skittered down her limbs, but the pain in her head reminded her how crazy fans could get. Her terror quickly flipped to rage. She wasn't about to let someone ruin her weekend.

The note had declared there were many people after her, but really, it came down to one jealous person.

They might not even have it right.

She'd been dancing with Eddie. This might be about him, and not Scott.

Mia crumpled the note, then smoothed it back out and tucked it in her purse. She paid her tab and headed for the elevator.

She was so wrapped up in her anger over the note; she didn't see the small crowd of girls until they'd surrounded her.

"Oh my God, you're okay!" one girl cried. "We were all so worried. Are you still gonna be able to go on the cruise?"

She scanned the small group.

They all seemed genuinely concerned for her. They must see her as just another RE fan that got lucky enough to dance with Eddie from *Next Step*, and unlucky enough to have encountered a jealous fan.

"Thank you for your concern. Yeah, I'm okay. I got eight stitches in my head, but Scott was super cool and went with me and stayed by my side. I got clearance to go on the ship." Mia made eye contact with the girl closest to her, trying to play up the fangirl aspect. "Do you think he will remember me when we get on the boat?"

"Oh, he better! He's my favorite, and I can totally see him doing something nice like that. Maybe he'll do something special for you at one of the events!"

The other girls started speculating what things could happen for her.

She smiled; glad she'd planted this seed. Hopefully, it would spread. If the crowds thought Scott was just being nice, there wouldn't be anything to worry about.

Mia chatted with the girls for a while, learning their names. She hoped she'd remember and see them on the boat later. She'd always aimed to make new friends, and these ladies seemed nice.

When the pain in her head got the best of her, she excused herself, explaining she needed to go take something for the pain.

Three other girls got on the elevator at the same time.

Mia didn't want them to see she was on the penthouse level, especially since one of them had on an NS/RE tour shirt. So she picked the next highest level that was lit up.

The three girls planned how to get the attention of their favorite band member.

The brunette was going on and on about how she was planning on hooking up with Scott.

Mia stifled a giggle as the girl explained excitedly.

She said she was going to corner him at some point and her kisses would be all she needed to say.

When they got off the elevator, Mia pulled out her keycard and selected the penthouse level. She was getting tired and wished for a nap.

Scott was still asleep, so she stripped down to her underwear, crawled back into bed, and snuggled against his back.

CHAPTER 18

The phone in the room rang, jerking them both awake.

It was on Scott's side of the bed, so he reached to grab the receiver. "Hello," he said, still half asleep.

"You gonna sleep all day?" Blaze drawled.

He glanced at the clock. It was just after noon.

"How's Mia doing? Is she still coming? Grace won't stop bothering me to call and ask," Blaze continued before Scott said a word.

He chuckled. "Gotta love that wife of yours. Mia's good. Eight stitches, and a mild concussion, but she's still coming. Can you ask Grace if she and the other wives would keep an eye on her? She's pretty much solo, and the doctor said to watch her for symptoms."

"Oh, you know they'll be thick as thieves by the end of the first day," the once bad boy said. "Hurry and get your ass to the dock."

"Dude, we have, like, three hours before the boat leaves. I'm good. Gotta go." Scott hung up before his friend could say anything else. He rolled over to look at Mia. "I can't believe you slept through breakfast."

"Um, I didn't." She sat up and wrapped her arms around her now bent knees. "I woke up a few hours ago. I've already been downstairs and eaten. But I came back up and fell asleep. So, what's the plan?"

An hour later, they walked through the now-empty lobby together, where the white limos awaited them.

When the automobile pulled up to the dock, Mia gasped and couldn't stop staring.

"I've never seen a ship that big up close. I feel like Rose walking up to the Titanic. Of course, hopefully it won't sink."

"It won't."

"That's what Mr. Andrews said."

Scott shook his head and tried not to laugh. "I have to let you go alone from here. We've got some band stuff to deal with." He kissed her softly, letting out a long held breath when she'd exited the limo. He kept his eye on her as a valet helped get their bags on board.

The limo took a turn around the parking lot and dropped Scott off right by another vehicle. He vacated the limo and joined his brothers in the latter. Eight people crammed into the over-sized limo, waiting for time to join the party.

It was tradition to all go in together. Not just the boys and their wives, but the entire entourage. There were friends of the band, their management and their friends. Hell, there were more people Scott didn't know, than ones he did.

The crowd screamed when they pulled up. Women wiped at tears that fell like they were still teenagers. He wanted to look for Mia, but knew she was already inside, probably getting settled in her cabin. It would be hours before he got to see her. Even longer before he could hold her in his arms. He craved her, like a drug. And almost losing her just hours ago, had almost been more than he could bear. He'd wanted a stiff drink then, but knew better.

He continued to wave at the fans as they entered the ship.

Their rooms were just doors apart, yet he wasn't granted that brief moment to check on her. They had to change into their Sail Away Party costumes and rush to the first sound check in the main theater.

It was going to be a long day.

THE VALET DELIVERED Mia and her luggage to her stateroom.

The suite was luxurious. It had a living room area, with a couch and two chairs. The king-sized bed had a mauve-colored bedspread.

The room had a tv and a small fridge, and the bathroom had a single stall shower with a jetted tub. She hadn't expected a tub at all, let alone one that big.

Mia fell in love with the cabin immediately, although she figured she wouldn't be spending much time there.

The ship's itinerary and an *All-Access* lanyard were on the bed. She was reading through the plans when a voice came over the intercom.

"Welcome, cruisers. I'm pleased to announce the party can start now. *Razor's Edge* has boarded."

Mia grabbed her phone from her purse, checking again to see if it would turn on. She was pleasantly surprised when the little apple appeared in the center of her screen. She set it down beside her on the bed to finish loading and glanced at the itinerary again.

Karaoke? Sounds like fun.

Her phone began to go crazy, sounding alerts for all the texts and emails she'd missed. Not wanting to deal with them, she dismissed them, and went straight to her thread with Scott.

MIA: Glad you're on the boat. Damn, this room is awesome.

. . .

SCOTT: Glad you like it. I'm gonna be swamped until late tonight. You gonna be okay?

MIA: I'll be fine. I'll see you tonight.

NO REPLY CAME, but she wasn't worried. He was on the boat. That was all that mattered. She'd see him later, at the themed party.

Mia explored the boat, avoiding the more crowded areas. She walked up and down the hallways, watching girls decorate their doors with pictures, notes, and other fun things. She was glad she didn't need to do that. These fans must've spent months planning their decor.

I wonder if it's a contest or something. That's a lot of work for nothing.

She'd have to ask Scott about it later.

She found the pools and where the karaoke would be. She went the opposite direction of the crowds.

They were having a sail away party on the lido deck, but she wasn't ready to party yet.

The boat was finally in open waters, and Mia found her sea legs with no problem.

There was a themed event planned for that night. She'd wait to jump into the crowds until then.

She was getting hungry, and the buffet was on the far side of the lido deck. Rather than taking the short way through the crowd of two thousand women, she went up a level, found another set of stairs, and made her way down to a mostly empty area.

She filled a plate and took it outside to sit on the deck overlooking the aft.

It was after eight p.m. when Mia finally made her way back to her room. She hung up all her dresses and costumes and sorted her bathroom supplies.

The itinerary stated the party started at 10 p.m. She didn't want to get in with the crowd. She hoped to find somewhere to sit.

Mia got ready for the 80s Hair Band Night party. She had thought long and hard about what to wear for the party. She needed to stand out, in a good way. She pulled the red and white checkered dress out of the closet. It was tiny, barely covering her ass; the buttons pulled tight across her breasts, displaying amazing cleavage.

She tied a white apron over it, a slice of cherry pie printed off-center. Then slipped on a wig cap and busied herself with makeup. Her black eyeliner was thick and her lips were fire engine red.

Mia pulled on the burgundy red wig, smoothing the fly-aways the mirror helped her locate.

Damn, even my mother wouldn't recognize me. Will Scott?

She grabbed her bag of costume accessories and pulled out a plastic, yet realistic looking, cherry pie. All she was missing was white roller skates with red wheels, but those weren't something she could wear on a cruise.

Mia stared at herself in the mirror. She looked exactly like the redhead on the cover of *Warrant's Cherry Pie* Single album. It had been one of her favorite songs from the hair band era.

Tonight she'd get into the crowd. She was gonna flirt hard with Scott, like a fan would.

He wants a secret love affair this weekend; I'm gonna give him one.

She grabbed her *All-Access* lanyard and tucked it in her pocket. She didn't want others to see, but carried it, in case she needed it.

When Mia stepped out of her cabin, she ran smack into a lady that looked a bit too much like the 80s popstar, Tiffany.

Her chestnut hair was crimped, and she wore a denim jacket covered with buttons with sayings, a short jean skirt, and yellow high tops. The woman had kind blue-green eyes that looked so familiar.

They stared at each other for a moment, and the Tiffany look-alike was the first to speak. "Mia?"

She could only nod.

"I'm not sure if you remember me, I'm Grace. Blaze's wife."

Recognition hit her, and her cheeks flushed with embarrassment from not recognizing Grace right away.

"Don't feel bad, I almost didn't realize it was you. If it hadn't been for my husband telling me what room you're in, so we could keep an eye on you, I wouldn't have recognized you either."

"Oh, good," she whispered. "I was hoping Scott wouldn't know it was me either."

"Why?"

She swallowed, mustering courage for the truth. "I want to get up and close with the fans, flirt with Scott like all the other girls. I need to blend in, so no one knows we are together." It was silly when said aloud, wasn't it?

Grace laughed and slipped her arm in Mia's, then headed for the stairs. "That sounds like fun, and I wish I could do that," the chestnut beauty said as they climbed the stairs from the seventh floor to the tenth. "Blaze would know me instantly, no matter how I tried to change my appearance."

They reached the lido deck.

"Scott will know right away it's you if we're seen together. But please, after he sees you, come visit us in the VIP section. You have your lanyard, right?" Grace asked.

She tapped her pocket, checking for her own peace of mind. "Right here."

"Good. Have fun, and I'll see you up there," she pointed to the VIP section on deck eleven that overlooked the lido deck.

Mia tried to make her way through the screaming fans to get as close to the stage as she could.

The crowd was brutal and didn't want to let her move any closer.

She understood; they'd been standing there for hours, but some girls were downright rude.

Mia had enough. She forced her way out of the mass of bodies, and headed for the bar at the back of the crowd. Maybe a drink would help.

She finally made it up to the counter to order something when the surrounding girls started screaming even louder.

Blaze, Nick, and Scott were to her left, coming out the galley door, aprons tied around their waists, trays of shots in their hands.

They were all dressed like 80s hair band rockers.

Blaze had on a yellow tiger-print jumpsuit and a long blond wig.

Nick was also blond, in a white artist smock, black tights, and a diamond-encrusted codpiece she could just barely see with the apron on.

Mia giggled when Scott came into view.

His black wig was long curled locks, with an orange headband around his forehead, keeping it all in place. He had a black long-sleeved top that opened at the chest and hot pink and black tiger-print tights. It was obvious he had nothing on under the tights.

Her secret lover was sharing way more than she wished he would.

Girls pushed up around her, pressing her into the bar, trying to reach the guys as they climbed onto the bar at various points.

Nick was right in front of her and held up one of the shot glasses. He licked the rim, being far too sexy.

All the girls around her were reaching high, trying to get him to give them the glass.

Mia was the only one not reaching up.

His eyes locked with hers.

Right away, she could tell he didn't realize it was her.

Nick pointed to her and handed down the shot.

She didn't want to give herself away, so she downed the shot, using the part of the rim he hadn't licked. That would've been wrong on so many levels.

When she tried to set it on the bar, the girl beside her picked it up and held on to it tight.

Mia had to fight not to laugh. She looked at Scott.

He was about six girls away from her on the right. On the bar, his head almost hit the lights. He leaned down to flirt with the girl in front of him, while all the ones around him were fighting to get his attention.

He turned toward her, and she held her breath.

Even though she could have him anytime, it was kinda thrilling to be acting like one of the fangirls, fighting to get his attention.

His gaze rested on her briefly, then he shook his head, like he was pushing away a thought. Scott continued to hand out shots to the women in front of him.

He took a step to his right, bringing him a little closer to Mia.

The bartender handed him another shot to pass out.

Instead of handing it directly to a girl, he took a sip before it left his hand. He did that a few times.

Knots formed in her chest.

They'd talked about his drinking in the past, and Scott had only had a glass of wine occasionally now, but never hard liquor. Not anymore.

It was only the first few hours on the cruise that would last four nights, and he was already succumbing to temptation.

It made her worry about what else could happen.

When Scott went to hand out another shot, she finally reached out.

He looked right at her and smiled, but handed the shot to the girl beside her. However, he maintained eye contact with Mia.

She held her breath from the briefest moment, worried he'd known all along it was her.

Then he looked away and was handed another shot.

He passed three more out before he took another step to his right, getting closer to her.

"Scott! Look at me!" She reached for it again, and tried to scream louder than the others.

He obeyed, and surprise washed over her.

Mia didn't want to smile, because it would give her away. So she held up her pie. "Wanna slice of my pie?"

He'd obviously caught on that she wasn't offering dessert. Scott smiled. Not his normal smile she knew so well. It was like he was trying to be nice, but didn't really care. "Maybe later, darling," he said before resuming passing out shots. He didn't look her way again.

Mia smiled.

He didn't know it was her, and hadn't really flirted back.

Actually, he'd ignored her after she'd been so bold. It might be shallow, but it made her feel good that he'd brush off a woman trying to seduce him.

They gave away hundreds of shots in a short amount of time, finally retreating through the galley door.

When they left, and the crowd dissipated slightly, moving to the main stage in the middle, Mia finally worked her way through the fans and headed over to the VIP section.

"How'd it go?" Grace asked.

She took the chair next to her, setting her pie on the table beside her. "Well, he didn't recognize me," her voice wavered.

"Okay, I'm confused. I thought that was what you wanted."

"Yeah, but…"

"But, what?" Her voice was laced with concern.

"He took a shot. A few, actually."

"Oh." Grace picked up her phone and began texting. "I just

sent Blaze a message to keep an eye on Scott. I'm sure he's just celebrating your here, but better safe than sorry."

Mia pulled her own phone from her pocket.

MIA: I'm realizing there are a lot of temptations on the boat. Please remember I am here for you if you need me.

She put her phone away, regretting the text. It could make him mad. He'd probably think she didn't trust him.

The more she worried about it, the worse she felt.

On the stage in the middle of the lido deck, the guys put on a show much like the after-parties she'd been to.

They did a lot of singing along to their own music.

The crowd went wild when they played all the favorites.

After a while, the DJ took over, spinning songs from the 80s.

Nick, Blaze, and Scott made their way up the stairs to the VIP area, leaving Thomas and Dwaine on the main stage, still interacting with the fans.

Mia moved over to the side. She leaned slightly over the railing on the opposite side of the stairs, so Scott wouldn't see her face.

The moment he passed her, she walked up behind him.

He stopped at the table where Grace sat. He was about to say something to Blaze's wife.

In one swift movement, she slipped her hands in between his arms and side, snaking around his chest, and pressing her breasts against his back. She hiked up her left leg around his waist, resting the heel of her red shoe just a breath away from his package. "Why, Scott Kay Ralston. You have been a very naughty boy," Mia whispered in a southern-belle accent.

He pushed her foot down and peeled her hands off his chest. When he whirled on her, his expression was tight, angry. "I'm really not interested," he said. He looked away, then did a double-take. He'd noticed the cherry pie on the table next to Grace. He looked back at Mia and shook his head.

She smiled, and couldn't hold back a laugh..

"Oh my God, baby. I didn't realize it was you," he breathed.

"I know. So, do you want some of my pie now?"

They both laughed.

Scott pulled her close, kissing her deeply. "Tell me about that pie," he teased against her mouth.

Grace picked it up and tapped it on its side on the table. "Um, Scott, sweetie, it is plastic."

Mia's cheeks seared, but she didn't answer Blaze's wife.

"I'd love to take you back to the room right this second, but I have to get back on stage with the guys." He kissed her lightly before getting a Red Bull at the bar and heading back.

The rest of the night, Scott only drank one more Red Bull and water. She kept a close eye on him, and it made her doubt what she'd seen when the guys were giving out the shots.

When Mia finally made her way back to her cabin, it was almost three in the morning.

The guys were still going strong, but she needed sleep if she was going to survive the cruise. Especially if all the nights ran that late.

CHAPTER 19

Morning rays spilled through the open curtain and woke Mia. She stretched like a cat. If this was day two, how was she going to survive the whole cruise?

She was a mess. Her body hurt from standing around and staying up well past her bedtime.

Her throat was raw from trying to get Scott's attention at the party. Mia was also starving.

She put on a lightweight, flowing summer dress, pulled her hair back into a ponytail, and put on some lip gloss before grabbing her lanyard and heading out to find food.

She hadn't even made it to the stairs when she heard her name.

"Mia! Mia! Wait for us!" Grace rushed to catch up with her, and two others trailed behind.

Mia recognized the other two from her disastrous night in Tulsa. It'd been a whirlwind then, and she couldn't recall their names, or what band member they belonged to.

"Are you heading for breakfast? Mind if we join you?"

She forced a smile. Did she have a choice?

The four of them took the stairs.

The two she didn't know chatted about what some girls on the boat had the courage to wear.

It put a knot in her stomach. She'd been one of the girls they were talking about. Before Mia could point that out, Grace grabbed her attention.

"We normally go into the sit-down restaurant, instead of the buffet. I hope that's all right?"

Again, she didn't feel as if there was really a choice, so she nodded for the second time. Not that she didn't appreciate their wanting to look out for her, but their presence reminded her of a night she wanted to forget.

They sat at a table beside the window, and Mia stared out to the ocean.

"Are you enjoying the cruise?" the petite woman with short chocolate hair inquired.

"I guess. It's only been one night, and I've hardly seen Scott, but I told him he needed to act like he was still single." She took a sip of her orange juice before continuing. "I'm sorry, and this will sound rude, but I can't recall your names." She looked between the dark-haired one and the stunning beauty with cranberry red hair.

"Oh, I guess it's been a while. I'm Hope," the tiny one said, extending her hand. "I'm Nick's wife."

"I'm Evelien, Dwaine's wife. Everyone calls me Evey. Like Chevy, without the 'ch'. I didn't see you at last night's party. Didn't you want to attend?"

Mia didn't think, just let the words vomit out. "I was there. Dressed like an 80s hair band whore, complete with my cleavage on full display. Even Scott didn't recognize me."

Evey's cheeks went crimson. "I'm sorry. I must've sounded like a jealous bitch back there. It's just…"

Grace saved her when she trailed off. "Think about it for a moment, Mia. You got the exact response we all hope to get from our men. Scott didn't know it was you, yet when you made advances, he politely declined you. The girls on this boat know about us; know we're here, on the boat. And even if we weren't, our boys are faithful. They can dress seductively all they want, it's not going to get them anywhere."

Mia looked down, and it was her turn to feel a tad overheated. "I wasn't trying to prove a point," she whispered, studying her glass of juice. "I wanted to play the part of a dutiful fan. I guess I took the themes a little too seriously."

Evelien barked a loud laugh, then grabbed Mia's free hand. "Oh, honey, I could tell you horror stories about my first cruise! I've never been more embarrassed in my life. Dwaine never lets me live it down. He brings it up every year, when I start packing our suitcases for the cruise. Trust me, you're not alone."

"This is mine and Hope's first cruise, too. I'm sure we can all make mistakes together. With Evelien's guidance, we just might survive this week."

They talked about the itinerary and which events they would attend, without too much fan backlash.

"I was looking forward to the karaoke contest. I'm not very good, but I love to sing," Mia said.

"Oh, that would be fun!" Hope said, "Grace is a professional singer!"

"No, I'm not."

"Yes, you are," the smallest woman pushed.

"I did one play where I sang. That doesn't make me a professional. And we agreed not to talk about that while on the boat." Her voice wavered.

Nick's girl didn't stop. "You have to start singing again, Gracie. Your therapist said it's important. And what better place than here, with friends?"

"The fans might not like it," the chestnut-haired woman said.

"They don't need to know," Mia said.

"What do you mean?" Evelien asked. "They know what we look like."

"So then, we change how we look," Mia retorted.

"And how do we do that?" Hope asked.

"Well, this overzealous girl packed like a fan. I went all out for theme nights. I have wigs in every color."

"And with Grace's theater background, she could do everyone's makeup to make us all look different," Hope said.

"I love this idea," Evelien grinned. "I've never been able to do fan stuff. I married Dwaine long before the first cruise."

"So, what should we sing?" Hope asked.

"I was reading the contest rules yesterday, and it says it has to be a *Razor's Edge* song. I'm the first to admit I don't know them all," Mia said.

"Rules? This isn't just for fun?" Nick's girl asked.

"It's a contest. They'll announce the winners of round one at the PDA Pajama Party tonight. The itinerary didn't say what the final prize was, though," Mia continued.

"What about *We Were Meant To Be* or *Designs Of Love?*" Hope inquired.

"Too obvious," Evelien said. "We need more obscure ones to choose from; something no one else will do."

"What about *How Did This Happen?*" Grace said.

"No, it's mostly a duet with Thomas and Dwaine. It needs to be more even. What about *Unfinished?*" Evelien said.

"Perfect!" Grace and Hope said together.

They spent the rest of the meal assigning parts.

The first round of karaoke started at four p.m.

"I think we need to meet up after lunch and find somewhere quiet to do a run through and try on wigs. Putting on a wig can change everything about you, from your posture to the sound of your voice. It'd be good to practice in our façade," Grace said.

They finished their meal and made their way back to their rooms.

IT FELT like it took all day before he spotted her. Scott watched as Mia stepped out from the interior of the ship, into the sunshine to lounge by the pool.

She'd put on an electric blue bikini that had a ruffle around the top edge of the bottoms.

He kept an eye on her, following her walk around until she found an empty lounge chair. She'd had a book in one hand and her phone in the other, setting them both at the foot of the chair to spread out her blue beach towel.

He grabbed his phone from where it sat beside him, at the edge of one of the pools, and sent her a text while she got settled.

SCOTT: Wow, babe. Nice bikini.

HE WATCHED her look around for him.

MIA: That message could be for any girl here. Look around at all the bikinis. How would I know that message was just for me?

SCOTT: I don't see any other beautiful women in a blue bikini, with a bald spot on the back of her head.

MIA: So you're telling me you spotted me from the bald-spot, not my cleavage?

SCOTT: Those nice round melons caught my eye first.

. . .

Her laughter filled him.

Scott and Nick were in the right corner by the edge of the pool, and had a large basket of water toys and guns. He picked up a super soaker and squirted the crowd. He got them all across the abdomen or legs. He avoided the chests.

When Scott leaned down to get another water gun after emptying the one he held, a brunette in a little bikini made a move, getting right in front of him.

Surprise hit him full on and he took a step back.

"Hi, Scott, I'm Victoria. I couldn't help but notice you're here alone."

He gestured to the people with his water gun. "Hardly."

She stepped closer, and he took another step back.

"So…" she drew out, in an attempt at obvious sexiness. "I was thinking we should hang out." The brunette stepped even closer.

Scott took a third step back. He'd never before felt as much like prey as he did in that moment. "We're hanging out. Let's go hang out in the smaller pool," he said, trying to move closer to his bodyguard.

She pretty much backed him into the wall. "I was thinking we could head to your room and…"

Scott felt his face flush with heat when she leaned in for a whisper.

"You'll never imagine all the things I am going to do to you. I'm very flexible."

Even before Mia came into his life, this was not the type of woman he would allow in his bed. He glanced at his security, knowing this was a time he would need some help. But security was dealing with two fans trying to pull Blaze into the pool, and were missing all of Scott's drama.

The tiny brunette couldn't have been over five foot-two inches, but she was intimidating him. He couldn't even say why.

She grabbed the front of his shirt, catching him completely off guard.

His hands went to her shoulders to steady himself.

She took it all wrong, more like he was accepting her advances than staving her off.

Her hands went around his neck, and she tried to kiss him.

Scott pushed her away before their lips met and sidestepped away from her.

He could hear Mia laughing.

At least she is enjoying this.

Although the kiss failed, the brunette's expression shouted that she was now more determined than ever.

The buzzing of his phone helped Scott to move a real distance from his suitor.

"Please, excuse me, I really need to check that." He grabbed the phone, waved at her, letting her know it was important, then scooted about ten feet away.

MIA: Looks like I've got competition. You okay?

SCOTT: Thanks. And no. No competition. Ever.

SCOTT HURRIED to stand close to his bodyguard, water gun still in hand. If the 'hunter' came back, he'd blast her.

CHAPTER 20

M ia had been out in the sun for over an hour and was getting overheated. A server stopped by to see if she needed anything, grabbing her attention off her man.

Alcohol was dehydrating, but a libation sounded fantastic. She ordered a fruity concoction, something sweet and strong.

When the server returned with her drink, he also handed her a small piece of paper. "Someone asked me to hand this to you."

Mia took the note.

The server walked away, ignoring her when she asked him to wait.

She glanced down at the small neat print.

"KEEP SMILING, *because soon enough, you won't have a reason to smile.*"

SHE LOOKED UP, trying to force a smile to trembling lips.

The server must've heard her, after all. He stood not far, but his expression was impatient.

"Do you remember who handed this to you?"

"It was the bartender. He said it was given to him for you, but he can't leave the bar. He asked me to give it to you."

"Any chance you can ask him where it came from?"

She glanced at Scott, who was halfway across the deck, still standing close to his bodyguards.

Maybe I should tell Scott?

"I'll go ask and be right back," the server said.

Mia couldn't take her eyes of the guy as he went back to the bar, and although she couldn't hear what they said, body language said it wouldn't be good news.

Grace and Hope came into view when the server made his way back to her, just in time to hear what he had to say.

"George, the bartender, said it was passed to him by one of the many girls that have ordered drinks. He really wasn't looking at her face." The server went pink, making it obvious he wasn't straight. "She just pointed you out and said the note was for you. I wish I could tell you more."

"That's all right. I still appreciate you asking for me."

He nodded and excused himself.

"What was that all about?" Hope asked.

Both women settled on the lounge chair on either side of Mia's feet.

"Nothing."

"Bullshit," Grace said. "You're family, now. We take care of each other. We came for you to get ready for karaoke, and the look on your face says it's something. Something bad."

She picked up her book and phone. "Let's head to my cabin, and I'll tell you."

I better tell someone, and Scott has enough on his hands.

MIA PULLED out the first note, then the new one.

Grace's face went white as she read the note. "Of all people, I know what dangers a note like this can bring," she whispered.

She was curious, but didn't press further.

"Have you shown this to Scott?" Hope asked.

"Oh, God, no. He never would've let me on the boat. Or he'd keep me locked in his cabin. He doesn't need to know. I can handle this."

Grace put a hand to her throat, her hands visibly shaking. "He needs to know. So do the others. Trust me when I say, something bad can happen from this."

"Nothing is gonna happen!" Mia paced. "I'm not gonna let some jealous bitch ruin my weekend."

"I think we should skip karaoke," Grace said.

"No! You're not finding an excuse to get out of that! You need to do it! Mia, where're your wigs?" Hope asked, her dark eyes sparkling with determination.

"I don't think so," Grace interjected. "We aren't going anywhere, or doing anything until this is taken care of."

They all turned and looked at Mia. She just wanted this to blow over. But it was clear Grace wouldn't let that happen.

"Fine. I'll tell Scott. When the time is right, we can deal with it together. Fair?"

Grace just nodded her head.

Mia pulled out the bag with her costume accessories. One by one, she pulled out different colored wigs, some sort, some straight, even one pre-set in a vintage style.

"Do we wanna know why you have all these?" Hope teased.

Her face burned with embarrassment. She wanted to lie, but told them the truth; these ladies were the only ones that would understand. "I thought it unfair to the fans if they found out that 'newly single Scott', wasn't so single. I brought all these wigs to make myself look different throughout the cruise, so if we got a few spare moments together, the other women wouldn't realize it was me each time."

"Damn. Why didn't I think of that?" Hope asked. "A lot of people still don't know about me and Nick."

"Bullshit!" Grace looked at the wigs. "The dumbass professed his love to you on national TV, *and* pulled you on stage. Then you had his baby while getting married! I think *everyone* knows about you."

"We got married while I was having the baby, get it right," Hope teased under her breath.

Grace glanced at Mia. "I get *why* you brought them. Did you buy them all just for the cruise? These are high-quality wigs, and had to cost you a small fortune."

Mia picked up the short black bob and slipped it on. "I own a pinup photography business. A lot of the women that come in want to look different, or they don't have hair that works with the vintage styles. I offer them a chance to be the bombshell they didn't know they had in them."

"That's pretty cool. You must love what you do. I know how much it can help overcome internal issues. Making yourself a little different." Grace picked up the platinum blonde Marilyn Monroe-like wig.

Hope stepped close to the cabin door. "You two try on wigs. I'll get Evelien, so we can practice singing while we get ready."

"Before you go," Mia stopped her. "Did you say you got married *while* having the baby?"

Hope laughed, moving a foot back into the room. "Yeah. You can blame Scott and Thomas for that one."

"Really? And how was it?"

"Messy," Hope said before she slipped out the door, without another word of protest from Grace; the note completely forgotten.

"Is it too personal to ask why you don't want to sing? It sounds like you have the talent to do it." Mia picked up another wig, this time the burgundy one, and handed it to Grace.

She was gentle with the blonde wig and when she put on the red, it was clear she knew her way around wigs, too.

"It's a long story," Blaze's wife breathed. "Better told another day. Let's just say, I had a traumatic incident that involved some singing, a lot of pain, and someone I thought was a friend. I haven't sung since. Not even in the shower."

Mia couldn't guess what could be that traumatic about singing, but Grace clearly didn't want to talk about it, and she wouldn't push.

Knock, knock broke the silence and she rushed to open it.

Hope and Evelien spilled into the room.

"I hope you're not going with that red wig, Grace. It's too close to your real hair," the woman with cranberry-colored locks said.

They were laughing and chatting while they all tried on wigs.

Mia glanced at her phone. She had a message waiting, and she hadn't heard the phone's alert.

SCOTT: Where'd you go?

MIA: Had to leave the pool. Got too hot. Need to get ready for the contest, anyway.

SCOTT: Contest?

MIA: Yeah. Karaoke.

SCOTT: Nice! What're you singing?

MIA: Not telling.

. . .

SCOTT: No fair. I wanna come watch, but they have us doing water games for the next few hours.

MIA: No worries. See ya later.

IT ONLY TOOK a few run-throughs of the song before they all felt comfortable enough to perform it.

Except for Grace.

She played the judge, letting each of them know where they could improve. She still hadn't sung a single note.

They left Mia's cabin decked out in wigs and full makeup.

They headed for the piano bar where the karaoke event was.

"I'm nervous," Evelien said. "This is the first time I've ever been able to enjoy fan activities. I only hope we make it to the next round."

Dwaine's wife filled out the form and handed it to the lady in charge.

They all agreed they needed to use false names to further throw off the fans. They went with the team name, *The Betties.*

The first *Razor's Edge* wife joined the other ladies at the table, as they waited for their turn.

A waitress came by and took their drink orders.

"I'll have a Moscato," Grace said.

"Me, too," Hope chimed in.

"White Russian," Evelien said.

"*Sex on The Beach*, please." Mia was a little embarrassed by her choice, but she hadn't had one on her trip.

No one said anything about it, though.

They finished their drinks before being called up.

When the music began, she leaned close to Grace, so only she could hear her. "I don't know what happened to you, but now is the time to find your voice. We need you."

The song opened, and three of them sang their hearts out. When it slipped into the chorus, surprise washed over Mia.

The voice of a tortured angel joined them. Grace was hauntingly beautiful. At the same time, she was gritty, like she hadn't used her voice in months.

Just like the lyrics of the song, without her vocals, they were unfinished. Grace completed their sound.

When they finished, there was a flurry of applause.

They returned to their seats, and agreed it was best to watch the other singers.

Common courtesy seemed to be lacking by others, who left as soon as they had sung.

When the last group performed, the beautiful blonde lady in charge stepped up to the mic. "Thank you all for coming, and for those that stayed behind to cheer on the other singers. We'll announce the groups that made it to the next round at tonight's party. We'll also hint at the grand prize. Start thinking about what RE song you'll sing if you make it to the next round! Have a great rest of your night."

The remaining singers filled out, but Mia and her new friends stayed behind to chat.

"Wow, that was amazing! Grace, you really shouldn't hide that voice," she said.

"I've been telling her the same thing for months. But trauma can do that," Hope said, dropping her voice on the second sentence.

"That went better than expected. I don't think anyone knew who we were," Evelien said, her relief evident. "Assuming we make it to the next round, what should we sing?"

They made their way to the dining hall, still talking out the decision they needed to make.

"I think it should be a fast song," Mia said as they found seats. "But I'll be honest, I don't know all their music, so it might limit my options. I catch on quickly, though. I do bad karaoke once a month at a local dive bar."

Hope poked Grace in the ribs. "See, we aren't the only ones that like karaoke. Maybe someday I'll get you to do it again."

"What do you mean, you don't know them all?" Blaze's wife ignored her friend and made eye contact with Mia. "We met you during the tour. At an after-party."

She tried *not* to remember the night they had all met. It wasn't a good night. "I, um...wasn't at the concert for *Razor's Edge*. I was there for *Next Step*. I didn't even like Scott when I met him." She clasped her hands over her mouth, then quickly added, "Please don't tell him. Only Eddie knows that."

Grace laughed softly. "You're in good company. I wasn't exactly a fan when I met Blaze, either. I didn't see the band perform live until after we were married."

That made Mia feel a lot better about not being such a good fan.

They kept going through potential songs while waiting for their food.

"I've got it!" Evelien said. "What about *Single Bullet?*"

"I love that song," Hope said.

"Is that the one with the vampires?" Grace asked.

"Yes," the first-wife replied.

"Vampires?" Mia cocked her head to the side. Maybe she'd never heard this one.

Evelien pulled her phone out. A moment later, she had the device propped against a glass of water. She kept the volume low, as to not disturb the other diners, but a girl at the table behind them asked her to turn it up.

She even came over to stand behind Mia to watch.

By the time the video ended, a small crowd had gathered.

"I love that video," one girl said.

"I don't know, the red eyes are a little creepy," another said.

They'd been so wrapped up in the video, and with their wigs

and makeup on, no one knew they were standing by the ladies with the band.

With all the comments around them, it confirmed the song would be a good choice.

"We should try to learn some basic choreography. Then we'd win for sure," Mia said. "I know exactly where to practice."

When Mia had been exploring the ship the first day, she'd come across a fitness class room.

There was a long wall with a mirror, and a CD player in the corner. The place was empty, and there was a piece of paper on the wall, listing class times.

There was no one there, so she checked the door. It was unlocked.

They quickly slipped inside.

Grace had gone back to her room and grabbed a laptop before meeting them there.

Using Evelien's phone, the three of them went over the song.

By the time Grace joined them, they had the song down well enough.

With her theater background, she was able to watch the video and pick up choreography quickly, then taught it to them.

After about an hour, she turned the sound down so they could barely hear it.

They sang along, using the mirror as a guide.

They ran through it one last time, when Hope pointed to a few girls hanging out by the door and windows, looking into the fitness room.

As much as they wanted to stand by each other when the groups going to the next level were announced, they'd all planned to attend the party looking like themselves.

They didn't want to give away the illusion.

Grace grabbed her laptop, and they headed out.

"That was awesome," one girl standing outside watching said.

"We really hope you're called to the next level. We watched

you sing *Unfinished*. There's no way we can win with amazing singers like you," another one said. "But we really wanna see you perform that on stage!"

"Thanks," Mia said hesitantly. Guilt swirled in her gut.

This was exactly why she and Scott were keeping their relationship a secret, so she wouldn't take away something from a fan.

They murmured thanks and kept moving.

"It's about damn time." Grace looked at her phone while they made their way back toward their cabins.

"What's up?" Hope asked.

"Blaze finally has some free time. I'll catch up with you later. I need my fix."

"Nick better be right behind him."

In the hallway, they showed their *All-Access* badges to security and made their way to their individual rooms.

Mia sighed, as jealousy replaced her earlier guilt. She wanted time with her man, too.

She'd hardly seen Scott, and only from a distance to boot. Regret about their secret relationship joined the envy in her tummy.

CHAPTER 21

M ia had just gotten to her cabin when another door just down the hall opened.

"Hey, sexy. You got any plans tonight?"

His deep voice resonated through her.

She felt like she hadn't seen him in weeks. She slowly whirled, trying hard not to smile. "Why, yes. I do have plans tonight. I'm gonna be in my pajamas, surrounded by half-naked, drunk women. Every man's fantasy." Mia took a step toward him, flashing a wicked smile.

Scott took a step closer, returning her grin. "Not my fantasy. All I need is you."

They almost touched, but stopped just short.

"Are you sure? There're some very beautiful women here and lots and lots of bare skin."

He closed the small distance between them. His arms went around her, and he pulled her body against his.

His lips were a breath away from hers.

"They may be beautiful, but they are not unmistakable," Scott whispered.

Mia kissed him, pushing her tongue into his mouth.

He always knew when to say the right things.

She ran her fingers through his soft hair.

They were deep in their kiss when she heard the security guy trying to explain to a group of girls that the area was secure and only those with *All-Access* lanyards could get them through.

"Well, how do I get one?" a girl asked.

"Have a cabin in this hallway. Or be married to a *Razor's Edge* guy," security said.

Mia broke their kiss and glanced over Scott's shoulder at the group. She didn't recognize any of them.

Unfortunately, one girl looked right at her.

If looks could kill, she'd be dead. Hatred, true hatred was stamped on the girl's face.

"Scott, I think we should get out of the hallway," Mia gestured with her chin.

The moment he followed her lead with a look, the girls realized who she'd been kissing.

They called his name and more, their individual words jumbled together, except one girl with long dark hair. She whirled away, so only the back of her head was visible.

Mia grabbed his hand and pulled him to her door. She didn't want to reveal which room he was staying in, even though it was only a few doors down. Hopefully she'd throw them off.

Once they were in her room, Scott burst out laughing.

Worry swirled around her, and he thought it was funny?

She didn't need word getting out that they'd been kissing. She sat on the edge of the bed and took a deep breath. Mia couldn't help but smile when she spared him a glance.

He didn't need to know what was going on in her mind. Scott had enough to deal with.

She didn't want to add worry over her to that list.

He stepped up to her, pushing in between her knees. His hands went into her hair, but he was still mindful of her stitches.

Scott kissed her forehead before their eyes met. "How's your head? Have you been taking your pills?"

She smiled again, this time at his concern. "Yes, I've been taking my pills. No, my head doesn't hurt...much."

He cocked his head to one side, as if he didn't like what she'd said. Scott kissed her on each temple, then moved down her face to kiss her lips with great tenderness. "I could show you the best way to get rid of a headache." He waggled his eyebrows.

"Tylenol," she teased back.

"Sex with your favorite *Razor's Edge* guy?"

She pushed him away and stood up.

He'd said the wrong words; used the wrong tone in his voice. He was being Scott, the big brother of *Razor's Edge,* and all she wanted was Scott, her sweet southern boyfriend.

There was still a very small part of Mia that disliked the band member of the most popular pop group in the world. *He* wasn't who she cared about.

The man that'd brought a stranger a bag of ice and kept her company since she was alone; *that* was who mattered to her.

The worst part was he didn't even realize what he'd done.

There was a knot in Mia's stomach.

The problem?

The reason for its origin was unknown.

"You probably should go. I need to get ready, and I'm sure they need all the *Razor's Edge* guys at the party on time." She intentionally used the band name instead of his, then stepped up to the door and opened it.

Mia stayed there, waiting for him to leave.

When he finally walked past, he leaned in to kiss her.

She shifted her head so his kiss would miss her mouth and land on her cheek.

"So, I'll see you at the party. Mickey Mouse jammies, right?"

She nodded.

He'd asked her to pack the pajamas during their very first night together. It meant something to him.

As soon the door lock clicked, Mia put her forehead against the cold door.

Her head was seriously hurting now. She stayed like that, trying not to cry.

Why do I even feel this way?

She finally pushed herself from the door and went to the bathroom.

Mia piled all her hair into a bun and tugged the provided shower cap on.

Tears would no longer be held at bay; she bawled as the warm water caressed her body. It was just a tad at first, but the more the cascading showerhead worked out kinks in her muscles, the worse she felt.

Tremors started by shimming down her spine, until they spread down her limbs and spread across her torso, until shaking wracked her whole frame.

Why was she crying?

The more she couldn't figure it out, the worse the internal earthquake got.

When her hands and feet were wrinkled, she finally stepped out.

Mia swiped a cloth through the moisture clinging to the mirror. Her face was red and puffy; no shocker there. Her headache had kicked it up a notch instead of being soothed by the heat.

She picked up the bottle of pain meds and swallowed it with a swig of vodka from the bottle Scott had delivered to her cabin on the first day. The fire of the alcohol burned her throat on the way down.

She stepped back into the main room of her cabin, and went to her suitcase. If Scott wanted a *Razor's Edge* fan tonight, she'd let him have one.

Mia picked up her Mickey Mouse pajamas and threw them across the room. Anger simmered below the surface of her skin, making her itch. The fabric landed in a small heap by the chair. She wouldn't crumple like Mickey.

She pulled out the matching bra and panty set she'd brought for the Prom Night theme party. It was a navy bra, with a little push-up—not that she needed it—and bikini panties. Both had a hint of lace at the edges.

Her shoes for her prom night dress even matched her undies. It was coincidence that her satin slip and robe she'd worn the night she'd given Scott her virginity, matched her set.

She left the slip in the suitcase and grabbed the robe, then made her way back to the bathroom and plugged in her curlers.

Once they were hot, Mia placed them in her hair and began applying her makeup, careful of the tears that kept trying to fill her eyes.

We haven't had sex since my house almost two months ago.

She tilted her head side to side, as she always did when arguing with herself.

It's not like I've had a lot of time with him so far.

He didn't even touch me at the hotel.

I did spend the night in the hospital, and the nurse said no sex.

Well, if he wants a fan, then I'll be one tonight.

I'm gonna walk out there dressed like every other skanky ho.

She styled her hair in perfect curls on top of her head, careful to hide her bald spot, grabbed only her lanyard, and headed out the door.

The party was already in full swing when she made it to the lido deck.

All five guys were up on the stage, dancing to the music and singing along.

Mia caught sight of Dwaine and Blaze's wives, sitting on one of the many couches placed on the stage for the event.

Grace waved.

She scanned the sea of girls. She'd been right. So many of them were dressed in very little fabric. There was red, black, and white, but not a single other girl was in navy or blue at first glance.

Mia made her way through the crowd, heading straight for the bar. She needed another drink. It didn't matter that her medication stated in bold print *not* to mix with alcohol. She didn't care.

She'd left her self-control in her room. She ordered a shot of tequila and a Long Island iced tea.

The shot was down her throat before the bartender could get her room key to charge her.

She went in search of somewhere to sit, drink in hand. She took a long pull, and the liquor already fueled her. Mia wasn't a big drinker, and the alcohol was hitting her hard and fast.

The DJ was spinning tunes, and it made her need to dance. There was an area up on the eleventh deck, overlooking the lido deck.

Mia let her body feel the music, closing her eyes, and moving with the beat.

When the song ended, she returned to her table, where she'd left her drink. No one had bothered it. She downed the rest, craving another.

The DJ stopped playing so the guys could perform a few songs.

They sang some unreleased songs.

Mia got into the thick of the crowd. She'd push her way through if she had to. She jumped up and down, acting like any other wild and crazy fan.

The crowd was still huge, but she pushed through an opening to get closer. There were now only a few girls in front of her, but she was still on the far-right side of the stage.

Scott had yet to see her, and when they got to the bridge of the song, he must've needed someone to sing to.

A redhead was in front of him, up against the stage, smiling his way.

He stepped to the very edge of the stage and sang to her. He leaned down to take her hand.

She was gorgeous, and Mia's gaze stayed on them.

Scott kissed the girl's knuckles when his part finished. He stood back up and winked before getting back to the rest of the band.

Mia's insecurities kicked in, full force.

Why would he want me when he can have any girl on this boat? Surely many of them have way more experience and can please him better. And far too many are better looking than me.

She pivoted, pushed her way through the crowd and headed back to the bar.

Two shots later, someone tapped her on the shoulder, interrupting Mia's order of another shot. She whirled, and came face to face with the dark-haired girl she'd seen in the hall when she'd been kissing Scott.

Her face looked far too familiar, but Mia's mind was fuzzy so she couldn't remember when she might've seen the girl before that day.

The black haired bitch shoved her without a word.

Mia wasn't going to take any shit. She stood her ground.

She wanted to shove her back, but what good would that do?

"What the hell is your problem?" Mia barked.

"Who do you think you are, kissing a man that belongs to someone else?"

She laughed. "A little jealous, are we?" The tequila was her courage.

The broad looked her up and down, disgust making her pretty face into a hard ugly sneer. "Jealous? Hardly. Look at you. You're nothing but a slut."

Mia laughed again. "Oh, yeah. You're just so jealous. Should I tell you how soft his lips are, or how strong his arms are? Or maybe how he'd never want you?"

She'd said the wrong thing.

The girl was petite and pretty, dressed in a cleavage-displaying red lingerie number that was made of lace and sheer material that covered and revealed at the same time. She looked beautiful, except for her dark expression.

Her face was now the same bright crimson of her sleepwear, and her slim shoulders were tight and slumped. She had her hands in tight fists at her sides, as if in an effort to keep her from becoming violent, but even Mia's muddled instincts told her she needed to be on edge for it.

It was a matter of time.

What Mia had accused of jealousy was rage.

The dark-haired girl pulled her fist back, to punch Mia.

Her waiting-time expired.

She ducked as the girl swung.

Mia had done enough dirty dancing the nights she'd gone to her favorite bar, so she could easily go low.

The other girl lost her balance and fell.

Mia straightened and laughed before she turned back to the bar, leaving the girl on the floor.

Trash to be forgotten.

Mia leaned up against the bar, a new drink in hand. She faced the crowd again, and gasped. Scott's green eyes were all she could see.

Where did he come from?

Her lover stood with his mouth half-agape as he took in her outfit. He was flanked by a bodyguard, who was holding a tray full of shots to give out.

She hadn't seen his approach. Had he seen her interaction with the bitch dressed in red?

Did it matter?

She plastered on a smirk. "I'll take one of those shots. And by the way, I'm your biggest fan," Mia said in a singsong voice.

Scott shook his head before he leaned in close to her, his elbows on the bar. "Baby? Why are you doing this?"

She straightened. "I thought this was what you wanted? A fangirl."

He shook his head again.

The girls were pushing their way toward him, reaching and screaming for a free shot, even though he had yet to pass out a single one.

"No, Mia. This is what *you* wanted. You told me to be the rockstar this weekend, so I am. What's your excuse?"

Mia blinked. His words were like a slap to her face.

She was suddenly sober.

He was *right*.

She was the one being stupid and cruel.

Mia took a step back, almost tripping over a girl behind her.

Scott's attention had been pulled away, so he was no longer looking at her.

She pushed her way past everyone and ran from the lido deck, tears streaming down her cheeks.

She'd been so wrong about everything.

Mia had no reason to be upset, but Scott had every reason.

Will he ever forgive me?

CHAPTER 22

Mia pulled out her *All-Access* lanyard and had her door open before she wiped away the blinding tears.

She took a deep breath and tried to center herself. Seeing him like that, and the things he's said had sobered her up faster than ten cups of coffee and a loaf of bread.

Mia had every intention to throw herself on the bed to wallow in self-pity, until Mickey Mouse caught her attention. Her pajamas were in a crumpled pile, like she felt on the inside.

She wouldn't blame Scott if he treated her like trash, tossed her away, unwanted.

Mia would never ever forgive herself.

She picked up her phone to turn on some tunes and make the silence go away.

It was as if fate had known what she had done.

It was still on the new RE playlist she'd made for the cruise, so she could learn more of their music and fit in better.

A song was already playing, but only the first few notes.

Mia sat on the very edge of the bed and really inhaled the lyrics. Scott's haunting voice sang directly to her.

I was deceived
A gift you always had
I'll fall apart
Like an egg dropped from up high
Never had someone like you
Not how I thought this would be, yeah
You're not the same, by far
Denying what the truth is
I wanna know

How bad do your broken wings hurt, just like this
Ever'thing displayed on the wall
How bad do your broken wings hurt, just like this
Could they ever grow back again?
So many things can change in the length of a heartbeat
You've taken everything away from me
So how does it feel?
How bad do your broken wings hurt, just like this

She didn't make it through the full song.

Mia switched the music off, and set her phone on the bed. She took a deep breath.

The words were so right. *She* was a fallen angel, a love with broken wings. How had she come to that?

She went to the bathroom and drank a large glass of water before taking the rest of the pins from her hair.

Mia let her curls rest against her back and cleaned off the dark, seductive makeup she'd applied for the party.

She grabbed her basic white bra and panties and her black

ballet slippers, changing into her Mickey pajamas. She brushed her teeth, and put on the barest of makeup.

All she wanted now was to look like Scott's girlfriend.

Before she left the room, Mia took another deep breath and sent him a text.

MIA: *I will understand if you never forgive me. I can't forgive myself. I don't know why I was being so shallow. Just know that no matter what, I love you. I'm leaving my phone in my room.*

SHE HIT SEND, then read what she'd sent.

I love you.

She'd never said the words out loud, never ready to say them.

She might lose him, so it hit her how true those words were.

He's not going to believe it, not gonna trust it's true.

Mia had chosen the wrong time, to reveal how she really felt. However, she couldn't take it back.

She plugged her phone into the charger in the bathroom and looked at her reflection one more time.

She couldn't help but let out a sigh.

Mia didn't want to go back to the party, but she needed to be there for the karaoke announcement.

She'd just stepped out into the heat of the night on the lido deck when the woman in charge of the Karaoke contest took the stage.

Mia took the metal staircase up to the eleventh deck where Grace, Hope, and Evelien sat in the VIP section.

The look on Grace's face said it all.

Mia hung her head in shame.

The woman introduced herself as Michelle. She praised the amazing groups that'd performed, but explained they'd had to get it down to five groups. "The finalists will perform tomorrow, on the main stage, as an opening act for the *Razor's Edge* Beach Party Concert!"

The crowd was in a frenzy over the news.

Grace drained of color, and Hope grabbed her hand.

Mia offered a smile she hoped comforted Blaze's wife, but Grace didn't respond. Her eyes were on the stage.

Michelle went through the list. There were three groups, but theirs was not among them.

The evening had already gone to hell, so this would just be the icing on the cake.

The fourth was announced, still not them.

Mia was ready to leave. The only reason she'd came back out was for this, and it didn't even matter. She'd say goodbye to the girls, and slip back to her room.

"And our last group moving on to the finals is four ladies simply known as *The Betties*," Michelle announced.

Her mouth dropped open. She really didn't think it would happen, after the way her night had gone. Mia was glad the crowd below was too busy watching the guys come on stage to notice them celebrating.

"I feel kinda guilty," Evelien said. "Like we're taking something away from the fans."

"From what I hear, you're Dwaine's biggest fan," Hope said. "Weren't you the president of his fan club, back in the day?"

The redhead's face almost matched her hair.

"You're a fan, and you're on the boat, so you have every right to do this, I think."

"It's too late now, to do anything about it," Mia said.

SCOTT SAT on one of the couches on the stage, watching the announcement. The wives had left the stage, moved up to the VIP section, and he watched for their reaction. Mia had joined them, looking like herself again. Finally.

It was Grace's face, turning white, that let him know, they were The Betties. He was happy Mia had made it to the next level.

The DJ was starting another set, and he stayed where he was. His buddies were around him.

"Grace told me to check on you. You okay?" Blaze asked.

"She was drunk, Blaze. She knows my past. Why would she do that? And did you see what she was wearing? This is worse than what happened at her house!" He made the mistake of glancing into his friend's face.

Blaze's expression was stamped with chagrin, and the guy dragged his hand through his hair.

Scott looked down and cursed. Of course, Blaze had seen Mia. They all probably had.

"What happened at her place?" Blaze asked.

He told him about the comment Mia had made about him not wanting her anymore. He kept out other details that were not important. He then told Blaze about Mia pushing him out the door earlier.

"What did you say?"

Scott sighed. "I'd asked her about her head, I could tell it was bothering her. Then I told her sex was the best cure for a headache." Realization bulldozed into his gut. "Ah, shit! What I said was something like, having sex with your favorite *Razor's Edge* guy…"

Blaze laughed and patted Scott's head. "Dude, are you really that stupid?"

He frowned and reared back, swatting his friend's hand away. "Excuse me?"

"Think about it. Mia wasn't in Minneapolis to see us. She was there for *Next Step*. Mia's the only girl on this entire boat that would take offense to being offered to have sex with a *Razor's*

Edge guy, and you said it to her. I'm sure it upset her when you said that. She loves the man you are, not the title you come with."

Blaze's words hit hard.

He'd been completely wrong.

Scott pulled his phone out and looked at Mia's text again.

She was feeling like *she'd* ruined everything, but he'd been the one to start it.

She'd finally said the words he'd waited so long to hear. But they weren't spoken.

They were typed.

Does it still count?

He stood up, spared Blaze one last glance, and walked off the stage.

SCOTT HAD an entourage of girls behind him, as he headed with speed toward the VIP section. Resolve was pushing him forward.

Before he could reach her, Mia said something to Grace and hurried away.

He didn't catch up with her until the hallway leading to their rooms.

"My room *is* in this hallway! I left my *All-Access* lanyard in the room, in the pocket of my robe. Look at my room key. It's got my room number on it." Her voice was rising in pitch as she argued.

"I'm sorry. No All-Access pass, no entry," the security guy stated.

He slipped his arms around her waist, and rested his chin on her shoulder. "She's with me," was all he said.

Mia squeaked and jumped.

He held her tighter.

The security guy moved out of the way so they could get past.

Scott stepped back from her but took her hand. He led her to his door, not even asking her if she wanted to go.

When he opened the door, Mia looked around, barely moving inside.

Scott dropped her hand.

She remained by the now-closed door, and he went to the edge of the bed.

He took a deep breath before he looked at her again.

She looked like she wanted to weep, red rimming her eyes. She took a step back. She looked down at her black ballet flats. "I'm so sorry," Mia whispered.

Scott darted back to her, lifting her chin to force eye contact.

"Are you upset about what I said, about having sex with a *Razor's Edge* guy?"

She trembled.

"I was just joking, you know." He was getting frustrated.

"I don't want someone from RE. I want Scott." Mia whispered shaky words.

"Mia, being a part of *Razor's Edge* is a part of who I am. And I'm sorry you misunderstood my intentions. But next time, you need to just talk to me. I'm not a mind reader."

Tears spilled from her eyes.

He reached up to wipe one away.

"I'm sorry," she said again, after seconds had ticked by.

"Alcohol is not the answer, trust me." Scott backed away slowly, retaking his seat on the bed. "It was hard to watch you do the same destructive things my friends and family had to watch me do."

She stepped closer, sinking to the carpet on her knees in front of him with her head down and eyes still on the floor.

He sat there silently, waiting for her to talk first. If he did, it wouldn't go the way he wanted.

She needed to be in control.

The turmoil in her eyes matched what was rolling in his gut.

"Do you remember when I got pushed in the pool?" she asked.

He blanched and swallowed. "I could never forget. I thought I was going to lose you."

"I don't think it was because I was dancing with Eddie." She paused. "The next morning, when I went down for breakfast alone, I was given a note. A rather unpleasant note."

Scott remained silent, and invited her to continue.

Where is she going with this?

"The note was threatening. But I blew it off as a jealous fan."

When he started to speak, she held up her hand. "I didn't tell you, because I didn't want to worry you about it. I thought it would just go away."

"But it didn't, did it?"

"No. I got another one today. Then, when we were kissing in the hallway, one girl saw us and… She confronted me later, at the bar. I don't know if she's the one that sent the notes. I was too drunk to remember her face."

"To me, that would say you need to be more alert, not drunk."

"I know. I could come up with a dozen excuses, but they're all just that. I think whoever's sending these thinks I'm just a fan, screwing a *Razor's Edge* guy. And what you said to me, made me think you wished I was just a fan, adoring you. I know, it's stupid. But that was what I was doing. Being a half-naked, drunk fan." Scott opened his mouth, but she kept going before he could get a word in. "And now I know I'm jealous of the fans. When I was there tonight, in my underwear, pretending to be a fan; it was thrilling to be like them, trying to get your attention. Then you sang to the girl and I…I lost it." Her voice trembled.

He moved off the bed, dropping down in front of her. Scott took one of her hands and kissed her knuckles. He looked into her intense blue eyes.

"This is why I love you. Because you're *not* just a fan. You're my Mia, my *Next Step* girl." He smiled. "But no more holding back, okay?"

Mia nodded.

"Do you still have those notes?"

"Yes."

Scott went to the room's phone, trying to hide his growing concern. His stomach threatened to bring up his dinner. "I need security to my room, please."

"Let's go. Your room. I need these notes."

He went with Mia to retrieve the notes from her cabin.

Once security arrived, she told men how she'd received them, so they could launch an investigation.

After security left, Scott could see Mia's nerves were raw. She was shaking. "How about a bath? Might help ease your muscles, help you sleep."

She rushed to his bathroom and started the water.

He came up behind her and poured a small vial of oil he'd picked out from a little basket of essentials on the edge of the tub. It quickly filled the room with the comforting scent of eucalyptus.

Scott turned the water off. He took the hem of her shirt in his hands.

Without speaking, and without breaking eye contact, he undressed her.

She stepped into the tub, pulling her knees up to her chest and wrapping her arms around her legs. She rested her forehead on her knees.

Scott quickly shed his own clothing before stepping in behind her.

He pulled her back against him until their skin met. He placed a warm wet washcloth on the back of her shoulders.

Mia rested her head back against him.

Scott kissed her gently, hoping she knew she was forgiven.

"I can't tell you how happy I was to see my Mia come back to the party," he whispered.

She lifted her head and their gazes brushed.

"When you came back for the karaoke announcement, you

were my girl again. The Mickey Mouse jammies," he smiled and picked the cloth back to wash her.

It was almost metaphoric, like they were washing away the night together.

His hands washed, but then became exploratory. He made her body sing. His ball tightened with anticipation and his cock jerked to life.

She sat forward and shifted again, splashing water over the edge. She slid her legs over his, so he had to scoot forward to accommodate her. She wrapped her arms around his neck, pulling him closer for a deep, powerful kiss.

Mia lifted up and came back down, taking him all the way in.

They both sucked a breath.

She rode him, and the water moved with their motion. It splashed over the side, but he didn't care.

Her body milked him, drawing them both to a fevered pitch.

Scott's mouth found her breast, and he suckled, bringing his woman to a fevered pitch, making her cry out in ecstasy.

He bucked beneath her, thrusting faster to get his own release while her body quivered around his cock.

When he came, he gripped on to her, pulling her mouth down to his. Scott shuddered.

They lay there for a moment, their bodies still one, but the water was chilling.

"I love you, Scott," Mia breathed.

It's about time.

"I know."

CHAPTER 23

Mia opened her eyes as the sunlight filled the room. She listened to Scott's deep breathing, and inhaled his scent. Her body was deliciously sore.

They'd done more than make up for the time they'd lost.

She didn't want to move; she could've stayed there forever, but she needed to get up and shower.

Mia carefully slid out of the bed and found her pajamas and room key. She dressed in silence, but something didn't feel right.

She couldn't put her finger on what, but she made as little noise as possible, and slipped out of the room.

It wasn't until she was in the shower in her own cabin that it hit her what was different. The boat wasn't moving.

Mia dried off and wrapped the towel herself before going to the window. Sure enough, they'd docked.

She selected a white flowing summer dress and matching sandals, then brushed her hair out and put it up in a ponytail before a little makeup.

Mia grabbed her phone and her *All-Access* pass. She remembered she'd brought a small hand purse for the day they docked. She stowed her pass and room key in her little bag along with her wallet and passport, and sent Scott a quick text as she headed out the door.

MIA: Scott, I love you. See you on the beach later. Don't forget, I'm one of your opening acts.

She headed out the door for breakfast. Mia didn't get far.

There were two security guards at the entry to her hallway.

One of them was very tall, with long black hair, pulled back into a ponytail at the nape of his neck.

The other guy was about Mia's height, with mouse-brown hair and a young face.

The tall man stepped over, blocking her way from leaving the hallway. "I'm sorry, Miss Lee. But we were told you aren't allowed to leave the secure area alone."

Mia blinked. Had she heard him right? She cocked her head to the side before she spoke. "And who told you I couldn't leave?"

"Head of security, Miss Lee."

She smiled sweetly at him. "Well, that's nice and all, but unnecessary. I'm just heading to breakfast."

"I'm sorry, Miss Lee. We have orders."

She narrowed her eyes and took a breath, trying not to make fists of irritation. With her luck, he'd think she wanted to punch him. She pulled her phone out of her purse.

Scott hadn't replied to her text but if she didn't eat soon, she was going to get really cranky. Hangry.

Mia looked up at the guards, trying to relax her urge to glare. "Scott, you know the guy in the band, and my boyfriend, hasn't texted me back, and I need to eat. It's barely eight, so it's not gonna be very busy. You can either let me pass, or one of you can come with me. Either way, I'm going to breakfast."

The younger man laughed. He gestured to the tall guy. "Dev,

she's all yours. Besides, how often do you get to go have breakfast with a beautiful girl?" He gave his colleague a light shove off, like he was trying to get him to go, but the other man stood his ground.

He looked between her and the other security guard. "That was not part of the deal," he mumbled.

"Guys, I don't wanna get you into trouble, but really? I don't need anyone to watch me eat. Just let me pass, and no one will know."

"I'm sorry, Miss Lee. But we have orders." He turned his back to her, but still blocked the way.

Mia huffed. Anger jumped up from her tummy, heating the back of her neck.

She didn't want to take it out on the one person who really cared about her, but this was ridiculous.

Since she didn't have a key to his room, she went to Scott's door and banged.

The noise she was making caused another door to open, just as Scott finally opened up.

Grace stuck her head out of her and Blaze's room, just across the hall. "Mia? What's wrong?" Grace asked before Scott had a chance to speak.

"Damn security won't let me leave unless I have someone with me. I just want to go to breakfast!"

Grace laughed. She looked over her shoulder to talk to her husband, while Mia glared at her boyfriend.

"Baby, I just want you to be safe. Besides, you and the wives are getting to know each other, so I didn't think there would be any problem. Grace said you've been having breakfast together. I'm sorry." He opened the door further, trying to urge her inside.

She wasn't mad at *him*, just the situation, but she stood where she was.

"Sweetie, just give me a few minutes, and we can grab Hope and Evelien and go down there together, okay?" Grace asked.

Mia nodded and begrudgingly stepped into Scott's room.

He shut the door, and she sat on the edge of the bed. "Why did you leave and not wake me up?" he asked.

"You needed sleep. I could tell you were exhausted by the way you were breathing."

Scott smiled and leaned in for a kiss. "Well, please keep close to Grace and the other girls today. Are you planning on going ashore?"

Of course, she was going to shore. The other *Razor's Edge* women were opening for them that night, as part of the karaoke contest. She smiled and kissed his nose. "Scott, I'll be fine. I think you're overreacting to this whole thing. It's gonna blow over soon."

He arched one eyebrow.

"It didn't seem like overacting last night. You're completely sober, and the sun is shining, chasing away all the bad dreams."

There was a knock at the door.

Scott opened it; Grace and Hope were standing in the hallway.

"Breakfast, then?" the chestnut beauty asked.

"Please!" Mia gave Scott one more kiss before heading out the door. She paused just as the door was closing. "See you on stage," she whispered.

IN A SHORT TIME, the girls sat in the restaurant with plates of delicious food before them.

They were coming up with ideas for their performance that night. They had to keep with the ruse that they were someone other than themselves.

"In Nassau, there's a shop called *The Girls of Brazil*. It's just off Legendary Bay Street," Grace said. "Because of all the colorful festivals they have throughout the year, they have a place where you can get costume supplies."

"Any chance we could get red contacts and vampire teeth?" Mia loved the idea of vampires.

"I would guess so. They have just about everything. We probably could even find some cute outfits that match what our men wore in the video."

"We better get our asses in gear then," Evelien said. "It's gonna take us a little while to get off of this boat."

Walking along the pink sidewalks of Nassau, they passed beautiful trees and charming lampposts.

They laughed about how fate had brought them all together.

When they got to the *Girls of Brazil* shop, all the colorful costume pieces the store had blew Mia.

They had no problem finding parts of what they needed. They would all wear something red.

She had a red crop top to pair with skinny jeans and red heels.

Grace said just about everything in her suitcase was red.

Hope was looking for something in the shop that would work. She checked out different styles of red shirts, but said she knew exactly what she wanted. She wanted a black leather jacket with a red stripe on the sleeves.

Nick had worn one in the video and since she was singing his part, she wanted one too.

As they explored, Mia's heart stopped. There was a full rack of petticoats in every color imaginable, including red.

She reached for a red one, pulling it to her chest like a child with a teddy bear. It'd been devastating when her petticoat had been ruined after the pool incident. She had to get this one.

A very flamboyant salesman approached Hope and Mia. "Can I help you find anything?" he asked.

"Do you carry red contacts, by chance?" Hope asked.

"Red? Let me check." He returned from the back room with two vials. "Yes, I do!"

"Great! Do you have three more pairs?"

He smiled. "Is this a vampire cruise?"

"No, we're just performing a *Razor's Edge* song tonight, and in the video they were vampires," Hope said.

"Oh, my goodness. That sounds like so much fun. But that means you're gonna need vampire teeth, too. I've got just the thing." The salesman opened a glass case, pulling out a little coffin-shaped box. Inside were two little vampire teeth.

"How do they work?" Mia asked.

He opened the box. "You have these little plastic beads you melt together then pour in the tooth and push it over your natural tooth. As the plastic cools, it molds to your teeth, so it looks natural."

"These are awesome." Hope must've been really excited, because she hugged the guy.

They all made their purchases, but Hope scanned the store one last time, wearing a frown.

"What's wrong?" Mia asked.

"I wanted a leather jacket."

"Yeah, and we still have to find you a shirt," Grace said.

"Sorry, did you say you were looking for a jacket?" the salesman asked.

"Yeah, I wanted a black and red one."

He pulled out a business card. "My cousin has a leather shop down the street. Tell him I sent you, and he'll give you a good deal."

About an hour later, the girls headed back to the boat, one beautiful black and red leather jacket in hand.

"I think we should grab some lunch quick, then go rehearse with the teeth in," Mia suggested as they entered the hallway to their cabins.

"Good idea," Hope said. "That way we can get used to singing with them."

Soon, they were back in the fitness room putting the final touches on their performance.

Once again, a small crowd built outside the room.

Mia wished there weren't three large windows that allowed people to see inside. At least, once they got on stage, people would still be surprised.

The girls watching had no clue how they'd appear later that night. They also didn't seem to realize three of the women were known RE ladies. No one had on a wig to hide their identities.

Grace picked up her laptop, and they headed out the door.

Most of the crowd were smiling and giving them praise.

However, one dark-haired girl with huge sunglasses had her arms crossed tight and her mouth was in a hard line.

She stepped through the crowd to get closer to them, staring at Mia. "If you win, everyone will know it's because you're sleeping with Scott, not because you have any talent," she barked, with venom in her voice.

Dammit, why can't I figure out where I know her from. This is driving me nuts!

Mia smiled at the girl.

The others in the area were speculated in loud whispers about her and Scott.

"I wish that was true, but you see the guys don't choose the winners. The girls on the cruise get to. And everyone knows that Scott isn't screwing a fan." She left it at that and spun on her heels, walking away with her new friends in tow.

They split up and went to their separate rooms to get ready.

Mia started doing her vampire makeup, starting with the contacts.

Oh, these make my eyes creepy!

They probably should wear sunglasses until they performed.

No sense in tipping people off.

She packed a bag with her swimsuit, a flowing summer dress and matching sandals, her makeup kit, and a contact case.

When the contest was over, Mia would want to be herself again. She grabbed her black and red-trimmed cat eyes sunglasses and headed out to meet with the others. It was difficult walking in the hallways of the ship with dark glasses, but it was going to be worth it in the long run.

They hurried to the skipper boat that would take them back to shore and the beach, where the event was happening.

They were supposed to be going on stage at three p.m.. The party was in a bay with the stage set up on the grass at the top of the beach, so people could sit in the sand and watch, or swim in the ocean.

It didn't surprise Mia to see the crowd was already pushing up against the stage, even though there was nothing going on yet.

When the girls arrived, Michelle, the leader of the event, informed them they would perform last.

Mia was grateful; this meant they got to watch the other groups.

She spotted the guys sitting in an elevated sound control booth in the middle of the crowd. They'd have a perfect view of the performers.

Michelle took the stage, and the crowd cheered with excitement. She introduced all five groups, and the order they'd perform. "The audience will choose the winner! Choose wisely. The winner will sing a song with *Razor's Edge* during the Main Theater Concerts!"

Mia's stomach lurched. She glanced at her friends, who all wore expressions shouting their collective nerves.

They couldn't back out now, though.

The show began, and the singing seemed to get better and better with each group. When the group before them sang a signature RE song, and incorporated dance moves, she let out a sigh of relief.

She personally wanted to win and go to the next level, but Mia understood why the others didn't. This group could win it.

Finally, they were called on stage.

They took off their sunglasses.

Hope slipped on her black and red leather jacket.

They all kept their eyes down while they walked to their starting locations.

Starting at stage right, Mia took her spot, going down on one knee, followed by Grace, then Hope, and Evelien.

The music began and Mia slowly stood; knowing the others followed up, one by one.

The people in the crowd started gasping as close people could see the blood-red contacts.

Mia started the song, performing Thomas's part, since they recorded it during the time Scott had left the group.

The other three girls moved into the exact choreography the guys had done in their video.

Hope stepped forward, singing Nick's part. They changed all the 'she's' to 'he's' in the lyrics.

When they got closer to the chorus, the dance had them switching places on the stage, so Hope was stage right, followed by Evelien, Mia, then Grace at stage left.

The dance moves for the chorus were like a country line dance, and Mia was proud of them. So far, they were making it look like they'd been dancing the choreography their whole lives.

They moved again, as Evelien sang Dwaine's part, the others were in a diagonal line, the tip closest to stage left, with Eveline at the head, then Grace, Mia, and Hope.

They spun around the stage while Evelien sang to meet back in the middle, breaking to opposite sides, as Grace stepped out to sing her solo.

Mia was blown away. She'd been holding back. Her voice was amazing. Her little solo alone would put them in the win.

When they moved to the chorus again, the crowd went wild, singing along with them.

They danced all over the stage, taking full control of their performance.

No one would've guessed this trip was the first time they'd spent any time together.

They moved like a perfect team.

Hope stepped forward to take the bridge, the others in a line behind her.

They stepped to her side, one by one, went down on one knee, except for Eveline.

She played with the audience.

They all stepped up to the edge of the stage, looking right at the guys in the band, for just a moment, instead of the audience.

They moved back into a line toward the back of the stage with Evelien stage right, then Mia, Grace, and Hope, to finish their choreography.

They pulled close together for their final notes.

The crowd went wild.

Each of them smiled, showing off the vamp teeth.

Listening to the screaming was breathtaking. It gave Mia a whole new appreciation for the guys.

She would have a big head if she was praised like that every night. She and the other loves of these guys were lucky they didn't have bigger egos.

Michelle took center stage, smiling as she walked past them. She had all the karaoke finalists come back on stage.

Mia watched out of the corner of her eye when the band left the VIP section with their security team, moving toward the stage.

The girls in the audience around them made a path but reached for them as they went by.

All of RE touched hands while they made their way through, and Thomas blew a kiss or two.

It only took a short time before the guys joined them on stage.

Just like the girls in the audience, the ones on the stage reached for them.

They made sure to touch every single woman's hand.

The men lingered just a little longer when they came to Mia

and her friends with the red eyes. The band moved to stand by Michelle for the announcement.

The woman in charge was handed one of the wireless mics the girls had just used. She stepped to the center of the stage, RE standing right behind her, the finalists behind them.

Michelle had an envelope in her hands.

CHAPTER 24

"Hello, everyone! Did you enjoy the performances?"

The crowd screamed.

"Like we announced in the beginning, the choice is up to you. *Razor's Edge* had no vote in this. I'm sure they would've chosen you all if they could. Our four judges based the decision on the reaction of the crowd. It came down to two groups. We couldn't tell which one you liked best. They both had equal screams, and each group had the crowd singing along."

Mia exchanged glances with the other RE loves. It didn't escape her notice that the other groups were doing the same. Their curiosity was palpable, like the crowd's.

"I'd like to ask groups four and five to step forward."

Grace turned to Hope and paled. "That's us, right?"

Nine women stepped forward, group four to stage left and group five to stage right, with Michelle between them.

"We've spoken with the judges and *Razor's Edge* and we all agree, the best way to do this is a kamikaze round. I'll give both groups a random RE song. They'll have 30 minutes to figure out how they want to sing it. *Razor's Edge* will take the stage to keep you entertained in the meantime. Once again, your screaming will choose the winners." Michelle finally opened the envelope, and read the contents to the crowd. "Group four will sing *Designs Of Love*, and group five will sing *I'll Be Your Shelter*. There are two empty fully enclosed cabanas on each side of the stage, you will go to. You have five minutes to get there and an additional thirty to practice. Good luck."

The two groups were escorted to their designated cabana.

When the door closed, leaving the four of them alone, Evelien sighed. "Let's be honest. This has been fun, but it's gone too far. We all agree we don't want to take things away from the fans. But this...this is too much. I'm having more fun than I've ever had on a cruise, thanks to the three of you. But I think we should step down."

Grace grabbed the cranberry haired woman in the blonde wig, pulling her into a deep hug, tears slipping from her eyes. "I should be thanking you. You ladies got me to sing again. I didn't know if I could ever get over what happened. You gave me the courage to do it. And now, I want to see this through. But only one more song. I have an idea."

THIRTY MINUTES LATER, the four of them joined the other team on the stairs to the stage, sans red eyes.

Group four went first and was amazing.

It was obvious they had people on their team with vocal training.

Mia watched Grace step forward. "We're hoping we can get RE to come join us on stage for our song."

Thomas stepped out from offstage first, a live mic already in his hands, as if the guys had planned this. "Anything for you."

"Can we get those stools you were using earlier?" Grace asked as the band joined them.

Three stagehands followed behind the guys, stools in hands. They set them in a line.

Grace motioned for the guys to take a seat on the bar stools.

Mia watched as Thomas moved to stage right, then Blaze, followed by Scott in the middle, then Nick, and last was Dwaine.

When the music started, each woman went to their man.

She couldn't help but chuckle to herself, poor Thomas had to sit alone.

Grace started off the song, even though the beginning was sung by Thomas.

Was it so long ago, when we tied the knot
The fire inside still burns the same
I hope every day that you see all my love
Or look in my heart and see the passion that can't be bought

EVELIEN WAS UP NEXT, slipping her arms around her husband's neck.

Our time together is unlimited
Useless words, I'll never use
And when the skies are dark, or it's inside of your head
Please know, I'll be your shelter

MIA MOVED to stand by Scott when the chorus began. She put her left hand on his cheek while she sang, and his green eyes burned into hers. She couldn't have looked away if she wanted to.

Hope stayed behind Nick, but wrapped her arms loosely

around his neck, holding the microphone to her mouth to sing the chorus.

> *I stand here, I'm your man*
> *I love you like the very first day*
> *When my days are getting dark*
> *You open up your arms like I do*
> *Please know, I'll be your shelter, too*

WHEN THE SONG ENDED, the girls stepped away from their guys to stand at the edge of the stage for the final lyrics to the crowd.

She tried to hide her surprise when Scott stepped up behind her and wrapped his arms around her. Mia glanced at the women that had now become her friends and saw the other guys had done the same with their women.

The guys then stole the show and sang the final chorus with the girls, over their shoulders.

> *I stand here, I'm your man*
> *I love you like the very first day*
> *When my days are getting dark*
> *You open up your arms like I do*
> *Please know, I'll be your shelter, too*

THE APPLAUSE WAS DEAFENING, even more than the shouts earlier.

Scott gave Mia a squeeze when Michelle returned to the stage.

"Well, I think we have a winner," she announced.

Grace broke from Blaze Looked over at the girls. "It's time," she mouthed to the other ladies.

The four of them gripped the front of their wigs and removed them in a flurry of colored hair.

Mia shook her long locks out, assuming the others did the same.

"Is that Grace, Blaze's wife?"

"Hey! That's Dwaine's wife!"

"Nick's girl?"

"Who's the blonde?"

Rather than looking into the crowd, acknowledging the speculations, Mia was glad when Grace stepped forward, bringing the mic up to her lips. "I'm sure most of you know, I'm Grace Solan, Blaze's wife. The four of us want to thank you for letting us be a part of this great adventure. We are fans, just like you and we wanted to see what it was like on your side of the stage, for just a little while. It was just for fun. We never expected to go further than the first round. But it has truly been a blessing and a great gift for us. Thank you. We want to step down now and let the other group move on." She waved at group four, bidding them to return to the stage.

RE opened their arms and hugged each other of the girls.

Mia overheard Scott whisper "Thank you for letting my girl do this with ya'll."

She frowned in his direction.

So much for keeping us a secret.

She tried not to be mad, but there were two more days on the cruise. Two more days of danger from angry fans.

Mia could only hope this girl didn't share what she'd heard.

Scott put his around Mia, and followed his bandmates, as they all headed off stage. "I want to spend the rest of the night wrapped in your arms, in your shelter."

Her irritation evaporated. She always melted when he talked like that. She loved how he tied in the song she just sang.

"But alas, my ass has to work. You'll stay close by, right? Or with the girls?"

"Yes, I'll stay with them. Have fun."

Mia stayed true to her word, keeping with the other RE women. She never would've thought when she first met them that awful night in Tulsa, they could come to mean so much to her.

The guys took the limelight for over an hour before finally mingling through the crowd with a bodyguard by their sides.

They slowly made their way to the roped-off section that made the makeshift VIP area.

"So, here are our little singers," Scott said, not revealing their relationship to the crowd following behind them. He offered a hand to Mia to help her up from the beach chair.

"Very impressive that you learned our moves," Nick said, pulling Hope to her feet and into his arms.

"I guess you've become a fan after all." Scott tugged her into a hug. His hands lingered on the bare skin of her back.

"Sweetie," she whispered into his ear.

He released her.

"Hey, you found them!" Dwaine shouted. He was trying to get through the crowd. "Well, part of them, anyway." He looked around. His own wife was missing.

"She went to grab us soda, but will be back soon," Mia said.

"Okay. It's good to see all our ladies here together," Dwaine said.

"Except poor Thomas. He hasn't found his girl yet." Mia giggled.

Thomas raised an eyebrow in her direction, then took a step forward, pretending to push Scott out of the way. "Are you laughing at me? Are you…laughing…at…me?"

Mia swallowed back another laugh. She made herself a little taller and put on her faux seductive face. "You're so adorable. If I wasn't already in love with someone else, I'd be all over you."

He blushed eight shades of red, and Scott burst out laughing.

Nick leaned in closer and whispered loudly to Thomas. "We all saw how you were looking at Mia at the pajama party last night." He was trying to be funny, but it hit a sore spot with Mia.

Hope must've seen her face fall before Mia brought a smile back. She grabbed Nick's forearm, forcing him to look at her.

Nick's expression sobered and he stepped over to Mia, pretending to congratulate her on their performance. He opened his arms for a hug.

She went to him, but hesitantly.

"Hey, I'm sorry. I shouldn't have said that. I feel bad about what I said; I was only trying to be funny," He whispered in her ear, then stepped back.

She nodded and offered a smile.

"Who wants to hit the water?" Scott broke the awkward silence. "It's almost six, and we gotta be back on the boat by eight."

"Sounds like fun," Evelien said. "You all could use a dip. You stink. Better grab security, though."

Even though they were playing games on the left side of the beach, distracting many of the girls on the sand, there were still enough surrounding the VIP area, they'd need the help.

Their group moved quickly to get to the water, but Mia lingered.

"I'm gonna run to the restroom. Go ahead without me. I'll be there in just a minute," she said to Scott.

He didn't move from her side. "I don't think so. You're still not going anywhere alone."

The others were far enough ahead, so she couldn't get one of the ladies to go with her.

"It's just the bathroom. I'll be fine. Please, trust I can take care of myself."

Scott pulled her to him and took possession of her soft lips. He tried to coax her to open, but she pushed him away in a hurry.

"Scott Kay Ralston! Are you trying to get me killed? You can't just kiss me like that out in the open. You did it on purpose, so I wouldn't go to the bathroom alone! Not cool!"

Before he could stop her, she turned on her heels and quickly pushed through the crowd, where he couldn't get to her.

CHAPTER 25

M ia was in a stall when she heard the door open, then some female voices.

"I still can't believe the wives tried to pull that shit. And who's the damned blonde? Why don't we know her?"

"Well, they were great," the second girl said.

"Yeah, but what the hell was up with Scott? Everyone knows he's single, so why hang on her like that?"

"Wasn't she the one that got pushed in the pool before the cruise started? Maybe he was just being nice to her?" a third chimed in.

"Maybe," the first agreed. "But he could do so much better. And I'm gonna prove it."

One of her friends laughed.

"It's not funny! I'll have that man naked and on top of me before the cruise is over. I almost kissed him once. This time we won't be interrupted."

Mia peaked between the cracks in the door to get a glimpse of the girls.

The boasting one was the same brunette as earlier, now in a pink bikini.

The other woman was a little taller, a little thicker, and had short brown hair. Her face gave the impression that she was kind.

The girls left the bathroom without even knowing she was there.

"We won't be interrupted, again."

The little brunette's words ran through her head.

Mia felt sick. Scott wouldn't cheat on her but now people had realized they were appearing together a lot.

It wasn't just that one girl, either. Outside the fitness center, the dark-haired woman had known about Mia and Scott.

Why did we think we could keep it a secret?

She stepped out of the bathroom and someone grabbed her arm. Mia screeched and made a fist, ready to swing, but stopped short when she saw the RE first-wife. "Oh my God, so sorry. You startled me."

"Sorry, too. Don't worry about it." Evelien's smile was warm and genuine and reminded her of what a big sister would give.

"Anyway Scott sent me to check on you. How're you holding up? You doing all right?" The concern in her voice had Mia worried.

"Yeah, I'm fine. I just wanted to use the restroom and change into my swimsuit. But Scott..."

Evelien stopped walking.

Mia got two steps ahead before pausing, since the woman wasn't right behind her. When they made eye contact, her stomach knotted.

"I want you to know, you can talk to me about anything. As the first-wife, I've done it all."

She glanced at her feet, shame washed over her. Dwaine's wife was probably referring to what she'd done less than twenty-four hours ago. "I hope you haven't humiliated yourself like I did last night."

"Oh, honey!" Evelien pulled her into a hug, running her hand down her hair like one would do with a crying child. "I think we all do something stupid like that at least once in our lives. But..."

Mia lifted her head and their gazes met again.

"Look at the bright side of this. Dwaine told me he'd seen Scott taking sips of shots, and after he saw you drunk, he immediately threw away the glass he had at the table. It was like a wake-up call for him. He saw through his eyes with you, what we'd seen with him."

They started walking again.

"Have you gotten any more notes?" her new friend asked.

"No, thank goodness. I think it's just some jealous fan. What I don't understand is how they figured it out. Scott and I have done nothing in public that could put us together."

Evelien sighed. "It doesn't take much. I'm surprised you've kept it a secret as long as you have. Didn't he visit you a few times? Some of these fans are pretty crazy; stalker-like. They know everything about these guys. We had to have cameras put up around our property. We had a fan come and sit at our house every day, watching us through the windows. One day, she tried to talk to our son, who was playing in the backyard. That was all it took."

Mia gasped. She put a hand over her mouth, and her friend laughed.

"That's what I mean. So, like I said, if you ever need someone to talk to, I'm here. Being a part of their lives means dealing with these types of things. We're strong women, and we can handle it. Because we have each other. Know you can come to any of us, at any time."

Mia hugged her, and Dwaine and Scott backtracked, probably to find out why they were taking so long.

Evelien kissed Dwaine sweetly. "We were just having a girl to girl chat," she said, looking over at Mia.

Scott pulled Mia into his arms. "Are you okay, baby? I was getting worried," he whispered.

"I'm all right."

He wrapped his left arm around her as they started moving again.

"You're all wet!" she tried to push him away.

"Yeah, I've been in the ocean," was his smart-ass reply. "Why didn't you come to join us?"

"Oh, I'm just getting tired and my head hurts," she said.

He turned her back toward the dock, his arm around her shoulders. "Are you not feeling well? Should we take you to the hospital?"

Mia rested her head against the shoulder. "No, it's okay. I just had things on my mind that were making my head hurt, but I'm better now."

"What things?"

"Oh, just some gossip I heard in the bathroom. But I'm over it," she said. "Oh, some brunette in a pink bikini is planning on shagging you before this cruise is over."

"Victoria," he said, laughing.

Mia frowned and tugged to another stop.

Scott's laughter died and when their eyes met. "Security just escorted her back to the ship."

She raised an eyebrow.

"She's drunk, and she thought skinny-dipping was a good idea."

She laughed.

"We weren't going to stop her, but when she tried to de-pants me... Well, it was time for her to go sleep it off."

Mia managed a smile, despite the subject and wrapped her arms around his chest. She noticed the setting sun shining on his face.

"Never doubt my love for you," Scott whispered.

"I don't," she said. She meant it. It wasn't him she was worried about.

She had to keep reminding herself that dealing with crazy fans was part of his life.

He took her hand, and they continued strolling the waterline, small waves crashing around their ankles.

♪♫

"Mia, maybe we should officially announce our relationship. It's pretty obvious people already know. Then we don't have to worry about it anymore." He was sick of hiding it. He wanted everyone to know. It might help keep the fans like Victoria at bay.

She sighed. "Yeah, it's crossed my mind. But it's only a couple more days. I think I'd like to be home before the press releases. A few fans knowing is better than a boat full knowing."

He could see her point. There were a few that wouldn't take the news well. "All right, we'll wait." Scott kissed her hand and led her further into the water up to their knees.

"Should we swim?"

She kissed his cheek. "I'd rather just head back to the boat, and skinny-dip with you. In the bathtub."

"Babe. I'd love to, but…"

Mia put her fingers on his lips. "I know. You gotta go be the rock star."

Scott pulled her close right when a bigger wave came at them. She lost her footing, and they both went down, water covering their heads.

Mia came out of the water laughing, rather than sputtering, like he expected.

"Well, since I'm already wet, guess we should swim."

She continued to surprise him by diving right into the next wave coming at them. Mia got about twenty feet ahead of him, treading water. "Are you gonna stand there with your jaw hanging open, or are ya gonna join me?"

He dived into the next wave, swimming right up to her. "Can we go back to our feet touching?"

She giggled. "Why? Can't you swim?"

"I'm loving how confident you are, showing me you've been practicing like you promised. But I want to wrap you in my arms and show you how proud I am." Scott grabbed her hand, doing his best to paddle just a few feet closer to shore. The second his feet could touch the sandy floor of the ocean, he stopped and pulled her in close, then captured her lips.

Their kiss was hot, heating them to their core.

His hands explored the body he already knew so well. He slipped his right hand under the tiny scrap of blue fabric that made up her bikini top, rubbing his thumb over her taut nipple.

Listening to her stuck in her breath caused his erection to jerk a demand. He wanted her, right there, in the ocean, in front of two thousand of his fans.

He didn't care.

"Scott," she whispered against his lips. "Is this a good idea?"

"Shut up," he stole her words as he took possession of her mouth again. He was lost in her, safe in her, he no longer felt incomplete.

She was everything he never knew he needed.

Scott wanted to shout it out to the world. Waiting another week to tell everyone was almost as much torture as holding her and not being able to do anything with her glorious body pressed against his. "Mia," he whispered.

"Shut up," she returned.

He didn't care about all the fans watching. He needed her, wanted her. He would've taken her right then.

"Scott," someone called from on a bullhorn. "Scott! We need you to return to the beach."

They were far enough out, they wouldn't have heard someone yelling, but the bullhorn made it loud and clear.

A small crowd of people started rushing to the shoreline, waiting for him.

Well, shit.

"Maybe I should stay back here, let you go back to the beach and I'll catch up later?" Mia asked.

"Um, no." He took her hand and practically dragged her to the shore.

"It's time to get you back to the boat," the huge black security guard stated while he escorted them back to the beach party.

"I'll just take one of the little skipper boats the rest of the fans are packing onto to get back to the ship. It's all right. It's what the wives and I had come on earlier," his woman complained.

"I don't think so. The wives were going back on the private skipper with their men. Therefore, so are you."

Within a short amount of time, they were back on the ship and heading to their cabins, fans still littering the hallway.

Scott held tight to Mia, not letting her go. He pulled her past her room, stopping at his own door. He opened it and dragged her inside, pressing her against the cold metal when the locked clicked.

He took her lips with the passion he'd had when they were still in the ocean, the fire heating them both. He pulled at her clothes, urging them off as fast as she could undress.

Mia moaned, as he ran his hands over her whole body.

Scott chuckled. "Baby, there's nothing I want more, then to make love to you, but…"

"I know," she interrupted him. "It's time to go be the rockstar."

"No, I don't care about that right now. You're covered in sand. I'm sure I'm covered in sand. I'm suggesting a shower."

Scott started the water while Mia finished undressing. She was just stepping in when his phone rang.

He growled on his way to answer.

"This better be important."

"Tick, tock, watch the clock," his brother from another mother said.

"Fuck you."

"No thanks. See you in an hour."

His beautiful woman stuck her head out the shower curtain and smiled when he took his shirt off. Water was dripping from her hair and he could see the outline of her luscious full bosom through the material. His balls tightened and his cock came to life, pressing firm against his swim trunks.

"What… you couldn't wait for me?" Scott teased.

She shrugged and went back to washing her hair.

He's never undressed so fast before.

He stepped into the water, letting out a happy sigh.

"Everything okay?" Mia asked.

"Huh?"

"The phone call?"

"Oh, yeah. Just Dwaine. Reminding me not to be late. I have a bad habit of being late." Scott massaged shampoo into his scalp. "Baby, the more I think about it, the more I think we should just come out. The rest of the boat will find out soon enough."

"I don't know. Did you see their faces when we revealed ourselves on stage? The death glares were unmistakable. When we'd been practicing, some dumb bitch said we'd only win because I was sleeping with you. I don't know how she knew we're together."

Scott rinsed the soap from his hair, but couldn't look at her. He understood where she was coming from, but she couldn't see his point of view. He wanted the world to know she was his. "You know I don't care what they think. Anyone in their right mind could tell you won from having talent on the stage, not in the bedroom."

Mia laughed, but stuck her bottom lip out. "Are you saying I don't have talent in the bedroom?"

Scott rolled his eyes at her pretend pout and wrapped his

arms around her, pulling her slick, wet body against his. His erection pressed against her hip. "Your talents are extraordinary, but for me only. No one else ever needs to know what you can do."

She kissed him. "How about I show you some of my talents?"

CHAPTER 26

S cott was going to be late, and Mia tried her best to feel bad. He'd taken time with her, and she couldn't feel bad that he'd taken time with her. He'd shown her all of the talents she'd promised to show him.

He was supposed to meet with the other guys at ten p.m., to all walk up to the lido deck together, in their matching Halloween costumes.

"What are you planning on wearing tonight," Scott asked while slowly circling the still-taut pink nipple of her left breast.

"I... um.." She couldn't speak when he teased her body. "Can't we just..."

He laughed. "You know I gotta get to work. But tonight, no matter how late I'm stuck on deck, we're spending the rest of it together. Naked." Scott stopped his delicious tortures . "So, what're you wearing?" He started up his gentle touch again, teasing her.

"Minnie Mouse!" she exclaimed. "I'm gonna be Minnie Mouse, now, please..."

He replaced his fingertips with his warm mouth.

Scott was going to be *very* late.

An hour later, she finally slipped away to allow him to get dressed.

Mia peered at herself in the mirror, proud of how she looked. It wasn't what she'd planned when she'd packed.

Originally, she was going to wear a pre-styled black wig, made to look like Betty Boop. Instead, she'd chosen her warm sand-colored hair in two pigtails. Her four-inch yellow heels stayed in the closet, her black ballet flats adorned her feet.

The crazy long eyelashes stayed in her makeup bag. Only black cat eyeliner, mascara, and fuck-me-red lipstick touched her face.

It was simple. She felt sexy.

Her black top had an off the shoulders boat-neck with cap sleeves. Mia tucked it into her red skirt with white polka dots, with a yellow belt around her waist.

She completed the outfit with white bloomers, the ruffled hem peeking out from under her skirt.

Mia picked up her mouse ears and slipped the headband on, setting it right in front of her pigtails.

She grabbed her yellow handbag and tucked in her room key, phone, and *All-Access* lanyard. She stepped out of her cabin and took a left. She'd have to wait for one of the wives to be able to leave the hallway.

Mia knocked on Grace's room; it was the first one.

The beautiful chestnut-haired woman opened the door wearing a smile.

Grace was stunning. She was dressed as Slave Leia, and she had the perfect body for the outfit.

"Come in, please."

Hope was sitting on the edge of the bed. The petite woman stood to show off her outfit. As the shortest in the group, her choice made sense.

She wore a pale green wig with white streaks. She'd dusted

her skin with a matching light green hue. She had on a dark brown wiggle dress, with a sheer tan kimono over it.

Yoda? Go figure. She makes it look so good.

"I take it you are all dressed from Star Wars?" Mia asked, suddenly feeling out of place.

"Yeah, we try to match our guys as much as we can. I'm surprised Scott didn't tell you," Hope said.

"I'm sure it's because I didn't want anyone to know we were together. I was worried it would cause trouble. Trouble found us on its own, I guess."

There was a knock at the door, and Grace moved to answer it. She looked over her shoulder. "Blaze! The boys are here!" she hollered.

The bathroom door opened.

Mia hadn't even noticed it was occupied.

Boba Fett stepped out. The man inside the helmet waved quickly, like a silly child, before revealing himself. Blaze wore a goofy smile, clearly proud of his costume.

Darth Vader was standing in the hallway. Towering over the others gathered there, revealed instantly it was Scott.

"I guess I've turned to the dark side," she teased when he lifted off his helmet. "Who else is out there?" She stuck her head out into the hallway to see Thomas dressed as Luke.

They'd dressed Dwaine as Han Solo with Evelien on his arm, dressed as Sexy Chewbacca.

Nick lingered in the back. His costume took a moment to place. He was A New Hope Leia, white floor-length dress and cinnamon bun wig.

Mia couldn't stop laughing. She turned to Hope. "Do you know what your husband is wearing?"

She joined her. "No, he wouldn't tell me. He made me get dressed in here, instead of our room. I can't believe you got to see him first."

The little Yoda pushed passed her and into the hall.

Mia didn't get to see her new friend's response to Nick's costume, because the Sith Lord got in front of her.

"I'm glad you have chosen the Dark Side. We have cookies," Scott said in a most Vader-like voice before removing his helmet. He leaned down and kissed her softly. "Tonight, you're arriving with me."

"Scott…" she protested, but he held up his hand to silence her.

"They've seen us all together, now. It doesn't mean they have a clue what is going on, but it won't come as a shock for you to walk up to the lido deck with us."

"Besides," Blaze said. "Your costume doesn't match, so no one will think you are an integrated part of us, but we know. And that's all that matters."

Grace's man's words hit her hard, and made her eyes tingle with unshed tears.

Mia was a part of them.

One of them.

They all accepted her.

It meant more than they'd ever know.

"Let's get topside."

The party was in full swing when they arrived on the lido deck.

Because of Scott, the band was over two hours late. It was their policy that they never went to a party until the entire group was ready.

He'd claimed his costume was hard to get into, and his face was red.

They all knew better.

Mia wanted to break off and blend into the crowd, but Scott held tight to her, keeping her by his side as they made their way on to the stage.

He finally let go of her when a microphone was shoved into his hand. "Let's get this party started," he screamed to the crowd, followed by a deafening scream of women, the sound drowning out the ship's engine.

"Welcome to Halloween Night." Dwaine stepped up to Scott.

"Look at all these love-aly costumes," Nick said, using a terrible sing-song voice.

The crowd screamed louder.

"I gotta know," Thomas said, moving to stage left. "Are you on the Dark Side…"

Women screamed.

"Or the side of the Rebellion?"

The noise was the same with each of his questions, making it clear everyone on the boat wanted to be a bit of both.

Good and Bad.

Mia watched from behind RE, and Dwaine stepped to the edge of the stage.

He pulled his gun from its holster and leaned down close to a girl and shot.

"Uh, Dwaine Solo? Whatcha doing there?" Thomas, aka Luke, asked.

"Well, they always say, Han shot first. So she got the first shot… of vodka." He chuckled at his joke.

Blaze strutted across the stage, his lethal swagger enough to kill any woman.

Damn, Grace is a lucky girl.

Boba Fett went to the opposite side of the stage as Solo and un-holstered his blaster. He leaned down and shot a stream of vodka into another girl's mouth.

The girls pressed harder against the stage, crushing the ones in front to get closer, to get a chance to have vodka shot into their mouths.

Mia felt so bad for the ladies in the front.

They'd waited hours to get their chance and now were being squished. However, they really didn't seem to mind.

All five men had water guns, painted black, filled with vodka. They were emptying them into as many mouths as they could.

When Scott ran out, he returned to the table at the back of the stage, where Mia and the other three women were standing.

The long table was covered with various liquors and almost as many funnels.

Scott handed his gun over to a cruise crew member, and the man replaced the vodka.

The Sith Lord didn't stand there and wait. He stepped up to Mia, keeping his back to the crowd. His costume was so wide at the shoulders and the cape long and full, she couldn't see around him at all. He pulled his helmet off. "How are you holding up, baby?"

"I'm good. Feeling awkward standing up here, but I'm okay."

"There's no reason for you to feel awkward. You belong up here. I know you heard Blaze. They see you as family, too. Just accept it." Scott kissed her cheek.

A very chaste and non-threatening kiss.

The crew guy handed him his gun and her tall, dark, and handsome man returned his helmet to his head and went back to shooting alcohol to the women who looked like fish out of water with their gaping wide-open mouths.

Mia really wanted a drink, but at the same time, had a feeling she needed to keep her wits about her. She was thirsty, and water didn't sound appealing at all.

She looked over at the alcohol-covered table. There were pitchers of soda, orange juice, and ice water.

Mia wasn't much of a soda drinker, unless it had liquor in it. Orange juice was a morning-only drink. She glanced at the other ladies. Hope was closest to her.

"Hey, Yoda. I'm gonna go to the bar behind us and get something non-alcoholic to drink. Do you guys want anything?" She had to almost-yell to get above the noise of the crowd.

"That'd be great! A pitcher of Peach tea! That's what Grace

usually gets. It's good on its own, or with a little something-something." She winked.

Before Hope or the others could stop her, Mia spun on the balls of her feet and took off the stage. She really appreciated their looking out for her, but all she was doing was getting a drink.

At a bar behind the stage, few people should be there.

She was about ten feet from the bar when someone gripped her upper arm and yanked. Hard. Intending pain.

The same dark-haired girl who'd confronted her outside the fitness room and tried to punch her at the bar the night before. "I know what you did." She glared, a promise of violence in her dark brown eyes.

"What? Won the karaoke contest, then gave it away?" Mia asked innocently.

"I know you slept with Scott, and that's why he broke up with Marissa." Her accusation was full of venom.

Mia didn't want to waste her time on something as stupid as this woman. She didn't deserve a reply. She shook her head and walked away, but the girl grabbed her again, spinning her back around.

"You better watch yourself. Your next trip into the water, you might not be so lucky."

She stood a little taller, lifting her shoulders. Anger made her ball her fists and she growled. "Do you really think I'm scared of getting pushed into the pool? Try again, bitch."

The shorter dark-haired beauty met her gaze again, pure evil in her eyes.

"There're other ways of getting rid of you. I wasn't talking about the pool." She stormed off through the crowd, leaving her threat trailing behind her like a dark ribbon.

Mia's imagination got the best of her. She could finally swim a little, but she still had a fear of deep water.

What if she manages to sneak up behind me and push me overboard?

How long would it take for anyone to realize I was missing?

Could I keep afloat long enough?

What if I hit my head going over and instantly drown?

She was shaking when she got up to the bar. She ordered the tea, trying not to let any fear show. She searched the crowd for the girl when she returned to the stage.

"Mia, what's wrong?" Hope asked. "You're white as a ghost."

Grace overheard Hope's question and peered their way. "Something's definitely not right." She went over to them, getting right in front of Mia. "What happened?"

She looked between the two of them. "Do you remember the girl yesterday, outside the fitness center, right after we were practicing our dance?"

Hope nodded.

"She found me again. I didn't really think much about it, and I tried to just walk away but..." Mia took a deep, still shaky breath. "I think she may have been the one who pushed me in the pool at the hotel."

Hope's eyes went as big as saucers.

"Did she threaten you?" Grace asked.

Mia nodded.

Grace waved over a large black man wearing a yellow shirt that said, "Security. We've had a threat," Blaze's wife told him, then turned back to Mia. "Can you describe her?"

"About 5'2" with long black hair and brown eyes."

"What's she wearing?" the security guy asked.

"A Playboy bunny costume. But there are at least ten of them in the crowd."

"Anything else you can remember?" he asked.

"Yeah, she has a tattoo on her right shoulder. A butterfly, I think."

"Don't worry, ladies, we'll find her."

She pointed out the direction the girl had taken off, and the security guy headed that way, radioing the rest of security.

Hope took Mia's hand and helped her to one of the wicker chairs. "Is there something you're not telling us? I get the impression you normally would've told the bitch to move on already, but you're still shaking. What else are you leaving out?"

"I... um... I have a great fear of drowning. I've been working on it. Then the pool incident happened the night before we boarded. I thought I was okay, I was getting over my fear, but what she said..." Before Mia could get out exactly what the girl had implied, she got herself worked up all over again. Pain spread out across her chest and back and she had trouble getting air in and out. Everything... hurt.

"Okay, now, deep breaths." Grace put her hands on Mia's knees.

She took a deep breath and let it out slowly.

"I think we'll take some extra precautions for the rest of the cruise," Grace said.

"Please, don't tell Scott," she begged. "He worries enough, and we can handle this on our own."

Grace just nodded.

Mia was a tad surprised she'd agreed so fast, but was grateful. "Maybe I'll just go to my room and rest for a little while." She stood, and Blaze's wife found her feet as well.

"Take security," the chestnut-haired beauty pushed.

"I'll be all right. I really doubt she'd do something right after warning me. She's gonna wait for me to let down my guard. That won't be tonight."

"Mia," the others chastised together.

"No. I'll be fine. If you send someone with me, it's obvious I'm *someone*. I'll text you the moment I get back to my room." She didn't wait for them to press the issue further. Mia raced down the stairs.

As she passed the pool on her way to the sliding glass doors that led into their hallway, she stopped cold.

There she was, the bitch who'd threatened her. She stood just to the right of the pool, her eyes on the stage.

Mia followed her line of sight.

The guys were all standing across the front, shaking their asses and having a good time.

The girl glared at Scott, menace rolling off her petite body in waves.

What's going on?

They'd all assumed she was a jealous fan, but the look in her eyes said something else entirely.

When the song melted into the next one, and it focused on Scott's vocals, the girl stormed off.

This is very curious.

Mia followed, trying to keep her distance. She was going to turn the tables on this bitch.

Right now, the other woman had her guard down, so she could get the upper hand.

The girl went to the bar and ordered a shot, then downed it quickly. She slammed the little shot glass on the counter before pivoting away.

Then she left the party.

Mia continued to follow her, still staying out of sight and silent.

The raven haired woman never even noticed her.

She left the lido deck, entering the sliding glass doors on the opposite side from where Mia had initially been headed.

She entered the buffet area, but didn't stop to get food. The girl went for a table toward the back of the room. One with a half-wall partitioner.

The woman sat and pulled out her phone, burying her face in the lit-up screen.

Mia slipped into a chair at the table behind her, the half-wall hiding her from view. She could still hear the other woman making a call. She leaned forward to listen better.

"Hey. It's me. No, he's still with her. Well, what am I supposed to do about it? I already threatened her, and if Scott finds out I'm on this boat, he'll have me thrown off."

Damn.

She wished she could hear the other side of the conversation.

"You know I can't get that close to him. No, Nick would recognize me, too." She sighed, her irritation sharp and obvious. "No, she's always with her friends now. The other wives. Stupid bitches. Being all, flaunty of their relationships! I'm kinda outnumbered here. I'll see what I can do but no promises." The black haired woman slammed her hand down on the table. "Damn it, Marissa! If you weren't my sister, I wouldn't be here."

Mia swallowed and blanched to her toes. She was dizzy for a moment, and she had to put her hands on the table to steady herself.

One part of her wanted to jump over the half-wall and give the woman on the phone a piece of her mind, and a piece of her fist for the one holding the phone. She forced a deep, quiet breath, got up and left before the bitch ended her call.

Mia rushed back to the party, her heart pounding and her limbs tingling.

"Mia," Grace called when she took the steps two at a time.

She ignored her new friend and reached for the first guy she could.

Nick was at the table getting a drink refill, while the other guys were at the front of the stage, keeping the crowd entertained.

"I need you..."

"All right, but I already have a wife." He winked.

Mia gave him 'the look', hoping he'd understand she was serious.

He set down his drink and stepped over to the side with her. "Mia, what's wrong? Do I need to get Scott?"

"Yes. Scott. I need him. I found out who's after me."

Nick went ashen. "What? Someone's after you? Who?"

"It's a long story, just know that it's Marissa's sister."

"Jazmin's on the boat?" he exclaimed. He started pacing. "I never thought she'd... why would..." he mumbled.

"What's going on?" Scott asked, appearing next to Nick and Mia.

Nick glared. "Jazmin's on the ship."

"What?" Scott exclaimed.

"Wait, who's Jazmin?" Hope asked.

"Marissa's sister," Scott said, looking from Mia to Hope. "And she always brings trouble. She's got to be the one sending you the notes. She'd do anything for her sister."

"How do you know it was her?" Hope asked.

"I saw her at the bar. Something wasn't right about the way she was looking at you." Mia gestured to Scott. "So I followed her."

"Mia!" he scolded "Why didn't you call security?"

"There wasn't time," she exclaimed. "Something wasn't right," she whispered. "She wasn't focused on me anymore; it was all about you. I was worried for you."

"What're we going to do?" Hope asked.

"We need to go talk to security," Scott said.

She shook her head. "No. We only have one more night on this cruise. Now that we know who it is, we must be diligent. Don't let her get the best of us. I don't know her, but I won't let her win."

He took her hand and kissed her knuckles. "Are you sure? We could have her put on cabin arrest, and have security keep her in her room until we dock?"

Mia squeezed his hand. "How will that look, hearing you've

got an unruly fan on house arrest? It's all right. Let's just enjoy the rest of the night."

"Speaking of which, I can call it quits now. I've done my mandatory two hours. Let's go back to our room and I'll show you my lightsaber."

CHAPTER 27

"I can't believe she's here," Scott ranted, his heart pounding with the fury burning inside.

"Do you think she was always planning on attending the cruise, or grabbed a last-minute cabin to..." Mia tried to keep up with Scott's brisk pace as they headed back to his cabin.

"I don't know. But I still think we should let security know." He couldn't let her try to talk him out of it this time. He understood her point regarding cabin arrest, but he could inform security and have a detail put on Jazmin.

He opened his door and led his woman in.

Mia took a seat on the bed and Scott went straight for the liquor cabinet.

He mixed them both up a drink.

The moment the glass touched her lips, he picked up his cellphone.

SCOTT: Sorry. You're not off work yet. I need you.

. . .

He waited for a reply, but instead of the text he expected, there was a harsh knock on the door.

The liquid in Mia's glass sloshed from her hand jerking in surprise.

He moved to open the door.

A huge black man with arms the size of boulders stood there, resolve all over his face. "Who's ass am I beatin'?"

"No one, yet. But come in." Scott stepped back to allow the much larger man into his room.

"Ms. Lee? How are you?"

Scott loved how her cheeks flushed pink when anyone acknowledged her as part of the family, like Johnny was doing.

"I'm okay. I think Scott's making a fuss. I can handle this."

"Mia, I love you, but shut up." He turned back to his friend and bodyguard. "We figured out who's sending Mia the nasty notes. You're never gonna believe who."

"All right, man. Stop with the suspense. Who am I throwin' overboard?"

He picked up his drink and downed more than half. "You want one?"

"Nah. It's after three, man. Some of us need to sleep. Let's get to the point, so I can deal with this shit and rest. You know photo day is the longest day for me."

Johnny was right. Over eight hours of standing in one room, taking photo after photo with small groups of fans, with only one break in-between Group A and Group B.

"It's Jazmin."

"Shit! Are you serious? Didn't she learn anything the last time she came around?"

Scott tried not to laugh. Johnny knew, better than anyone, how determined that girl could get. They had history. It went back a few years, but it was the kind no one forgot.

"I need to have a team on her. Distance, but always aware of her location. I wanted to have her banned to her cabin but

Mia," he glanced at his blonde sitting on his bed, slowly sipping the jack and coke he'd given her. "She thinks it would look bad, for us to lock a fan in their room. So I'd like it if we could keep an eye on her and make sure she doesn't get anywhere near Mia."

"Agreed. Good plan. I also think you should give Ms. Lee an escort as well. Just in case."

Scott laughed when Mia glared up at the man that was three times bigger than her.

"I already told Scott, I don't need a bodyguard! Now that I know who it is, I can be on the lookout. Stop treating me like I'm gonna break!"

Johnny laughed. "Man, you sure you can handle a woman like her?"

He offered his beautiful girlfriend his hand. He helped her stand, then pulled her in tight, then looked into her intense blue eyes. "No mortal man could handle this woman. But I'll be glad to die trying."

She stole his breath with a kiss not meant for public viewing.

The door clicked with Johnny's hasty retreat.

$$\text{🎼♩}$$

Buzz, Buzz.

"Damn it," Scott mumbled at his alarm.

Mia was curled up against him, her bare skin keeping him warm.

He wanted to stay there forever, safe in her arms. Unfortunately, he had a job to do.

Reluctantly, he slipped from the bed to take a shower.

The heat from the water washed away the aches. Not only in his body, but his soul.

He couldn't tell Mia how scared he was. Stalkers were not something to take lightly.

Almost everyone in the band had first-hand knowledge of how bad things could get.

Blaze and his wife had had the worst of it, though. The stalker in the Solan's life hadn't been a *Razor's Edge* fan, he'd been someone close to Grace. Even worse, he was Nick's little brother.

Grace had almost died.

Scott wouldn't let something like that happen to Mia. He'd do everything in his power to keep her safe. He didn't care if she got angry.

Johnny would be on top of things. The man was part of the family, another brother, and he'd help keep Mia and the others safe.

Scott wrapped the towel around his waist and did his best to wipe the moisture off the mirror. He examined his reflection. There were dark circles under his eyes.

The fans wouldn't notice. They never seemed to notice when something was off. They only saw what they wanted to see. Another reason he was so grateful his girl didn't start out as a RE fan.

"What am I going to do?" he asked the man in the mirror. "I know it's only Jazmin, but she is a little crazy. I can't let anything happen to Mia. I'd be lost without her."

Scott ran a comb through his hair, brushed his teeth, and began dressing for the day.

The fans loved their costumes, so management had decided they'd, once again, dress for the occasion. The year before, they'd dressed them as seamen, but this cruise, they were going as pirates.

The costumes were horribly cheesy. Thomas, Blaze, and Dwaine had terrible wigs. He and Nick could get away with no wigs at all.

His costume was the simplest.

Thank goodness.

Scott wore a white linen, long sleeve shirt that was a size too big. It had lace on the cuffs, and the collar was ruffled. It was unbuttoned halfway down, and tucked into his black pants.

The pants had a button up crotch and buttons on the outer side of the legs, from the hem to the knee. He tucked them into knee-high boots, the cuff folding over to give that authentic 'pirate' look.

He had a red cummerbund with a black belt over that, the gold buckle was bigger than his hand. Another leather belt crossed his right shoulder to sit on his left hip. They'd even supplied him with a golden 'pistol'.

Scott took one last look at his beautiful girl, still passed out, and slipped out the door, ready to take on the day and every single fan on the boat.

His brothers all collected and made their way to the large dining hall where the photos were being done.

Justin, the photographer, was putting last-minute touches on the lighting, and the line of fans was all the way down the hall.

There had to be a thousand of them, all dressed in their best; hair and makeup spot on.

Scott wished he could 'see' them like Mia had told him to. He saw adoring fans, but couldn't focus on a single face. He didn't want that. He appreciated every single one of them, and what they'd done to get him where he was.

He was in love with Mia. *She* was all he could see when he closed his eyes. Her scent still lingered in his senses.

Hour after hour he smiled, hugged, and played the part. Not one woman knew his thoughts were elsewhere.

They were with a beautiful blonde, a woman with the most glorious breasts he'd ever seen. A girl who held his heart in her hands and contained his soul within her own.

"Scott!" The dark-haired woman was throwing herself at him.

His heart stopped, but for only a moment. This girl had a sweet child-like voice, not the snobbish tones of Jazmin. He tried to swallow away his concern, and calm his pulse.

He took the photo with the cocoa-skinned beauty.

When she and her friends walked away, he flagged down Justin and Jillian, the woman in charge of keeping the line going.

"I'm sorry, but I need a break. Just a few moments to gather myself."

"Hey," Thomas said, "I think that is a great idea."

"I could use a second to go check on Grace," Blaze chimed in. "I think she's seasick."

"But..." Jillian tried to interject. "We've still got..." She didn't get to finish.

Scott, along with his brothers, bolted for the stairs, their security team running to catch up.

MIA SAT on the balcony of Scott's cabin, the first time she'd taken advantage of the beautiful view. She slowly sipped orange juice, flavored with a little tequila.

Sure, it was called a screwdriver, but she'd always told herself if drinking alcohol before three in the afternoon, calling it a *flavoring,* rather than the official name, it made it less... lush.

She couldn't believe she was drinking orange juice. It was well after noon, but she'd slept in, thanks to Scott, so technically, it was still 'morning' for her.

A knock on the cabin door had her sighing but pushing herself off the lounge chair.

Mia peeked through the peephole.

Grace and Hope were in the hallway.

She grinned and opened things up. "Good morning, ladies."

"Morning? Mia, honey, it's almost two in the afternoon," Grace said. "We were getting worried, since you didn't come to get us for breakfast."

"Oh, sorry. I didn't realize how tired I was until after I slept so hard. Scott didn't wake me when he left, and my body got what it needed. Since I woke so late, I just called for room service. I figured you'd all gone to eat already."

"Oh, you should've called. Gracie here has been throwing up all morning and can't keep anything down, so I had to go to breakfast alone."

"Where's Evelien? And why were you throwing up?"

"She got a text from Dwaine and took off to go deal with something. So we thought we'd come to find out what happened with you, how you're holding up," Grace said, not commenting on her own issues.

"I'm fine, as you can see. Are you okay?"

Blaze's wife just nodded, but Hope was almost vibrating.

Nick's woman was clearly excited about something but wasn't sharing her thoughts.

"Are you all right?" Now Mia was getting concerned. She stepped closer to her two new friends, reaching out for the tall chestnut-haired beauty.

"I'm fine. I thought it was just seasickness, so I went to the ship's doc to see if they had anything that would help," Grace said.

"But you weren't sick the first few days. Isn't that when it's usually at its worst?" Mia downed the juice from the glass still in her hand, the 'flavoring' burning as it slipped down her throat.

"Well, I learned something while I was there."

The lock clicked and the three of them collectively glanced that way.

Scott entered the room, his brothers in the hallway behind him, all on their way to their own cabins. "The ladies are in here," he called over his shoulder.

Blaze pushed past his 'older brother' and rushed into the room, pulling Grace into his arms. "How are you feeling, baby?"

"I'm fine. Actually, I'm more than fine. Can everyone please come in here?"

Mia scrunched her brows together as the room became very

crowded. She was still in her pajamas, and didn't want the others to see her in skivvies.

"I've got some exciting news," Grace said. She reached for her husband's hand. "I wasn't feeling good this morning, so I went to the ship's sickbay to see about getting something for my nausea. They gave me something, all right."

The chestnut-haired beauty had every eye in the room.

"Grace, honey, spit it out," Hope said.

"I'm pregnant!"

The small cabin was immersed with joyful glee.

Blaze swept his wife into his arms and kissed her with a passion not meant for the masses.

Mia's cheeks seared.

"Three down, two more to go." Nick looked directly at Scott.

"Dude, seriously?" He shrugged.

She went to him, running her hand inside his opened-chested pirate shirt, splaying her fingers over the soft skin. "Well, we might not be ready for kids, but I'm up for practicing."

"And *that's* our cue to leave." Nick laughed, grabbing Hope's hand and dragging her out the door, the others quickly following.

CHAPTER 28

Thomas stopped at the door, holding on to the frame to look back. "Bro, we still have a line of fans waiting to take photos. You're gonna have to practice later."

Once the door clicked closed, he pulled her hard against him, feeling his belt buckle digging into them both. "I don't want to go back. I *need* to stay here in your arms."

Mia kissed him, her tongue encouraging him to open. He moaned at the taste of her.

Orange juice and tequila.

He was emotionally drunk from her.

They were so far away from even thinking about babies, but it was still in the back of his mind. Scott could still remember to glow on Nick's face when Hope was about to bust at the seams with his child.

Someday, he wanted that. Not yet. But some day.

He released her, holding her out just enough to look deep into her amazingly blue eyes. "How did I fall so hard, so fast? Mia, what did you do to make me fall in love with you?" The words in his heart slipped out of his lips in a whisper.

"It wasn't intentional, I promise," she teased. She kissed his nose. "But you wouldn't be where you are, here in my arms, if it wasn't for your fans, who got you where you are. So go be a good rockstar, and finish taking your photos. I'll be here when you're done. Getting ready to be your Prom date."

She was right, and Scott reluctantly let her slip from his arms. "Just a few more hours, Mia. Then I'll be all yours." He stopped just outside the cabin, leaning his head on the closed door.

On the other side of the cold metal was his world.

The joy on Blaze's face at the news he was going to be a father, filled him with an unpleasant mixture of happiness and envy.

That will be me someday. Soon.

For what he wanted to do next, he'd need the wives' help.

First, he had to get through photos.

SCOTT HAD THOUGHT the first four hours were grueling. He'd had no idea.

The girls seemed to be much more enthusiastic than the first group.

It wasn't until Blaze pulled him aside when they were heading out, done for the day, he was clued in to why.

"Dude, I know why I have a reason to be grinning from ear to ear. What's your excuse?"

"Huh?"

"Ever since we came back to finish our photos, you've had this goofy smile on your face. Even the fans noticed. I know you didn't get some, there wasn't enough time. So what's up?"

"I need your wife," Scott said.

"Excuse me." His buddy reared back.

"And Nick's, and Dwaine's."

"Are you starting a harem? I don't think you could handle all the estrogen."

"Who's starting a harem?" Nick asked.

"Scott is, with *our* wives," Blaze teased.

"Excuse me?" Nick's eyebrows shot up.

"Good job, dumbass." Scott shoved playfully at the bad boy of the group. "Now Nick will never let Hope out of his sight." He glanced at the youngest member of the band. "I need the wives' help with something I want to do for Mia, if that is okay with you."

Nick cocked his head side to side, like he was trying to figure Scott out. "What are you gonna do?"

"You'll just have to wait, like Mia, to find out."

They had reached their hallway, and Scott went straight to Blaze and Grace's door, knocking harder than he'd meant to.

Grace opened the door, and she was alone.

That was a surprise. He'd assumed the others would be with her.

"Can I borrow you for a few minutes? And Hope and Evelien?"

"Is everything all right?" Her sweet voice was laced with concern.

"Everything's great. I could use your help with something."

"Let me slip on my sandals. I think the others are in their rooms."

In the time it took Blaze's wife to get ready, Nick had already rounded Hope up and Evelien in the hallway.

"So, what's up?" Hope asked.

"We need to head to Deck Seven. That's where I need your advice."

With Johnny in tow, they stepped into the atrium, and Scott directed them to the left. To the ship's only jewelry shop.

"What are we doing here?" Evelien asked.

"I want to propose to Mia tonight."

The three women began exclaiming words he couldn't keep up with.

He held up a hand, but instead of silencing them, they threw their arms around him, surrounding him with their joy for him.

"You can't tell her," he tried to say as they crushed him.

They finally released him, and the four of them walked up to the counter to look at rings.

The salesman looked at Scott before glancing at the three women. "So when is the big day? Which one of you is the lucky lady?"

Scott cocked his head to one side. How had the man known?

"I saw you through the window getting mauled by these ladies, so I just assumed."

He hated when people assumed things. "Oh, I'm marrying all three. Plus one more." He gave it back to the man. He glanced at the three wives. "Which one do you think Mia would like? And how the hell do I figure out what size?"

Evelien slipped an arm through his, bringing him over to a case she'd been looking at. "I'd go with platinum. I've only seen her in silver jewelry this week. And platinum is a study material, so she's less likely to misshape it when she punches you."

Scott blinked at the first-wife.

Evelien just smiled big at him, revealing her tease.

On the other hand, she was probably right.

Mia would need something she wouldn't break.

He pointed to one in the platinum section. "What about that one?"

"Oh, no." She wrinkled her nose.

"Too small of a diamond?"

"Too big. That's gaudy. I can't see her wearing that one."

Grace pointed to a small half-carat, in a simple setting. "What about this one?"

He tsked. "I want to give her something more special than that."

They whittled their way down to three rings.

One was a floral design around the band with a circle stone.

Another was a twisted band, also with a round stone. And the last had a textured band and a teardrop shaped stone.

"Which one, ladies?"

"That's a decision only you can make," Grace said. "We'll leave you alone to think about it. Get it in a size seven. Her hands are pretty close in size to mine."

Scott watched the three ladies retreat.

Damn. How did my brothers' and I get so lucky?

He returned to his final three, trying to imagine each one on Mia's hand. That helped.

Scott made his decision, paid for the ring, and headed to his room, the blue satin box tucked safely in his left boot.

MIA WAS PULLING her navy-blue dress over her head when Scott stepped out of the shower.

He wrapped a towel around his waist and ran a hand through his wet hair, sending droplets of water to run down his bare chest.

He looked her up and down, admiring her floor length dress. It covered one shoulder, and it dipped low in the back. "Do you need help with the zipper?"

"Sweetie, it zips on the side."

"I think I should help you with that," he pressed.

She laughed when his knuckles slid over her skin, but he closed the dress.

Scott kissed her bare shoulder when he was done. "I better go back into the bathroom to get dressed. Otherwise I may strip that dress off you."

"Scott! You know you can't be late tonight. Dwaine already gave me shit about that!" She kissed him before slapping his ass through his damp towel.

Mia worked to pull all her hair up into a semi-French twist.

She had a visible part on the left side and the very ends of her hair were tufted upward in the twist.

She finished her make-up and went to the closet to get her jewelry.

The door to the bathroom opened again, and she sucked in a breath. Scott's tuxedo was a beautiful Armani suit with a satin lapel and white hankie. His buttons were onyx, set in silver and his black bowtie was satin.

What I wouldn't give to get him out of his tux.

Behave, girl.

She stepped up to him, handing him her sapphire necklace. She gave him her back so he could clasp it for her. Mia didn't expect it to be his lips that touched her skin first. She let her eyes slip closed.

He kissed her neck, sending goose bumps over her skin, all the way up into her hairline. His kisses moved to her bare shoulder.

There was a tingle of interest between her legs.

Mia took a step forward, forcing herself out of his reach.

His green eyes had darkened with desire.

"No, Scott. You can't be late. Again." She kissed the tip of his nose. "But I'm all yours after Prom." She took her necklace from his hands, not letting him finish *'helping'* her.

She grabbed her matching shoes and purse that sat on the bed, and headed out the door.

Mia took a deep breath to center herself before knocking on Hope and Nick's door.

Nick looked sharp in his black tuxedo. He wore a satin yellow vest and yellow bowtie that matched Hope's dress.

She had to give the woman kudos, Nick was a hottie.

He stepped to the side to allow Mia into the room.

"Wow, you look breathtaking, Hope! I can't believe you have a five-month-old baby." She watched the petite woman's face blush.

"I worked really hard to get into shape, not only for the cruise, but so I would have the energy I'd need when she starts crawling."

"Where's Scott?" Nick asked.

Mia tried not to laugh, recalling the state she'd left him in. "I think he's taking a cold shower."

"Shit! He's still in the shower! We are supposed to be..."

She held up a hand to stop his rant. "Nick, I mean he was in need of a cold shower. He was dressed when I left."

"Damn it," he mumbled, then slipped into the hallway.

"Let's get the others," Hope encouraged, leading her out.

The party was in full swing when they arrived.

The party goers were all dressed in their finest. The gowns were all so very different; no two girls had the same style.

There were hot pink and red, blue and green, and lots of black.

There were some that were very short and others that were floor length, like Mia and Hope's. There were super tight and super flowing.

The only thing missing at the prom was dates.

The guys were already on the stage singing. As if sensing their presence, Scott and Nick looked back to the entryway when the four women walked out into the night air on the lido deck.

The light behind them lit them up.

Scott missed a step and smacked into Thomas.

Mia covered her mouth, half wanting to giggle, and half wanting to be horrified. She didn't want him to have an accident on stage.

Thomas covered his mic and whispered something to Scott, and the other guys exchanged looks that seemed sheepish, even from their distance.

Grace shook her head when Mia spared her a glance, so she'd seen the misstep, too.

The song ended, and the guys went right into the next one, without missing any more choreography.

Mia liked this one, and she got sucked into the words.

Scott kept looking directly at her.

Don't ask, It'll never happen
There's promises I'll never make
Too scared, you'll never want me
It's something that I can not take
Doesn't matter to you
You're still here by my side
Am I acting the fool
Still Better, you see
Da da da de da
There is no fear
I see you're hanging around
Don't tell me I'm not a clown
Still Better,
You see
Da da da de da
Da da da de da

THE BAND PERFORMED a few more songs before they had the DJ take over. They worked their way through the throng of girls to find one to dance with.

Each RE member had a security guy, to prevent other girls around trying to interfere with the one they were dancing with.

Scott hadn't joined the guys, but Blaze was dancing with a short robust girl in a pink frilly dress.

. . .

MIA ENJOYED WATCHING the fans in the crowd getting a chance to be a prom date, as RE made their way through the groups of ladies, dancing for a few moments, with as many ladies as they could.

"I could use a drink. Would you come with me?" Grace asked.

"Uh, we have drinks on the table," she said.

"I know, but there isn't Peach Tea."

If the woman hadn't announced she was pregnant, Mia would've told her to deal with what they had. She really didn't want to go through all the fans pushing to get closer to the guys.

The look on Grace's face said it was important, so Mia nodded.

"Something tells me we need to go to that side," she said, taking Mia's hand, almost dragging her into the crowd.

As they moved through the mass of finely dressed females, Mia spotted Thomas from the corner of her eye. He'd just thanked the girl he'd been dancing with and was trying to move on to another.

Scott wasn't far either, and he was looking at them; she had no doubt about that.

Grace tried to maneuver them a little closer.

"I thought we were going for tea," Mia said.

"We are, but I think Scott's trying to get to you."

They moved a little closer, but were halted when a tall, big black guy stood in front of them.

Mia tried to get around him, but he kept moving to sidestep her. She was about to ask him to move him when Scott peeked out from behind the guy.

He beamed.

When *he* stepped around the big guy, Grace moved to the left so Mia was right in front of him.

He offered Mia his hand as the words to the next song began. It was, *I'll Be* by Edwin McCain.

"I could really use someone to dance with. Do you mind?" Scott asked.

"I don't mind, but there are about three thousand other girls that might," she teased.

"They'll get over it." Scott smiled at her.

Mia nodded, and took his hand.

He pulled her to him, bringing his right hand to her lower back.

Their eyes locked, intense.

She had to use all her strength to not kiss him.

Scott seemed to be fighting the same battle.

CHAPTER 29

S cott pulled Mia closer, inhaling her scent.

These last few days had been so hard on both of them. He'd understood her desire to be secret during the cruise, and it's already been proven to be a wise choice, but all he wanted to do in that moment was get lost in her.

His desire to keep her safe was ruling his mind.

His heart was making his decisions.

Scott ran his hand up her back, caressing her soft bare skin. He leaned in, toward her ear, so only Mia could hear him. "Have I told you tonight how beautiful you are?"

She smiled, and her eyes shone a little brighter. "Have I told you tonight how much I love you?" she whispered back.

"I could spend all night right here, in your arms and be complete."

"Me, too. But you need to pick a Prom Queen."

When the song ended, he gave her a squeeze, bringing their bodies as close as he could. "I'll see you soon. Love you." Scott reluctantly let her go. It took everything in him not to turn and look at her one more time.

The evening wound down, and the guys assembled onstage.

"And now the part of the evening we've all been waiting for," Dwaine said into his mic.

"It's time to announce our Prom Queens," Scott said, although he couldn't bring who he really wanted on stage yet.

The band dispersed into the crowd to select their queens.

They all return to the stage, leading a female fan by the hand.

Thomas's girl was short and heavyset. She was wearing a pink ball gown with spaghetti straps. He retrieved her tiara from a table on the stage.

Her smile was massive when he placed it on her head.

The delicate tiara had *"Razor's Edge"* spelled out in rhinestones.

"My queen, Brittany," Thomas said into the mic.

There was applause for Brittany, and she blushed as pink as her gown.

Blaze's queen was gothic. Her red and black dress and dramatic makeup made her look like a vampire. Ironically, her name was Angelique.

Nick chose a girl with the wildest dress. She wore a leopard print, spaghetti strap top and a red frilly skirt that looked like a short version of Mia's petticoat.

Dwaine chose a Hispanic girl, wearing an orange micro mini dress.

Scott took a long time finding a girl in the crowd.

She stood alone, with her hands crossed in front of her and her head low. This fan was tall and gangly, dressed in a turquoise short tea dress that looked like it was from 1988. She beamed when he offered her his hand.

The Prom Kings and Queens danced in a circle in the center of the dance floor to, *I've Had The Time Of My Life* from *Dirty Dancing*, before opening it back up to the other girls.

A half an hour later Blaze, Thomas, and Dwaine made their way to the stage, while Nick and Scott remained to work the crowd.

BLAZE TOOK his mic from a tech and went to the center stage, with Dwaine right behind.

Mia laughed as the bad boy of the group squirmed. It was a sight she'd never seen before. What was about to happen to make him look like that?

Dwaine had the same look on his face.

"Since tonight's Prom Night, and our last night on the boat, I want to share something special. Well, we all do. But I get the pleasure of going first." Blaze looked over to the VIP area, where his wife sat with the other girls. "I'd like to ask my beautiful wife, Grace, to join me on the stage."

Grace looked shocked as she obeyed. She worked her way through the girls, who were trying hard to make a path for her.

Mia exchanged looks with Hope and Eveline

Blaze continued while Grace joined him. "So many people in this world never find love. I've been so blessed. I not only married my best friend, but my soulmate. She's always stood by me. No matter what happened, I could always count on her love."

Scott and Nick were right behind Blaze's wife. As they put in their earbuds and were handed mics, Blaze took Grace's hand.

"I still can't believe what Fate did to us to bring us together. I wish I could take the nightmares away, but I'm so grateful to have you in my life. To call you my wife. You knew my past, who I was, yet you stood by me. You've always been there for me. I haven't had the chance lately to tell you how much I love you. So here I stand, ready to tell you."

Grace wiped tears away as they fell.

Music began, and he sang to her.

It was a song Mia hadn't heard before, but it clearly was about their relationship.

Everyone teared up as Blaze sang his heart and soul to his wife. When he ended, Grace took the mic from him.

"There's never been a moment where I ever doubted your love for me, but it means so much to have you sing it, to remind me of it. I didn't think I could've loved you more but..." She touched her belly, ever so slightly, not letting the crowd know her little secret, but Mia did. "I love you more than I ever thought possible." She stepped into Blaze's arms and he kissed her with a passion that wasn't meant for public eyes.

Her cheeks flushed red when they broke apart, but he didn't let her go.

They stood there for a moment in each other's arms.

Obviously not wanting to waste any time, Dwaine stepped forward and called his own wife forward.

Evelien glanced at Mia and Hope before she stood. She rested a hand on Mia's shoulder as she walked past.

Once again, the crowd made way for her to get to the stage.

Dwaine waited at the top of the steps for his wife.

She kissed his cheek when he took her hand.

They took only a few steps before Grace reached for Evelien. She hugged the first-wife then she headed to the side of the stage.

Dwaine brought Evelien to center stage, where Blaze and Grace had been just moments before. He took a deep breath. "There aren't enough words in the world, nor enough notes in music, to express everything I feel for you. This song, we all wrote together, years before I met you. But somehow, it was always meant for you."

This was something the crowd didn't expect, to have the guys singing to their wives.

Many of the girls in the crowd were wiping at tears, just as Evelien was while Dwaine sang to her.

Even Mia had to swipe at her face. In her heart, she wished one day Scott would sing to her.

Hope wore a similar expression. She was dabbing at her eyes with the cloth napkin she had had in her lap, right before she was called to join the others on stage.

"Hope," Nick began once she was by his side. "Our life started out a little rocky, and I had some really dark days. But you were always the light in my life. I wrote this song when we were apart, but somehow it gave me... well... hope. That things would work out."

The love that was on that stage would drive anyone to beautiful tears.

Mia had no doubt the men of Razor's Edge loved deep and hard, with every fiber of their being. She zoned in on Grace, who was still on stage, and she smiled when they locked eyes.

Scott stepped forward.

Her stomach knotted, and nausea swirled there. "He wouldn't, would he?" She mouthed at Hope.

"As many of you know," Scott said. "I was engaged, but things didn't work out. We said goodbye. I never thought I'd ever find love. But one night, when I was least expecting it, the woman of my dreams came into my life." He looked right at Mia.

More tears welled, but she blinked them away. Mia didn't want anything to blur her vision. She didn't move, except to wipe away tears.

"I've been an alcoholic."

The crowd gasped, as this wasn't public knowledge.

"But to her, my angel, I'm just Scott. She's brought me down to earth and made me see I can be loved for who I am. I know many of you have met her this weekend, and the first thing you need to know, she's a truly talented woman, who's given up being with me most of this weekend, because she didn't want *you*, our fans, to feel like she was taking time away from you." Scott looked right at her, gesturing to show everyone where she was. He wanted her to stand. "I want to introduce you to my girlfriend, my angel, Mia. Mia, please, come up here."

She shook her head, but he laughed and called her up again.

Mia took a timid step forward, followed by another. No matter how slowly she walked, the stage got closer and closer.

Her heart was thundering—it hurt—as she took the steps up the stage.

Grace and Evelien smiled from their husbands' sides.

Scott met her at the top of the steps. He took her hand and pulled her to center stage. Then kissed her knuckles and dropped to one knee.

He pulled a blue velvet jewelry box out of his pocket. "Mia, I know we haven't been together long, but you're my heart, my soul, the air I breathe. Without you I'm unfinished, incomplete. Would you do me the honor of becoming my wife?"

The noise in the crowd was a deafening mix of joy and anger.

Why can't people just be happy for us?

Mia tried to block the sound, and focus just on Scott.

It only took the breath of a heartbeat to get back to him.

His eyes were piercing, waiting for her answer.

She put one hand to his cheek. "I'm the one who would be honored. Yes, Scott Kay Ralston, yes!"

In one swift movement, he was upright and lifting Mia off her feet, spinning her around with a passionate kiss.

Her arms snaked around his neck, not caring about the thousands of people watching. She never wanted to let him go.

The crowd cheered for them, but the sense of selfishness inched up from her gut, chasing away the warmth.

She broke their kiss, and Scott set her back on her feet.

"May I?" he asked, pulling the ring out of the box.

Mia held her hand, and he slipped the ring on her finger.

It was a beautiful twisted band with a huge round diamond in the middle. "It's too much," she whispered.

"It's not enough," he said without missing a beat. "I want you to always know you are loved."

"I don't need a ring for that. I only need you. By the way, you're in *so* much trouble." Mia frowned, since her back was to the crowd.

"You don't like the ring?" he asked.

"We weren't even going to announce we were dating, and you *proposed*!"

"Good thing we have eyes on Jazmin. Now, I don't have to keep you a secret." Scott kissed her again, pushing away any thoughts of danger.

"Hopefully no one else goes postal on me for this."

He pulled her aside, away from the front of the stage. "Do you not want to be my wife?" There was pain and confusion in his voice; it wavered slightly.

"It's not that," Mia said. "It's just…"

Blaze grabbed Scott's arm before she was done, pulling her *fiancé* back to the front of the stage. "Hey, loverboy," he said into his mic. "These lovely ladies out front need our attention right now. Your new fiancée will have to wait."

Scott glanced over his shoulder, his eyes still revealing the hurt his voice had held.

She'd hurt him.

Something she never wanted to do.

He'd put her in danger. Again.

Even if Jazmin was being watched, she wasn't the *only* fan upset over this news.

Mia had heard them in the crowd. There were more angry fans than happy ones. She loved Scott, more than she wanted to admit. It didn't negate the fact she had every right to be upset.

Tears stung her eyes but she didn't want to shed them in front of anyone.

There was a small restroom just past the food court that was rarely used, so she headed straight for it.

The band and the wives were busy on stage, which insured no one saw her leave.

Cold water on Mia's wrists helped draw the heat out. She brought her wet hands to the back of her neck, willing her tears to stop before they could fall.

It took everything she had, but she kept them in check.

Minutes clicked by, and it felt like she'd been in the tiny restroom for hours. She opened the door to step out.

Someone shoved her backward, and she lost her balance. Mia fell; her back slammed into the sink and hands tightened around her throat.

CHAPTER 30

"You can't have him! He doesn't belong to you!" Jazmin let up on Mia's throat to throw a punch, which caught her left cheek.

Stars floated before her vision, and the tears she'd held back moments before, came flooding out.

But it gave her a chance to catch her breath.

She screamed.

No one could hear her over the noise of the crowd.

Jazmin grabbed a handful of her hair, ripping it out of its French twist, and dragging her out of the tiny restroom, toward the sliding glass doors that lead back out to the lido deck.

Mia's hands clawed at air to get a grip on the woman assaulting her. When she touched skin, she pulled with all her might.

The woman's fingers were entwined in her hair, and pulling didn't free her.

Moist ocean air blew over them both when Jazmin slid the doors open, then continued to pull Mia outside.

"Scott belongs to my sister, not some blonde slut!" the girl yelled over the music playing just one hundred feet ahead of them.

The music and screaming fans was almost deafening, making it hard for her to hear what the cocoa-skinned woman was yelling.

Mia was glad they were now outside. Surely someone would see them fighting. Until it hit her where Jazmin was dragging her. "Let me go, you stupid bitch!" She struggled, twisting around to break her attacker's grip. It caused her more pain. Her stitches were likely popping open and another bald spot forming.

That was better than going overboard. Mia spun like a fish on a hook, breaking from the death grip Jazmin had on her hair. She'd barely gotten upright before the crazy woman flung herself forward.

Jazmin slammed Mia's back against the railing.

She made the mistake of glancing over her shoulder to see the dark waters below; the waves were rough against the side of the ship as it cut forward.

A hard punch to her abdomen brought her face forward and she doubled over.

Jazmin grabbed Mia's head and brought it down to her raised knee.

Blood exploded from her face when her nose collided with the denim. Mia had never been in a fight in her life, but it was obvious Jazmin had. She fought to remain conscious.

Bet she was the schoolyard bully.

Another blow brought Mia to her knees; her beautiful navy gown crumpled around her.

Someone has to see this... please let someone see. I can't do this...

She swayed with the motion of the boat, finally falling onto her left side, then curled into the fetal position.

Jazmin got down on the deck next to her, leaning so close, Mia could smell liquor on her breath. "He broke my sister when he left her. Now, I will break him." She put her hands on Mia, one on her shoulder, the other on her curled up knee. "Losing you will break him. And the fall should break you." She shoved Mia to the very edge.

The railing had a two-inch lip, to prevent towels and trash from going overboard.

It wasn't meant to stop a body.

Jazmin gave another heave forward, pushing her over the lip and through railing.

Mia grabbed the two-inch lip. She screamed as loud as she could, fearing no one could hear her. She'd fall into the dark water of the ocean and die.

Scott would never know what happened.

Her last moments with him played through her mind while her high-heeled shoes scrapped the edge of the ship and she tried to get her feet on anything that could hold her up.

Mia's dress whipped wildly around her, like the sail of a boat, gripping at her and pulling her hard. The tips of her acrylic nails cracked and broke as she dug her fingers into the small piece of metal she clung to.

"Jazmin!"

Mia's heart soared when she heard Scott's voice over the noise of the party, and the roaring of the blood in her ears.

"Scott," the woman said curtly, and took a step closer to the railing, trying to hide Mia hanging there.

"What the hell are you doing here?" he asked.

"I had tickets for the cruise and I thought it a shame to miss it, although it would be better if my sister were here. I see you found a new slut to fill your bed."

"Where is Mia?" he demanded.

Mia screamed again.

He has to hear me!

How she managed to be alert to her surroundings while hanging on for dear life, she could never explain.

One more scream, and Scott threw Jazmin out of the way. Then he hung over the rail.

♪♩

SCOTT HAD TURNED his back for only a moment, and Mia had disappeared.

She knew better than to go off on her own, didn't she? Even with Jazmin on watch, she should stay put.

He'd put her in danger from the fans.

"I think she went to the restroom," Grace said. "I can go check on her if you like."

He nodded, and Grace stepped away, just as Johnny pulled him aside.

"Bro, she gave us the slip."

"I know. Grace just went to check on her in the restroom."

"Jazmin? Why would Grace…"

Scott's friend and bodyguard's words sank in. "Oh, shit! Jazmin isn't being watched?" Bile rose, burning his throat.

After his announcement, his ex-fiancée's sister was likely to go atomic.

"We've got to find her." He didn't bother to address the crowd. Scott ran off the stage, in the direction Grace had gone.

Three steps away from the stage, he found Jazmin, not his love.

She was just to the side of the sliding glass doors next to the food court, and she had her back to him.

"Jazmin!"

"Scott."

"What the hell are you doing here?" he demanded, moving closer.

"I had tickets for the cruise and I thought it a shame to miss it, although it would be better if my sister were here. I see you found a new slut to fill your bed."

"Where is Mia?" he demanded, the blood running cold through his body.

He heard her scream, barely audible over the noise of the party and the ship.

Scott grabbed Jazmin, throwing her to the side, then flung the upper half of his body over the railing.

He couldn't reach her from there.

Her grip was on the deck itself.

"Help," he screamed over his shoulder before dropping to his knees. He slipped through the lowest railing, trying to grab Mia, and hold her in place. He couldn't see who grabbed his legs, only felt the weight of someone holding him in place. "I've got you, baby," Scott cooed to his love, gripping her wrists as hard as he could. Even if he bruised her, she'd be alive.

Out of the corner of his eye, Scott spotted Johnny on his left, flat on his stomach, reaching through the railing to grab Mia by her waist.

"Don't let go," she screamed, pure terror filling her voice. "Please, don't let go."

Scott held tight while Johnny used his massive upper body strength to lift her up, and he pulled her back through the rails. He finally let go of her wrists and threw himself over her, taking her whole body to his, crushing her with the fear that racked his body.

She was safe.

"What the hell happened?" Nick pushed his way through the circle of people watching the drama unfold.

"Nick please, help me," Jazmin brought attention back to her. "She attacked me; I was only defending myself."

"I'm not stupid. We already know you were out to get her!" Scott spat.

His friend grabbed the girl's arm. "Johnny, we need to get her locked up somewhere. She tried to murder Mia," Nick exclaimed.

The surrounding fans murmured their comments and replied to the allegations.

"I-I was doing it for us. If Scott and Marissa get back together, then things can work out for us too," she said.

"There is no *us!*" he shouted. "There never *was!* I put you in your place years ago! I'm married, and I have a baby. Why the hell would I want you? You and your sister can take a long walk off a short pier."

Hope stepped up beside her husband. Her face was a deep shade of red. Without a word, she punched Jazmin's face before Nick could stop her. "That's for Mia! And stay away from my husband!"

Nick yanked Jazmin's arm, trying to get her away from the scene.

Jazmin threw herself against him to cry on his shoulder, giving no notice to the blood flowing from her nose.

Both Cruise and Band Security had surrounded them by then, giving Nick the opportunity to shove the offending woman off him, and into the strong grip of Johnny.

"Get her out of here!" Nick said. "And make sure we never see her again." His expression was disgusted.

"She'll go to the brig," one of the cruise line security pointed out. " We'll hold her there until we dock and can get Miami Police on scene."

They led Jazmin away, and her screams could be heard throughout the area, bringing plenty of RE fans to see what was going on.

"We'll get you back! She can't have you! Nick, Scott! Come back here!"

SCOTT CARRIED MIA TO SICKBAY, much to her protest.

Blood covered not only her face and chest, but the dark color stained part of her dress. There was blood in her hair too, but it wasn't clear if it was from her face, or her previous injury.

"I'm okay to walk," she tried again.

"Stop arguing." He walked so fast through the corridor, he had to keep her feet from hitting the wall.

Only one shoe remained on. It could've been lost to the sea or left on the deck after her rescue.

His mind kept going to the most trivial things, to keep his thoughts off her near-death experience.

The ship's doctor used a warm cloth to clean up her face and chest, then examined her nose; it wasn't broken.

Her stitches, on the other hand, were another problem. Of the eight, four had popped. The tissue had been healing nicely, but the attack on her scalp had ripped it open.

The doctor didn't think they needed to be replaced, but recommended seeing her personal doctor as soon as she got home.

"Can I take her back to our room, now?" Scott asked.

"Yes, but be mindful of her head, and try to keep her awake for another hour or so, just to make sure."

"I can do that," he said.

"Only if I can walk back to my room," Mia said, her mouth set in a stubborn line. She crossed her arms over her breasts, too.

"*My* room. You're not spending another minute without me by your side."

CHAPTER 31

"Will you ever forgive me?" Scott asked when they were back in his cabin.

Mia sat on the edge of the bed, and he paced. "Forgive you for what?" Her whole body hurt, and she was having a hard time concentrating on anything besides the pain. He was making her dizzy, with his quick back-and-forth.

"You could've died, and it was all my fault."

She got up and made him stop moving. "It wasn't your fault. It was a psycho fan. You couldn't have done anything differently. I hear psychos are part and parcel of being a star, or dating one."

"Not dating. Engaged. That is… if you still want to marry me?"

Mia put her hands on his cheeks, bringing him closer to her. "I want nothing more," she whispered against his lips.

He sighed, like she'd taken the world off his shoulders.

"Okay. I lied," she said.

"What!" Scott's face drained of all color.

Mia laughed. "There is something I want more."

"Anything, baby."

"Can you get into my room and get my pain pills?"

He chuckled, and his broad chest heaved with relief she could feel. Clearly, he could concede to this demand.

"Um, one thing. I have no idea where my handbag is, with my room key."

"Shit. Let me check with the others. Maybe a wife grabbed it." Scott pulled his cell from his pocket.

Mia stretched her back while she waited for him to finish his text. Her dress was becoming stiff from drying blood. She wanted it off, and had just reached for the side-zipper when Scott stepped up beside her.

"Let me help you with that," he whispered in her ear.

Goosebumps erupted all over at the feel of his warm breath on her bare skin. Mia gave him better access.

The zipper wasn't very long, yet he took forever to get it all the way down. He helped to slide the fabric off one shoulder and the dress fluttered down to pool at her feet, like deep water.

Mia stood before him in her navy-blue panties and bra. The strap went across her chest from the inner side of the left cup and over her shoulder to hook on the back-right side.

Scott looked hungrily at her full breasts, as they almost spilled out of her bra. He shifted closer, capturing her lips, as his hands worked to free her bosom.

Mia let out a sigh of relief as her breasts were released.

He laughed against her mouth before kissing her again.

As the bra fell to the floor, he helped her step out the fabric piled around her.

She reached for his jacket, intending on helping him out of it, but he gently grabbed her hands, pulling them away. She frowned.

He chuckled, not saying a thing, and went for his phone.

Mia arched an eyebrow, as he replied to a text. She sat on the edge of the bed.

Scott smiled, but still said nothing. Of course, he was concerned, but the doctor said she was fine.

So why do I have to be mostly naked, while he messes on his phone?

She went to the bathroom. Mia wasn't trying to be mean; she just didn't want to sit there without clothing. She'd been getting hot and bothered, despite her physical discomfort, but the mirror reminded her of the blood in her hair.

She turned on the shower and let the hot water wash away the night. Mia didn't stay in long. She grabbed the bathrobe hanging on the wall and put it on.

Just then, there was a knock on the door. Mia didn't open it; she just took a deep breath in, and let it out. "Yes?"

"Baby, everything okay?"

He'd sounded concerned, so she opened the door just a crack. He was still fully dressed. He even had his shoes on.

"Yeah. Everything's fine. Just needed to get the blood out of my hair."

Scott put one hand on the door, giving it a little pressure.

Mia leaned into the door, stopping him from opening it.

"Babe, let me in."

"I don't think so."

"What is going on?"

"You tell me. You undress me, then ignore me. You wouldn't even let me get your jacket off."

He laughed, and it was a deep, really amused, belly chortle.

Mia frowned and wanted to curse at him.

He reached into the bathroom just enough to put one hand on her cheek. "Come out, and I'll explain. Please."

She sighed, but opened up, the rest of the way.

He laughed again when he saw the bathrobe. "Really?"

"I told you, I needed a shower. A cold shower." That wasn't really the truth. The water in her shower had been hot. She *had* needed to cool off.

Scott had turned off the main room light and only had on the small lamp on the desk.

The curtains were open across the sliding glass doors, and the moon was shining bright; the light spilled into the room.

Her bottle of pills was on the nightstand.

"Evelien brought them over. She'd grabbed your purse off the table on the stage, where you left it. Please, take one." Scott must've followed her gaze.

Mia didn't hesitate. Normally she needed water to take a pill, but she didn't care, just needed to get it into her system.

He came up behind her, catching her off guard when he reached for the ties of the robe.

She gently pushed his hands away.

He reached for her robe ties again, but she pushed him away again.

She met his eyes and held his gaze. "I thought you were going to explain why I was mostly naked, and you were fully dressed."

Scott took her free hand. "When you came out of the bathroom, right before the Prom, I saw the hunger in your eyes. I could see how much you liked my tux and you told me that after Prom, you were all mine."

Mia nodded; she remembered.

He still looked so good in his tux, but that didn't explain why she was the only almost-naked one.

"So when we came in here, I had a plan, since you promised to be all mine. I wanted you to see me in my tux while I did things to your body you would never forget."

Her face heated, just thinking about what he would've done to her.

"After almost losing you tonight, I couldn't wait to make things right with you. I didn't care if you had blood in your hair, or smudged on your chest. I just needed you." He kissed her hot cheek, moving to her lips.

Mia's protest died as he untied her robe, letting it fall to the floor.

They held each other close and the passion consumed them both.

Without missing a beat, or breaking the kiss, Scott walked them toward the bed, sitting on the edge when his legs met with the mattress. He pulled Mia down. He leaned, and suckled her right breast.

Mia moaned as he feasted on her flesh.

When he took the other nipple into his mouth, she took the moment to slip her hands over the silk of his collar, trying to remove his jacket.

"Baby, don't you..." he asked.

She put her finger on his lips to silence him, then offered him her hand. Mia needed him skin to skin.

The tux was hot, but his naked body was hotter.

She struggled with his bowtie, but had it fluttering to the floor promptly.

One-by-one, she undid the buttons of his soft while dress shirt. Mia ran her hands up and over his abdomen, which was covered by a white undershirt. She slipped the dress shirt off his arms, not caring that it now lay crumpled on the floor.

The white undershirt swiftly joined it.

Just as seductively as he'd done with her dress, she took her sweet time unzipping his pants, letting her knuckles graze the protrusion of his manhood.

Mia lowered her body as she slowly slid Scott's pants down his long, lean legs. She gently pushed him back, so he returned to the edge of the bed.

She'd never taken a man's shoes off before; it was oddly sexy.

She completed removing his dress pants, tossing them over her shoulder to join the other clothes, and stood between his legs.

Scott gripped her waist, bringing her sensitive skin within kissing distance. He returned to her right breast, followed by the left, all the while holding on to her like she'd float away.

"Scott," she breathed his name in a revenant whisper.

"Step back," was his reply.

Mia obeyed, expecting him to stand, but he moved to the floor, landing on his knees.

His hands returned to her waist, and without warning she almost lost her balance when his tongue assaulted her in a most delicious way.

He gently coaxed her legs apart so he could taste even more of her.

She buried her fingertips in his soft dark hair, to keep balance and ground herself. Her body was so close to release that her knees locked and her body went rigid.

Scott wasn't going to let her finish just yet. He must've known what was happening to her body, because he quickly stood. He moved them to the bed and gently urged her back.

Mia adjusted on the bed so she was up on the pillows.

He went up her body, and she wrapped her legs around his slender waist. He began his slow invasion of her body. He sucked in a breath when he filled her completely. Scott didn't start to thrust.

She looked into his eyes, and without words knew why. Mia threaded her fingers through his hair and brought him in for an intense kiss.

They'd almost lost each other that night.

It was a lot to take in.

Neither of them spoke, as their lovemaking intensified.

Everything was heightened, because they were relying on their emotions rather than words.

There were so many emotions.

Mia wriggled beneath him, then lifted her hips, encouraging him to start the motion that would bring her pleasure.

Her hands slid down to cup his beautiful ass when he finally pushed forward.

With each gentle thrust up, she mapped his working muscles.

Scott moved slowly at first, his back curving softly as he moved inside her.

Mia's hands trailed up his back, stopping when he pressed in a little harder, a little faster.

Her breathing became ragged, her body growing tight.

He slid his hand down her leg, catching right behind her left knee, hiking it up to give him deeper access.

He was hitting places inside her body she'd never felt before. Stars shot behind her eyes; her explosion was near.

His hips dug into her as he pressed on.

Scott pushed harder and deeper than he ever had before, like he was trying to bury himself inside her forever.

He took possession of her mouth, devouring her with the intensity that took them both.

Mia's lips would be swollen, her chin would be red and chaffed from his goatee. She didn't care.

The sounds that came from his throat, let her know he was as close as she was. She undulated again, trying to match his rhythm, needing them to finish together.

A few more deep thrusts had Scott shouting as he came inside her. He made a guttural sound before collapsing onto her, both their breathing raspy.

Scott rolled to the side, separating their joined bodies, but didn't keep his hands to himself. He began circling her taut pink nipple, making her womb contract.

His fingers trailed down her body to find her core, still hot and wet with need. One finger gingerly touched her clit and her body responded.

Mia gasped from the simple touch, closing her eyes to maximize the sensations.

He brought his whole hand in to play, teasing and caressing her sex, making her wiggle beneath his touch. He slipped one finger inside, finding the spot she most needed him to touch.

The intensity was almost more than Mia could bear.

When Scott shifted so he could massage inside and her clit, her body betrayed her.

In one instant, she exploded. Her body squeezed around his finger, pulsating as the orgasm affected so much more of her body than ever before.

When she opened her eyes, Scott was watching her. The green orbs said more than words ever could.

She'd never doubt his love for her. More so, she couldn't deny her love for him.

Because of that, Mia needed to tell him the truth. Before she went home.

He deserved to know she'd hated him. Once upon a time.

CHAPTER 32

A light knock on the door had Mia scrambling to slip on the robe she'd left on the floor.

She barely had it tied when the knocking was harder, more insistent.

Not wanting to wake Scott, she cracked the door open.

Blaze stood in the hallway, his beautiful wife right behind him. "Oh, good. You're still alive," the dark-haired, tattooed bandmate teased.

"Why wouldn't I be?" Mia frowned.

"Well, sweetie," Grace said from over Blaze's shoulder, "we docked over two hours ago, and you both should've vacated the ship by now. We had to get special permission to re-board to come get you."

"Oh, shit! Scott!" She called over her shoulder. "Scott, get up! All my stuff is still in my cabin. I haven't started packing yet. I don't even know where my key is."

Grace stepped around her husband and reached for Mia, pulling her into a hug. "Didn't Scott tell you? When I brought over your meds, I also packed one of you little bags with just the essentials, to get you off the ship. Then Hope, Evelien and I packed your stuff, so you wouldn't have to worry about it. After the night you had, it was the least we could do."

"Thank you," she could only whisper, her heart overflowing at the love these people had shown her. She'd always wanted sisters. Now she had three.

"Get Scott moving. We'll meet you in the hotel. The Police have Jazmin and we've all given our statements. Blaze smooth talked them into letting you two give yours at the hotel. They are meeting you in an hour. The driver knows you'll be out soon. Just hurry." She grabbed her husband's hand and rushed him down the hall.

Scott was stretching his back, the sheet bunched up at his waist.

It fell away to reveal his hard, naked body when he stood up, making Mia's core tighten.

All she wanted to do was wrap herself around him once again. However, they had to leave the ship, and she had things to tell him.

"What was that all about?" he asked in between two yawns.

"Um, I guess we should've disembarked a few hours ago. You worked me over so hard last night, I slept through it all."

He tugged her against his hard chest, his erection pressing against her hip. "*We* slept right through it, you mean. They can wait just a little longer." Scott leaned down to kiss her, but she stepped away from him.

"No. We need to get packed and off the ship. The cops are waiting for us. Let's go." Mia found the bag Grace had spoken of, but screeched when he lifted the hem of the robe and lightly smacked her bare ass. She whirled with a glare for her fiancé.

Scott beamed. "Five minutes. Give me five minutes, then we can pack." His voice was husky and he moved closer.

Mia put her palm up. "You and I both know it would take more than five minutes. You are no one-pump-chump kind of man."

He chuckled. "All right. You win. But as soon as we get settled into the hotel, I want you naked, for the rest of the night."

"Just get packed."

There wasn't time for a shower, so Mia took a washcloth and wet it with warm water to clean all her vital parts. Her bag was under a chair by the TV and she quickly dressed, glad the girls had thought to pack her clean underwear and soft pink summer dress.

It was her favorite because no matter how it was packed, like the hasty tossing of it into a small bag, it never wrinkled.

She ran a brush through her hair, pulling it back into a low ponytail, before turning to her ruined dress, still crumpled on the floor. Her eyes burned as she looked at the once exquisite piece of clothing.

Scott stepped up behind her, kissing her shoulder where the straps didn't cover it. "I can have it cleaned. It's just blood."

"I know. But I don't think I could ever wear it again. My chest is tight just thinking about it. It holds memories I never want to remember, and ones I never want to forget."

He scooped up the gown and took it into the bathroom with him.

"Can I help with anything?" she asked after she was ready, standing around with nothing to do.

"Nah, I've got this. Almost done."

Less than ten minutes later, they emerged from the ship and into the bright afternoon sun. There were still a few fans lingering, mostly Scott's, waiting specifically for him; to say goodbye.

Many of the ladies congratulated her on their engagement, wanting a closer look at the ring. It was a pleasant surprise.

Mia had learned firsthand, there were some crazy women out there, but there were even more that genuinely cared about the band, wanted them to be happy.

Those were the ones she'd focus on in the future. She couldn't let one psycho ruin her forever.

♭♪♩

SCOTT LET OUT a sigh of relief the moment the door to their hotel suite clicked shut, the two of them tucked safely inside. They'd met with an officer and a detective, gave their statements and promptly headed upstairs. It was something they would be dealing with for a while. But not the rest of the night.

That belonged to them alone.

Scott knew the cruises would never be the same after this one. His life had changed forever in the course of a few days. He'd almost lost his true love, in more ways than one.

He'd never let something like that ever happen again.

He stepped up behind his beautiful blonde fiancée.

Fiancée.

Scott could say that word now and not cringe; not like he had with the last one. Mia filled him with such joy he might burst.

They'd teased him when he was younger because he wasn't afraid to show emotion. He cried. He shared his feelings. There was nothing wrong with that.

He had so many feelings flowing through him now, expressing them would be a challenge.

Scott kissed her shoulder. Then her neck.

Mia turned in his arms and he captured her lips.

He'd show her what his words were failing at, everything he wished he could express.

But instead of the response he was expecting, Mia slipped her hands in between them and gently pushed him back.

"Scott," she began. "There's something I need to tell you."

The tone of her voice had his stomach dropping to his feet.

Those words were never good to begin with but how she'd said them, made him ill.

The blood rushed from his head. He sat on the bed so he wouldn't fall over.

Mia put her hands on his knees, spreading his legs so she could slip in between them, like last night.

Her hands continued up his body, sending heated spikes through him.

She stopped at his face, holding him captive. She leaned in, giving him a chaste kiss. "You know I love you, right? It took me a long time to say that. I want you to know why." Mia kissed him again, this time with more fire, coaxing Scott to open so their tongues could dance.

Her hands slipped into his hair, giving a little tug, and making him growl deep in his throat. His cock jerked with anticipation, pressing hard against his far-too-tight jeans.

He slid his hands under her dress to reach the creamy soft skin, inviting her to go further.

But instead, she backed away. "Scott. I'm serious. I need to get this off my chest."

"Whatever it is, we can handle it, together."

"I need a drink," she mumbled.

"Mia?"

When she faced him again, her blue eyes rimmed with red.

"Baby, what is it?"

She buried her face in her hands and cried. Through the noise, he could barely hear her words. "I hated you, okay. I hated you for years. And the guilt is eating me up."

Scott jumped from the bed, pulling her into his arms, letting her soak his shoulder with her tears. His hand found its way into her hair, where he held her like she was the most precious thing in the world.

Because she was.

"I figured as much," he whispered.

"What!" Mia pulled back to look at him. She glared, seeming more angry than relieved.

"Well, think about it. The first time we met, you were less than friendly. Even *Next Step* fans usually blush or swoon when they meet one of us. But you were almost cold. And only to *me*. So, I figured there was something in my past you didn't like. I never did figure out what it was, and in the end, it didn't matter."

"It matters to me!" She pushed out of his embrace and started pacing.

Scott had to try hard not to laugh.

She ran her hands through her hair in agitation. "I could've loved you years ago, and because of a stupid TV show, I missed out on so much!"

"Baby, come here." He moved to sit on the bed, patting the spot beside him, waiting for her to join him. "Please."

Mia let out an audible sigh and joined him, but kept her distance, selecting the far side of the bed.

"Mia, come here." He patted the bed again.

"I'm good here."

"Tell me, why did you hate me? You just said something about a TV show? I honestly don't know what it is."

"MusicOne," Mia said, burying her face back in her hands, her elbows resting on her knees.

Scott racked his brain trying to figure out what she meant, but nothing came to mind. They'd done a good job of keeping his alcoholism hidden, since Blaze was the one that held the focus of the media with his drug and alcohol abuse. So it wasn't that. He'd been a pretty squeaky-clean guy. His parents had raised him well.

What could I have done for her to hate me for years?

He waited for more from her, but it wasn't forthcoming.

"Damn it, Mia. What the hell did I do?"

Her answer was laughter. She lifted her head and threw it back, laughing so hard it shook the bed.

He cocked his head to the side. Confusion made him frown.

What the hell?

"I can't even say the words now. It's silly really. I don't know why I've let it bother me for so long."

Scott had had enough. He moved to stand in front of her. He

grabbed her face. "What. The. Hell. Did. I. Do?" He emphasized each word.

Mia placed her smaller hands over his, but didn't pull from his grip. She held his gaze. "You talked shit..." she giggled again. "You talked shit about *Next Step*, saying they made your life hell."

"What?" He couldn't recall ever saying something like that. Those guys were like brothers to him now. "When did I say that? *What* did I say?"

"It was a documentary about boy bands. You said they made things hard for you..."

"They did. They set standards we all had to meet and surpass. We did, but it was hard. I *never* said I hated them."

Her face fell.

"Baby," Scott kissed her nose.

"It was stupid of me, to take it so personally. Missed out on everything with your band. Now we've lost so much time..."

"No, my love, we haven't. If you'd been a fan, I may never have found you. We wouldn't be where we are now. I'm glad you hated me."

"You are?" Mia's blue eyes went wide.

He kissed her again, this time capturing her lips, tempting her. "I am," he whispered against her skin. "Let me show you."

THE END

SNEAK PEEK

Read on for an excerpt from
Andrea Hurtt's novella, from the *Razor's Edge* Series.

UNDONE

Now available from Piece of Pie Publishing

ORDER IT NOW

OR

GET IT FREE

Sign up for Andrea Hurtt's Newsletter
and get the ebook at no cost!

https://dl.bookfunnel.com/n9we1apx9k

UNDONE

CHAPTER ONE

"Breathe. Just breathe." Grace took a deep breath as she entered the community hall's recreational room. This was where she was going for her life-changing event?

The lights were bright, harsh old fluorescent tube bulbs. The room smelled like a locker room.

She took in the less-than-impressive view.

The bleachers were closed and pushed up against the walls, giving the room a large cavernous feel. If anyone yelled, it would echo off the walls.

It made Grace smile.

That slice of joy only lasted a moment.

Her new costar, was about ten feet away, bouncing a red dodge ball like it was a basketball.

She cringed inside.

Those balls were made of nightmares!

"Gracie! You're here! It's about damn time! We can't get started without you. Hey! Catch!" The good looking, well-built twenty-one-year-old man threw the ball at her.

She stepped out of the way before it could collide with her. The flying red rubber hit the wall behind her only to roll back her way. Grace continued to ignore it, walking closer to not only him but the others in the room.

"Seriously, Grace. Would it really hurt that much if it hit you?" Charles crossed his bare muscled arms over his chest, looking at her with mock disapproval.

If you only knew.

She forced a smile and stood by the other actors. Grace, for all her name implied, had always been clumsy.

In middle school, they'd given her the nickname, Graceless. One time in gym class, she tried to dodge one of those red balls. She'd slipped and broke her left arm when she'd hit the wooden floor.

She'd screamed like the world had ended, and everyone had laughed. The horrible teasing was born. That was the day she lost her voice, not just physically, but emotionally. She'd become an introvert, caving in on herself.

If Grace talked with no one, no one could hurt her.

Years later, theater had helped change all that. Taking on characters, *becoming* someone else, her whole body changed.

She had poise and grace she'd never had before.

Her new addiction.

She always needed more.

"Everyone please take your seats, I don't care where. Just sit and I'll pass out the scripts," Jason, the man in charge said. He was an amazing man with a vision. At six foot, five inches, his height alone made her uncomfortable. His sun-bleached hair and copper tone shouted he spent more time outside than in a dark theater. When he smiled, and those pearly white teeth shone, it set her at ease.

Jason had been on a massive search throughout the theater communities everywhere, for actors looking to spread their wings. He needed people that could act, sing, and dance and weren't afraid to leave their homes for an extended period.

That was what'd caught her eye, and motivated her to drive the long distance to audition.

Grace took a seat next to her new costar, as she tried to push back memories she didn't need at the moment. She *had* to focus.

The script in her hand took on a permanent curved because she kept rolling it and squeezing, then unrolling and smoothing it out.

Her nerves were getting the best of her.

I still can't believe I am here. This is really happening. Mom, I'm doing it. I'm doing this for you.

The younger man bumped her shoulder, bringing her back to the moment. "Are you ready for your life to change?" he whispered in her ear, his breath warm from his earlier exertion with the damned red ball.

ALSO BY ANDREA HURTT

Razor's Edge Rockstar Romance

Masquerade - Book 1

Undone - Book 1.5

Unmistakeable - Book 2

Incomplete - Book 3

Love Under Lockdown Series / Short Stories

Acting the Part in Lockdown

Coming Soon

Razor's Edge Rockstar Romance

Drowning - Book 4

Inconsolable - Book 5

The Sealgaire Saga

A Slice Of Hell - Book One

Prince Cove Curse

Under The Sea - Book One

ABOUT THE AUTHOR

Andrea Hurtt is an emerging author of various romance categories. She enjoys writing a little bit of everything.

She's still deciding what she wants to be when she grows up. Andrea has been a dental assistant, a stay at home mom, owned her own clothing store, was a clothing designer with a vintage inspired clothing line, Amaryllis Designs, even won Omaha Fashion Week for Top Designer in her category, and Top Boutique for Cancer Survivor Night.

Andrea currently spends her days either writing books or making #EmotionalSupportPillows and traveling around the USA and parts of Canada with the cast and fans of the CW TV show Supernatural.

She is the mother of two children, two cats and a dog, and is a proud Army wife; currently residing in the MidWest.

For more books and updates:

www.pieceofpiepublishing.com
www.facebook.com/andreahurttauthor
www.Twitter.com/atomicbombshel1
www.Instagram.com/AndreaHurttAuthor
www.Amazon.com/author/andreahurtt

Made in the USA
Middletown, DE
13 January 2025